# REBECCA STUBBS
## THE VICAR'S DAUGHTER

# REBECCA STUBBS
## THE VICAR'S DAUGHTER

Hannah Buckland

# AMBASSADOR INTERNATIONAL
GREENVILLE, SOUTH CAROLINA & BELFAST, NORTHERN IRELAND

www.ambassador-international.com

# Rebecca Stubbs
## The Vicar's Daughter

ISBN: 978-1-62020-543-3
eISBN: 978-1-62020-451-1

Scripture quotations taken from The Authorized Version.

Cover Design and Page Layout by Hannah Nichols
eBook Conversion by Anna Riebe Raats

AMBASSADOR INTERNATIONAL
Emerald House
427 Wade Hampton Blvd.
Greenville, SC 29609, USA
www.ambassador-international.com

AMBASSADOR BOOKS
The Mount
2 Woodstock Link
Belfast, BT6 8DD, Northern Ireland, UK
www.ambassadormedia.co.uk

*The colophon is a trademark of Ambassador*

ACKNOWLEDGEMENTS

I would like to thank my father-in-law, who encouraged me to write in the first place, and Christine for seeing potential in *Rebecca Stubbs*. Hartelijke bedankt! Thanks also to Helen for her observant reading and special thanks to Dad, who ploughed through the story for agricultural or historic accuracy.

# INTRODUCTION

*For eleven months of every year, the picturesque oast houses that are so much a part of the Kentish landscape stood silent and still, their only inhabitants being farm machinery and field mice. But as August gave way to September and the hop bines in the field swayed heavily with green flowers, the oast houses became the centre of agricultural activity. Their heavy doors were swung open, the rusty machinery was dragged out, and the field mice fled. The farm labourers swept out the oasts to a standard any self-respecting housewife would be proud of, and huge charcoal fires were lit, ready to dry the newly picked hops.*

*Harvesting the crop required a large workforce. The coarse, scratchy hop bines had to be pulled down and the precious green seed-cone flowers picked off by hand and then gathered into big sacks called pokes. These pokes were transported to the oast houses, where the fresh, damp hops were carefully dried in kilns over a charcoal fire until crisp and brittle. Once packed into large bags called pockets and stencilled with the farmer's name, the hops were ready to be collected by the brewery, where the bitter pollen of the hop would give the beer its uniquely tangy flavour.*

*A large number of seasonal labourers was needed to harvest the hops, so year after year Londoners from the East End descended upon the rural villages of Kent in order to gain employment, a few weeks of country air, and a few shillings to put aside for winter expenses. Most farmers saw the*

*Londoners as a necessary evil. They provided rows of hopper huts and cook houses to accommodate the multi-generation crowds. Some of these were solid, water-tight brick huts, but others were merely wooden shacks. Straw and sacks were provided for mattress making, and faggots for fires.*

CHAPTER 1

SLEEP EVADED ME. THE BED was cosy, the temperature agreeable and my body tired, yet my whirling thoughts refused to rest. Why, oh why had I decided to leave my native village of Pemfield to work in a faraway manor house? Why had I not listened to the wise advice of my seniors and stayed put? At the crack of dawn I was to leave my dear friends, those who had lovingly supported me after my parents' untimely deaths, to become a housemaid among strangers. I—who had never set foot even in the grounds of a stately home and had no idea of the daily life of their inhabitants! My ignorance would be plain to see and the housekeeper was sure to detect it within seconds of my arrival. She would send me straight back with a flea in my ear for wasting her time, and all of Pemfield would be talking of my inadequacy and silly ideas. So much had happened in the last seven months of my life. Was I about to add to its drama by my ill-advised decision? My restless mind reviewed again the sad events that had catapulted me into this situation.

September of 1857 had begun like any other: with commotion and chaos, laughter and lice, hordes of EastEnders from London descending on our rural Kent village—Pemfield—for hop-picking. As usual my father, the vicar of the parish, wholeheartedly welcomed his temporary parishioners and sought to do them good for both soul and body. His normal, rather staid parish became a hive of activity, gossip, scandal, and friction between villagers and Londoners—and Londoners against each other. The East End invaders were treated with great suspicion by the locals, who blamed them for any vegetables missing from their gardens, clothes from their lines, or apples from their orchards. The Londoners thought the locals were an ignorant bunch and could not appreciate the wisdom gained from living near to the soil and being dependent on the weather.

Pa went from one hopper hut to another, meeting old friends and new babies. He caught up with the news of another year and—amid friendship and warmth—he would try to recommend Christ to everyone he met. His message was usually received with politeness, thanks to his kindness and office, but most of his words were choked by the cares of this life. Getting pokes filled with hops, cooking meals over smouldering fires, dealing with teething babies, and keeping leaking hopper huts dry occupied most of the daylight hours of the busy workers. Any spare time was spent catching up on the latest scandal or with singing around the campfire with a stiff drink, rather than with reflecting on a distant eternity ahead.

Ma and I were equally busy in the garden and along the hedgerows picking berries and apples for jam and jelly. This was our favourite time of year, the chilly morning mists breaking into gloriously sunny days ready to be filled with harvesting the abundance of nature. Our cool kitchen floor was littered with baskets of fruit waiting to be chopped, boiled, and sugared. The stove worked overtime, bringing sweet, sticky liquids to gelling point.

"Before we know it, October will be upon us, and we will be organising the wobbly and precarious display for the Harvest Thanksgiving service," Ma said as she chopped up some apples.

"I don't think any of Pa's carrots and potatoes will be suitable for display," I replied, stirring the bubbling jam. "The few the rabbits and slugs haven't eaten are so misshapen they are not fit for public inspection—we'll have to hide them behind someone's prize marrows."

"Don't talk to me about hiding veg!" Ma replied with a smile. "There is no easier way of falling out with a parishioner than by placing his prized product behind a cabbage or cottage loaf!" She sighed and shook her head. "Your poor father, he works so hard in that vegetable patch."

"It's more a labour of love than hard work, isn't it?" I suggested. "Anyway, he says it is there that his sermons take shape."

"Then, my dear, it might be more fruitful than we think."

The thought of Harvest Thanksgiving must have been on her mind, for Ma started humming "Come Ye Thankful People Come," and before long we were singing it together, with Ma singing the melody and me harmonising with the alto. The words, "All is safely gathered in, ere the winter storms begin," gave a warm and cosy feeling of food stored in the loft and in the cellar whilst whirling snow drifted outside. But this year we had no inkling of how close the safe gathering would reach.

That evening Pa arrived late for supper, accompanied by a gust of chilly autumnal air.

"It smells like a sweet shop in here," he said as he removed his boots.

"Damson jam and elderberry jelly," I explained.

"What delayed you this time?" Ma asked after grace had been said and as we tucked into beef stew.

"Zaphnath-paaneah!" Pa said without looking up from his plate. We immediately knew what he meant. By not providing adequate housing, Farmer Joseph Smith was the cause of many problems amongst the hop pickers.

"So what was it you provided today, which Farmer Smith should have arranged?" I asked.

"Buckets," answered Pa. "Buckets to catch the drips in leaky hopper huts."

"I thought I was missing a few pails from my wash-house!" exclaimed Ma.

"And from the state of the row of privies, I doubt if rain-water will be all they are catching," continued Pa, digging into his dumplings.

"Oh, Frank," ejected Ma as I giggled. "Then I will not be wanting my buckets back, thank you very much!"

"My darling, you may have full peace of mind about that. Have we ever had anything returned which we 'loaned' to the hoppers?"

We continued our supper, after which Pa read a passage of Scripture from the well-worn family Bible and ended the meal with prayer. Then we lingered at the wooden kitchen table, reluctant to get up and start the work of cleaning the dishes, each filled with the lazy contentment that comes from eating good food after a busy day.

"An infant of a hop-picker is feverish," Pa announced, breaking the silence.

"Is he teething?" asked Ma. "I have a lotion for that."

"The mother doesn't think so."

"It could be sunstroke; those hop gardens become a sun-trap come noon, and there is so little shelter for the little ones. I can find some calamine for that."

"Thank you, my dear apothecary, but the child has been well discussed by the London women, and they do not think it is sunstroke. Between them, those women have more wisdom than. . ."

He paused for a suitable simile.

"All the colleges in Cambridge?" I suggested.

"Exactly!" he replied with a laugh. "And a good deal more common sense too. And by the way, my dear," he said, turning to me, "it is good to have you back to your normal self again."

Indeed it was good to be back to my normal self. The previous week I had written a letter to a young man, ending a four month long courtship—or rather, entanglement. As a young seventeen-year-old, I had been flattered by the attentions of Raymond, a serious and sober-minded church warden ten years my senior. During my infatuation and under his influence, I began to think cheerfulness and humour were signs of a shallow mind and sinful heart, and that a melancholy approach to life befitted true Christians. I held myself aloft from Pa's humorous comments, which I had previously enjoyed, and tried to cultivate an air of thoughtful silence. Raymond thought I had too much "book learning," so I stopped voicing my opinions. Raymond thought women should look to their husbands for answers and not trouble their pretty little heads reasoning things out for themselves, so I tried to look decorative, pretty, and receptive to his wisdom.

The spell was finally broken when I was invited to his parents' house for Sunday tea and saw the appalling way his careworn and nervous mother was treated by her husband and sons. I suddenly had visions of myself becoming such a down-trodden, unpaid servant with a wedding band. Of course, Raymond managed to get the last word, for I received a reply to my letter stating that I was "an unsuitable partner for a man of his standing." Indeed, I was most unsuitable, for once again I could run and skip, laugh and chat, and enjoy my father's humour in a way that I had denied myself for far too long.

"Oh, Pa, it is good to be back to normal, and thank you for not being sullen like your esteemed church warden."

"My pleasure, my dear," said Pa, "but why should Christians be sullen? We have so much lavished upon us here by our heavenly Father and a wonderful future in glory to enjoy."

"You are quite right, Pa," I replied, "and I hope I never forget that!"

"Then just be careful who you make sheep's eyes at next!"


The following evening, Pa came home looking pale and exhausted.

"More children are feverish," he announced as he sank into his chair.

"Then do let me come to the camp and help you," pleaded Ma.

Pa shook his head: "No, my dear, I don't want you running into danger. Not after all you have suffered recently with your rheumatics."

"Then I shall come, Pa," I said.

"No. You two stay away and respond to requests from here. But I would appreciate your prayers. Finally, now there is danger, the hoppers are wanting my prayers and are asking the right sort of questions, so I need much wisdom. And stamina."

It was not until Pa came home with the sad news of two deaths in the camp that we realised the seriousness of the situation and of Pa's selfless care for the Londoners.

The following day, through grief, fear, and some superstition, many of the hop pickers hastily returned to London, leaving the frantic farmer to rally a local workforce. Even the gypsy families, who came to the village as soon as there was any seasonal work to be done, shut their bewildered children into their wagons, put their squawking poultry into baskets, and left the neighbourhood as quickly as their straining ponies could pull them.

Pa's workload returned to normal, but he was left exhausted and drained. Within days he himself was confined to bed with a raging fever. Dr. Skinner was suspicious of typhus and with a heavy heart warned us that it could be mild or fatal. He recommended to us a trusted nurse from the neighbouring village, but Ma declined, insisting on attending to Pa's every need herself. She would not leave the bedside, day or night, and with great intuition seemed to know if Pa's restlessness indicated a need for a cold compress or hot-water bottle, fresh air or a window closed. Her expressions of love to Pa and her dry, gnarled fingers caressing his pale face brought tears to my eyes.

Some days Pa was more responsive and communicative than others, and during those times he often wanted us to sing his favourite hymns. Ma and I tried our best to oblige, but when Pa's once-strident voice joined in as a weak croak, it brought such a huge lump to our throats that we could hardly conceal our emotions. He also wanted us to read from the Scriptures, especially from St. John's Gospel, so we took turns sitting next to him, holding his hand and reading, particularly concentrating on Christ's High Priestly prayer. Pa knew it by heart, and his lips moved with ours as we went through the chapter.

The days when Pa was well gave us hope that he would recover, but this was not to be. In early October, Pa died in his sleep, as easily and comfortably as a worn-out child falls asleep on his parent's lap, and was taken to his eternal reward. We knew with all certainty that he was now with Christ, which is far better—the Lord he had served faithfully and recommended so warmly, but we sorely missed him. The grief affected us in different ways: I busied myself from dawn to dusk with replying to condolence messages and running the much neglected house, whilst Ma was paralysed with grief and seemed to have given up the will to continue. I nursed Ma day and night, desperately pleading with the Lord to spare her to me. I clung to her frail body as if my hold on her would prevent her departing.

"Ma," I said as I stroked her tangled hair, "do you remember the time you got rid of Uncle Hector by serving him over-cooked beef and boiled cabbage for days on end? He was always recommending Ramsgate as a place to convalesce. Maybe I could take you there when you are strong enough. Can you remember the time Bessie and I fell into the stream and you found tadpoles in my bloomers?"

Sometimes I was rewarded with a weak smile, but mostly she seemed unreachable.

"Ma, the hedgerows are still full of blackberries, and the trees laden with elderberries, so as soon as you are well, we can start making jam and jellies again. Won't it be lovely to fill our picking baskets with the juicy gleanings and smell the sweet mixture as it bubbles in the pan? You always say it is your favourite smell. Oh, Mama, please stay with me; please don't leave."

The thought of being left alone without either of my parents gave my prayers the raw urgency of the psalmist. But Ma had neither the strength to fight the illness nor the will to live on earth any longer. Ten days after my father's death, she joined him, slipping quietly away from me and from this life to her heavenly home and to joy unceasing, leaving me alone and comfortless.

My grief and desolation were indescribable. The only life I had ever known had been swept away, and I was left to pick up the pieces, but there did not seem to be any pieces left to be picked up. I struggled to comprehend the finality of my parents' departure and could hardly grasp the fact that I would never see their faces, hear their voices, or embrace them again. I longed to hear Pa's whistling and see Ma hobbling about the kitchen humming to herself, but they were gone forever, leaving only silence and emptiness. Time and time again the reality of it all hit me afresh, the punch never decreasing in strength or painfulness.

Throughout my parents' illnesses Mrs. Brown, our washerwoman, had been a valuable support, visiting every day and preparing meals. Now she became my mainstay, helping with all practical arrangements, shielding me from visitors and even moving in so that I was not alone. Mercifully, I became ill myself and was forced to spend a few days in bed, mainly sleeping, and thus I was rather detached from the organisation of funeral affairs. Sleep was a welcome escape for me and I prayed that I, like my parents, would wake on a brighter shore, but I always awoke in my own room at the vicarage and the awful reality of my bereavement would hit me again with fresh pain and clarity.

Uncle Hector, my father's one and only sibling, but with whom he had nothing in common, took over funeral arrangements and stayed in the village for a week to help sort out my parents' affairs. He informed Mrs. Brown that he wanted to take me back to London with him, but I was well enough to realise that this would be an awful prospect.

"Please, Mrs. Brown, don't make me! I don't want to live in a stuffy town house in the middle of London where I know no one except awful Uncle Hector."

"But what is so awful about 'im, my dear?" asked Mrs. Brown. "He seems a very obliging man to me."

"He never spoke one good word about Pa, always belittling him and his work in the parish and always boasting about his own achievements in local government."

"'E must be a clever man."

"Humph, only in his own opinion! And then I would have to accompany him to Bath, Ramsgate, or Tunbridge Wells for him to drink the waters or inhale the sea air for his much talked about and fussed-over chest complaint."

"So you would meet lots of wealthy people."

"But they are not my type!"

"And 'e be rich, and you will lack for nothing," continued Mrs. Brown.

"I will lack! I will lack Pemfield, I will lack my old friends, and I will lack you," I cried. "Oh please, don't make me go! I won't be a nuisance here, I promise."

"Then you will stay, my child, and I am right glad you want to," said Mrs. Brown as she hugged me tight.

So Mrs. Brown somehow persuaded Uncle Hector that I would be better off among old friends and in familiar surroundings and he returned alone—probably much relieved—to London.

I regained my physical well-being, but my emotions were in turmoil. I felt guilty for letting Pa work himself to death, for not nursing

Ma more expertly, and for not dying myself. I felt let down by the Lord, Who allowed all this to happen to me and then I felt guilty for feeling such rebellion. I could not understand what God was doing to me, yet I clung to Him as my only hope of recovery. I knew that He never gave Job an explanation for what happened in his life and He was under no obligation to give me one either.

I missed my parents and our life together so much that it was a physical ache. I found some comfort in the text "Underneath are the everlasting arms," as support was promised however low I sank. I desperately wished I had a sibling for comfort with whom I could reminisce about home life and share old stories and jokes. But I was an only child, due to the fact that my parents met comparatively late in life.

Ma had been the local school mistress and was secretly seen by the locals as too old-fashioned and religious to ever marry. She had come to the same conclusion herself and had tried to bury the sadness it gave her by being a diligent and kind teacher to all children that came to her small school. She had been well liked and respected by both pupils and parents alike. The elderly vicar of the village retired to live with his daughter in Sussex, and my father became the new incumbent. His evangelical zeal came as a surprise to the villagers who had been used to a vicar who worked only on the Lord's Day. He began giving a Bible lesson once a week at the school and soon recognised Ma's virtues. Before long the pair started walking out and then married.

The rather reserved school mistress blossomed into a smiley and friendly vicar's wife, showing a side of her that had been kept under wraps for many years. My father's monkish establishment was transformed to a regulated and loving household. At last he had found a companion to share his dreams and sorrows, and to laugh with him about the various foibles of his parishioners. To my parents, marriage was an unexpected blessing, and the subsequent arrival of a baby was their cup running over.

But now the cosy union of this trio was severed and I was left alone. Mrs. Brown kindly listened to my tearful, incoherent recollections of daily life and held me in her arms as I ended up sobbing. She decided it would be best if I went to stay with her in her little cottage and I reluctantly agreed. From there she could carry on her normal daily routine and mother me as best as she could. With tender intuition she gave me time to grieve but also involved me in her chores and socialising as she felt appropriate, so I was not left to sink into the whirling pool of my own thoughts and sorrows.

Miss Miller, the school mistress, frequently called around in the evenings to chat about her day, invite me for a walk or invent some other way of distracting me from my grief. Miss Miller and I had not always enjoyed a good relationship: when I first started school Miss Miller seemed to demand a higher standard of behaviour from a vicar's daughter. I was supposed to be a beacon of virtue and an example to other girls, but instead I behaved just like the rest of them. Thanks to Ma's teaching, I found the work rather easy, so had plenty of time to draw silly pictures (often of Miss Miller) on my slate and share them with my row of friends. More than once I was caught and had my knuckles severely whacked. But as the work became more demanding I began to appreciate Miss Miller's knowledge.

My best friend Bessie left school at the age of fourteen to help on her family farm, but my parents thought that I should stay in schooling longer and learn as much as possible. By this time I was enjoying the challenge of studying and, due to a common interest in geography, had a better relationship with Miss Miller. Each morning I helped her teach the infants and then in the afternoon continued my studies independently. Seeing the little ones progress from total ignorance of their ABCs to reading and writing at a reasonable level was rewarding, but it required such repetition and patience that I vowed never to become a governess or school mistress.

This classroom arrangement lasted only a year, for Ma's rheumatism had progressed at an alarmingly rapid pace, and it was decided that I should stay at home to care for her and the household. This I did willingly, and much to our relief, Ma's condition stabilised. Miss Miller continued her contact with the family by having tea with us once a week and amusing us with surprisingly witty tales from the classroom. She kept herself aloof from the villagers and lived a very solitary life but enjoyed a warm friendship with my parents and appreciated Pa's preaching. Whether out of compassion for me or a sense of indebtedness to my parents, Miss Miller made it her job to support me, and she proved a good friend and an excellent shoulder to cry on.

I gained great comfort from the many letters of condolence I received. Various villagers and even people I had never met wrote to me, expressing their gratitude for my parents' kindness and generosity; they paid tribute to my parents' thoughtfulness and the usefulness of my father's ministry. Pa had been very quick to see where there was a need and quietly supplied what was lacking: a bag of coal, a bottle of tonic, or in one case, a pair of working boots. As I read of how my parents had touched so many lives with their kind words and gifts, I felt privileged and thankful to have been their daughter. I had been greatly blessed in having these two loving people nurture me to adulthood and instill in me some of their values and beliefs. The letters helped me begin to slowly acknowledge that "the Lord gave and the Lord hath taken away, blessed be the name of the Lord."

Mrs. Brown and I realised that sooner or later a new vicar would be appointed, and the vicarage would need vacating. We set about this task in a business-like manner, enlisting Miss Miller to help. I allowed myself to keep only small mementos and books as I had nowhere to store bigger items. All our furniture was sold at an auction. I could not bring myself to go and watch the familiar, old items being inspected and prodded by strangers who had no idea of their preciousness. The furniture was neither new nor antique and therefore worth very little in monetary terms. Mrs. Brown insisted in going to the auction to make sure "all was above board."

While the auction got underway, Miss Miller took me off to draper's shop to buy a length of material for a new spring dress. We were soon engrossed in comparing various yards of beautifully-printed cloth, enjoying the unique smell of fresh cotton, and were almost able to forget that my family furniture was under the hammer. We finally emerged from the draper's, each triumphantly hugging a parcel of material, thread, and buttons, ready to begin our new sewing projects. When Mrs. Brown was satisfied that all had been done decently and in order (apparently she had stood, arms folded, near the auctioneer, giving all who dared bid disapproving stares, as if they were trying to get something for nothing), she joined us for a cup of tea and piece of cake at the Tea Rooms. The auction had gone "as well as could be expected" and had generated a small profit, once the auctioneer had claimed his hefty fee.

After all my parents' goods and chattels had been sold and their savings calculated, it was found that I was the heiress to a modest inheritance. I had imagined that the smallness of Pa's stipend, matched with the largesse of his Christian charity, meant he never had any money to save, so I was pleasantly surprised. Now I had a new dilemma of knowing what to do with the money and my life. I could live off the money for about four years and then find a way of earning my keep, or I could deposit the money and start work as soon as possible.

## CHAPTER 2

DURING THE FIRST FEW MONTHS following my bereavement, the quiet life with Mrs. Brown suited me very well, but after that I began to feel restless and ready to stretch my wings. I wanted to leave Pemfield, meet new people and, most of all, earn my own living. I was anxious not to become a burden to Mrs. Brown or an object of pity to those I met with. I broached the subject with Mrs. Brown one evening.

"Mrs. Brown, I think it is time I got a job."

"Why, my dear? You are busy enough 'ere with me."

"I mean one where I could earn a living."

"Then ask in the village, but there ain't much for a girl around 'ere."

"I mean a job away from Pemfield."

"Now, why would you want to leave dear old Pemfield, my child?"

"To stretch my wings a bit and be independent."

"And what do you have in mind?" she asked cautiously.

"Someone offering board and lodging," I replied. I could tell Mrs. Brown was hurt and puzzled.

"Maybe domestic service," I continued.

"You would make a good cook," she ventured.

"But kitchens in big houses are normally below ground level. I would feel like a holed-up rabbit."

"With your nice up-bringing, you would make a good lady's maid."

"But I would have to agree with all the lady's views and keep mine to myself!"

"Well then, what about an 'ousemaid? Your ma certainly made sure you know how to clean. I remember all those times you rushed through your chores, and your ma caught you just as you were escaping through the door to play with Bessie. She called you 'Slap dash' and made you do them all over again properly!"

We laughed together at this, and that is how it was decided that I should look for a housemaid's position. I wanted the Lord to guide me to the right household and prayed that He would open up a suitable door for me.

I bought *The Morning Post* and intently studied the "Situations Available" pages. I wrote to various housekeepers in reply to adverts, but my inexperience seemed to go against me, and I received many polite refusals. At seventeen years of age, I was probably considered too old and unmalleable to be a suitable servant. Mrs. Brown could not hide her satisfaction as refusal followed refusal, maintaining that domestic service was beneath a vicar's daughter; but I, knowing that my parents never looked down on hard work and being ignorant of what the job might entail, continued to hope. Then one day a new advert appeared, one for a housemaid for a large household at Barton Manor, East Sussex. The place name rang a bell with me as Pa had known the vicar there, many years ago, and esteemed him highly for his evangelical preaching. This seemed ideal, and as I wrote to the housekeeper, I prayed that this would prove to be the right post for me.

About a fortnight later I received the reply, and to my delight and Mrs. Brown's dismay, the housekeeper of Barton Manor requested my presence for an interview in a week's time. I should be prepared to stay on after the interview, if deemed suitable, in order to start work immediately. My excitement at the imminence of my new adventure was only matched by Mrs. Brown's disappointment. I felt sorry that I was clearly going against her wishes, but knew I needed to start ploughing my own furrow in life.

I wanted to give Mrs. Brown a sum of money as a thank-you gift for all her love, support, and hospitality to me over the past half a year, but of course she would not hear of it. After some thought, I visited the butcher and the baker, put in a small weekly order for her, and paid ahead for a year. The first delivery would arrive after I had left the village. I hoped this would help to stretch her limited income and lessen her burden.

I had only a week to pack my belongings, finish making my new spring dress, and say good-bye to my dear friends, including Bessie. We had not seen much of each other for a few months due to her all-consuming romance with the blacksmith's son, Rob. She had made many errands to the blacksmith for her father, but on one occasion whilst waiting for Rob to repair her pruning hook, she got too close. As Rob stoked the fire, a hot coal shot toward her and landed on her skirt. Rob saw the situation and flung a bucketful of icy water over the skirt, causing a shocked, shivering, and soaking Bessie. Her forlorn state seemed to touch his heart, so he handed over his work to another man and took her home to dry by the fire and have a reviving cup of tea. During that informal tea break in the blacksmith's kitchen, it was decided between them that they should meet up more often. Thus a new romantic attachment was formed. She was now excitedly preparing for marriage but was at a loss regarding how to communicate with me over my parents' deaths. Our friendship seemed to be slipping away as our paths divided.

As the week quickly sped by, my excitement turned to nervousness, and I began to have cold feet. I wondered why I had ever thought of leaving the only friends I had ever known and my village, full of happy memories. I visited the church and sat silently weeping in our old family pew, almost hearing and seeing Pa in the pulpit.

Oh my dear pa, he had been so helpful to me and so wise in dealing with my spiritual struggles. For a few years I had been a little Pharisee, thinking I (being a decent and respectable citizen) was good enough for God, but Pa's sermon on the text *"I came not to call the righteous, but sinners to repentance"* hit me powerfully. I gradually realised I was despising God's one and only way of salvation—the gift of His eternal Son the Lord Jesus. As Pa read John 3:16, *"For God so loved the world that he sent his only begotten Son, that whosoever believeth in him should not perish but have everlasting life"* and then later verse 18, *"He that believeth on him is not condemned; but he that believeth not is condemned already because he hath not believed in the name of the only begotten son of God,"* I realised that the greatest sin in all the world is not murder or committing some other gory crime, but not to believe and trust in Jesus Christ as the one and only Saviour of sinners. I pleaded with God to forgive my sins of unbelief and self-righteousness and asked Jesus to come into my heart.

Then one Easter, when I was fourteen years old, during the Good Friday service on the crucifixion, I was struck by how loving Jesus Christ was, to die a death He did not deserve and take our punishment for sin. I knew that my sins added to the heavy load He was bearing and my heart was filled with love and gratitude to Him. Now

I knew He was my Saviour; that He had taken my punishment for me and that I no longer had to face condemnation and hell. I had done nothing—He had done everything.

I knew He was strong and trustworthy enough to look after my soul for ever, and without a great thunder bolt from heaven or amazing religious experience, I just relaxed my weary soul onto Christ. My relief at having my inward struggle resolved was clear to my parents, and they were overjoyed.

I was keen to be confirmed and to declare my faith in Christ; when the day, a few months later, finally arrived, I hoped for a real sense of the Holy Spirit in my soul, confirming the step and filling me with joy and peace, but I felt absolutely nothing. I went through the motions, but inside I was as unfeeling as the pew I sat on. I thought more about my new gown and shoes than my God and Saviour. I was very disappointed and worried that I had been mistaken, but when I confided in Pa he assured me it was not unusual, and that we have to learn to trust God's unchanging Word more than our changing emotions. Oh how much I missed my dear parents' wisdom and prayers. I wondered how I could carry on without their wise, practical advice and their cheerful Christian example.

Then I visited our old garden (the forlorn vicarage now being locked and empty). So many happy hours had been spent there weeding the flower beds with Ma or harvesting the knobbly potatoes with Pa. I dug up Ma's favourite rose bush and transferred it to her and Pa's grave. The old cherry tree was just beginning to bloom, so I took some flowers to press and dry, and to keep forever in our old family Bible.

During that busy week, I walked around my favourite fields and paths. Pemfield village was situated on the Greensand Ridge, a gentle escarpment overlooking the beautiful Medway Valley, and my favourite paths were the ones offering an extensive view of the woods and fields below. I drank in the familiar sights and smells: the stream through the village that Bessie and I had dammed up so many times, the trees we had fallen out of, the bracken covered slopes we had made dens in, and the paths we had cartwheeled along. I gazed at oast houses, bare hop gardens, orchards, and meadows of Romney sheep and their skipping lambs. The scenes I had taken for granted all my life now seemed so beautiful and precious. I did not know when I would see them again, and I wanted to have a clear picture of them in my mind's eye as I travelled out of Kent for the first time. The thought that I would not be around to see spring turn into summer nearly brought fresh tears to my eyes, but I reminded myself that the seasons change even in remote East Sussex.

I must have slept for a few hours during the restless night before my departure, for I was startled by Mrs. Brown's wake-up call. My nervous excitement created the energy that a good night's sleep normally supplies and I, up with the lark, put on my new dress and finished packing my trunk. Mrs. Brown wanted me to eat a big, sustaining breakfast, but as I could hardly face a mouthful, she parcelled up some bread and cheese for the journey. Mr. Hicks, the local haulier, was going to town for market that morning, and it had been arranged that I would go with him and from there, get the stagecoach. He arrived all too soon, and I bade Miss Miller good-bye and then hugged and kissed Mrs. Brown. With wet eyes and a heavy heart, I climbed up beside Mr. Hicks. His mare began plodding along, carrying me away from my dear friends. I looked back at the ladies and waved and watched until we turned the corner and I could see them no more.

## CHAPTER 3

MR. HICKS WAS OBLIVIOUS TO the momentousness of the occasion and talked incessantly about his sow that was soon to farrow. As he warmed to his subject, I heard about the various pigs he had reared: which ones produced the best bacon, which one was an escapist, and so many other facts that I wished all his pigs were already sausages. I was only half listening, but my vague responses seemed to act as an encouragement for him to wax lyrical on his theme, and he was soon extolling the virtues of pig manure. When we finally got to the place where we parted company, he suddenly gained favour in my eyes for he was the last familiar face I might see for a long time. I bade him farewell with rather more reluctance than anticipated, half wishing I could travel back with him to our village and learn more about pig rearing.

I had never travelled by stagecoach before, so the novelty of the ride soon perked up my youthful spirits, and the whole trip once again seemed like an adventure. I wanted to sit outside in the fresh air but thought it might leave me looking too dishevelled for my forthcoming interview, so I sat inside and gazed out the window at new and interesting scenery. The rolling hills of Kent disappeared, and we rode through Ashdown Forest, then out the other side onto moorland. At last we came to Barton, where I alighted.

The village seemed much larger than mine, and I had no idea which way to go to reach Barton Manor, so I asked a woman who was getting in her washing. She pointed me in the right direction, and I soon came to the imposing gates of the estate. The drive seemed never ending and my trunk increasingly heavy.

At last I saw the manor and gasped at the size and grandeur of the house. It was built to impress—but my first thought was of the vast amount of dusting such a house would need—and the number of windows to clean! I hid behind a bush, rearranged my hair and bonnet, dusted off my shoes with the hem of my dress, and sent up a prayer for help before taking the path around to the back of the house where the servants' entrance was sure to be positioned.

I found the door and before my nerves failed me, I wiped my clammy hands on my dress and pulled the bell chain. I waited what seemed a long time and was just deliberating on whether to pull the chain again when a housemaid flung open the door. I was immediately impressed by her smart, neat uniform, and she seemed to be noticing my scruffiness as she slowly looked me up and down. I suddenly wished I had brought a small looking glass with me and had tidied myself more thoroughly.

"Err, good morning—" I began.

"Good afternoon," she corrected curtly.

"Yes, indeed, good afternoon. I have come to be interviewed for a housemaid's post."

"Name?"

"Rebecca Stubbs."

"Stubbs, you mean. Christian names ain't for the likes of us," she informed me as she let me through the door. I trotted along behind her as she led the way along a dark corridor smelling of boot polish. "Ya'll have to impress our 'ousekeeper, and that ain't easy."

"How can I impress her?" I asked, seeking some inside information.

"By working 'ard and not breaking nothing."

"I'll do my best," I assured her as we stopped at the housekeeper's door.

"Humph!" snorted the housemaid. "From the look of ya, ya won't last a week."

With that less than reassuring comment, she ushered me into the presence of the woman who was to determine my future. The housekeeper greeted me and offered me a seat at a table. She was a slightly plump, middle-aged woman with greying hair. She wore a white blouse with a lace collar and a long black skirt. From her waist hung a large set of keys, a mark of authority and responsibility. Her rather stern, lined face belied the fact that she had a warm smile, and I was sure that, given the correct circumstances, her eyes would twinkle. She introduced herself as Mrs. Milton.

Much to my surprise, she offered me a cup of tea, which I gratefully accepted. As she was busy pouring the water, I had the opportunity to look around me. Her room was clearly her little haven; a small range gave pleasant warmth to the room and nearby sat a couple of armchairs. She also had a desk under a window, where I assumed she did the household accounts. We sat up to a small, round dining table with a lace cloth, and under our feet was a tired-looking red carpet. As the tea brewed Mrs. Milton got down to business.

"So, Stubbs, I see that you have no experience whatsoever in domestic service, is that correct?"

"Yes, Mrs. Milton, I'm afraid it is," I admitted, wringing my hands under the table.

"So what makes you think you are suitable for this post?"

"Well, my mother instructed me fully in household chores and insisted on a high standard."

"Are you used to hard work?"

"My parents seemed to consider idleness a sin, ma'am, and worked hard from dawn to dusk in their parish and home and made sure I did the same."

"I think you will find it a bit different here to a cosy little parsonage," Mrs. Milton said witheringly.

"But please try me, ma'am. I will work hard and do my best for you," I pleaded.

As the conversation progressed it became increasingly obvious to both of us that my limited experience of domestic work at the vicarage was inadequate and pathetic. I realised I was unconvincing, but I was desperate to get the job and prove myself. I did not want to return to Pemfield and Mrs. Brown, having failed.

After drinking the last dregs of her tea, Mrs. Milton put down her cup with the conviction of one about to pronounce her final verdict. "Well, Stubbs, you definitely do not have the experience I would wish, and I fear that training you up will take some time—time we can scarcely afford." I nodded my agreement. "But you do seem fairly sensible," she continued, "and on the strength of that, I will give you one month's trial as the second housemaid." I started to smile and thank her, but she silenced me with a wave: "If you prove unsuitable, you will leave with just one week's wages, the rest having been deducted for your uniform, the effort you have cost me, and your board."

Once she had established that I knew the terms of employment, she went on to the rules of the house.

"What I am looking for is obedience and humility. Never forget your servile position in this house. Only speak to a member of the family if they speak to you, but never give your opinion. If you do speak, be brief and quiet and keep your hands behind your back. If a member of the family comes into a room whilst you are working, be as invisible as possible: stand next to the wall with your eyes to the floor. If, for some reason, you need to follow a member of the family, keep a respectful three paces behind them. Do your work as silently as possible."

I tried to look humble and willing as her voice droned on, but inside I was saying, *Well, Rebecca, wave good-bye to your name, your own will and desires; you are now a nobody, paid to work but not to think.*

"Am I making myself clear, Stubbs?" asked Mrs. Milton.

"Most clear, thank you, ma'am," I replied, rather startled (did she have powers over my mind already?).

"Good, then I will tell you about your position."

I would take my orders from Mrs. Milton and the first housemaid; under me was the third housemaid, but we were all to help each other for the smooth running of the household. Mrs. Milton emphasised that we were to take pride in our work, remembering that the standard of cleanliness and efficient running of the house reflected directly on the family we served.

The first housemaid, Emma, was called to show me to my room. I was relieved to hear Mrs. Milton calling her by her Christian name and soon learnt that in this household, surnames were rarely used among the female servants, in fact, only when you were in severe trouble. Emma was the girl who had opened the door to me. As I followed her up the long tiled staircase, she looked over her shoulder and said, "I still reckon you'll last only a week."

*Oh dear,* I thought. *This is the one that I need to be friends with, for she could make my life easier or harder at will, and we haven't exactly got off to a good start!*

Furthermore, it turned out that I was to share a bedroom with her. As I slung my trunk onto the bed and opened it up to unpack my few possessions, Emma exclaimed, "Wow, ya've got a lot!"

"I didn't know what to pack," I replied somewhat apologetically.

"I 'ad nothing to pack, so it made it easy." Emma laughed and then asked, "So 'ave ya got lots more at 'ome?"

"I haven't really got a home," I blurted out before I could think of a less dramatic response.

Emma sat down on her bed with a plonk. "No 'ome? A nice girl like ya? Wiv all them nice dresses?" Her lively eyes danced with the idea of scandal. "Were you chucked out?"

I hesitated, reluctant to share my story with a stranger and become an object of sympathy, but I equally did not want to become an object of speculation in the servant hall, so I briefly explained about my parents' deaths.

"And ya've got no sisters?" Emma asked, her brown eyes now filled with pity.

"No," I replied, "nor brothers."

"No grandparents ta take ya in?"

"No, only a stuck-up uncle," I answered, trying to lighten the mood whilst wiping my damp eyes.

"Well then," declared Emma as she put her arm around my shoulder, "ya just stay right here wiv us, cos we're more fun than any stuck-up uncle."

"But I'm here only for a week," I teased shyly.

"And so ya are," she laughed, as she left me to unpack. "But I am willing to be proved wrong."

## CHAPTER 4

THE FEMALE SERVANTS WERE HOUSED in attic rooms, which were light and airy with basic, functional furniture. I soon realised that the position of the rooms meant they were hot in summer and freezing in winter. Our small window had an extensive view—of the roof. The house was designed to hide all evidence of the servants' quarters, so our bedrooms looked out onto the gully between gables. The kitchen, scullery, numerous cold rooms and servants' hall were below ground level.

I soon learned that there were ninety-four steps between the lowest level and our bedrooms, and they were the last thing we wanted at the end of a long day. The male servants' quarters were in the basement, as far away from our quarters as possible. They did not have all the stairs to contend with, but were nearer the noise of the kitchen and they also suffered from rising damp and mildew during the winter.

I had the rest of the afternoon and evening to unpack and alter my uniforms so that they fit me. I was to wear a pink and white candy-striped dress with a large white apron and a white bonnet in the mornings, then change into a black dress with a lacy white apron and lacy bonnet for the afternoons. I quickly let down the hem and took in the seams to fit my long, slender frame, thankful for the first time that Ma had insisted on me laboriously acquiring dress-making skills. I buttoned myself into the afternoon uniform and looked in the looking glass. The blackness of the dress drained my eyes of their blueness, making them look grey. The severe, scalp-pulling bun I was forced to screw my wavy brown hair into, in order to perch the bonnet correctly on my head, produced an effect that could hardly be described as becoming. Bessie and I were once thought of as the beauties of the village. *You're on your own now, Bessie,* I thought ruefully as I resigned myself to my new, austere look. Then, getting back down to business, I wrote as promised to Mrs. Brown, describing the journey, the interview, and letting her know that I had the job (I did not feel she needed to know it might be only for a month).

I presented myself to Mrs. Milton for inspection, and after giving my uniform a few sharp tugs here and there to make it hang better, she was satisfied with the fit.

"But I can still see too much of your hair," she observed as she looked in her desk drawer for even more hairpins. "With bouncy hair like yours, you'll need a whole pack of pins."

Mrs. Milton proceeded to stab around, thrusting in her hairpins, ignoring my wincing, until she was satisfied and my scalp was sore.

My first meal in the servants' hall was daunting. Mrs. Milton ushered me in and introduced me to a sea of faces before taking her seat. At the top end sat Mrs. Milton, Mrs. Patterson the cook, and Mr. Carter the butler, and then going down the table in rank sat the master's valet and two ladies maids, the footmen, the housemaids, the laundry maids, then finally the scullery maids and house boys. I sat down next to Emma and was pleased when the food became the centre of attention rather than the newcomer. The conversation was stilted and mainly confined to the top end of the table; we were only to speak when spoken to by the upper servants. But at pudding time, the top trio retired to Mrs. Milton's room, leaving us lesser mortals to eat unsupervised. Conversation soon flowed, gossip of the day was exchanged, and the atmosphere lightened. But soon "them upstairs" began ringing the bells, and the servants attended to their evening duties.

I retired early, feeling rather shy and unsure of what was expected of me. Emma was still busy, and I was grateful to have the solitude to read my Bible and pray. I was thankful for journeying mercies and my new job, and I pleaded with the Lord to help me to do my work well, get on well with my fellow servants, and stay faithful to Him. After committing myself and my faraway friends into His hands, I fell asleep in my new bed.

At a quarter to six the next morning, with as much noise as she dared, Sarah, the third housemaid, brought Emma and me a cup of tea and a jug of hot water, thus announcing the beginning of our working day. We stumbled out of bed, had a quick wash, and struggled into our uniforms whilst sipping the hot, sweet tea, which would be our only sustenance for the next two hours. My first task of the day was to take a jug of warm water and a cup of tea to the first lady's maid. I tried to do this quietly and kindly, but I soon realised that I would be blamed if she went back to sleep, so I had to ensure she was properly awake. I had to put the saucer over the cup and walk briskly upstairs to ensure the tea was still warm after the long ascent. It did not take me long to conclude that the designer of the house had had a grudge against women.

Emma, Sarah, and I were to clean downstairs when the family was still upstairs and then prepare the dressing rooms for their ablutions and dressing; when they had vacated their chambers, we were to clean upstairs. Emma introduced me to the housemaids' closet and laughed as she saw my eyes widen at the array of equipment. It contained brushes for every situation: stove, banister, closet, curtains, furniture, and shoe brushes. Velvet and oil brushes. Carpet, wall, and bed brooms. Lotions and potions for all manner of cleaning. I was to learn all their uses and woe betide me if I used the wrong brush on the wrong surface!

Sarah and I went from hearth to hearth, removing yesterday's ashes, re-blacking the fireplace, and laying a new fire for the day. We lugged coal and logs from downstairs to each room, and once a fire was lit, it was our responsibility to keep it going for the day. Each room was to have a fire going, regardless of whether the family would use the room or not. We first crept quietly into the bedchambers and attended the fires to ensure the family had warmth when rising. It was hard in the dark not to bang the fender or the cinder pail, and while I was still learning the task, my inept clatter often resulted in an expletive from the slumberer. Once that rather tense task was completed, we hurried downstairs to prepare the house for a new day. Curtains and shutters were opened, letting in the pale morning sunlight. Rugs were removed and shaken—a job that I came to enjoy as it gave me a few breaths of fresh air and a brief excuse to be outside. Floors were swept and furniture dusted. Emma was responsible for cleaning all the precious ornaments, which obviously could not be touched by inferior hands. All cushions were pumped up to be soft and airy for the next person who sat on them.

By this time of the morning, the family members were beginning to stir, and we would tidy ourselves up and set about our next task of supplying vast amounts of hot water for bathing. Twice a week the tin hip bath was warmed by the fire, and then we struggled up three flights of stairs with large jugs of steaming water to the lady's maids, who prepared the baths for their mistresses. The lady's maids—Eliza and Jane—would be reprimanded if the quantity or heat of the water was substandard, or the timing was not as desired, and they in turn would berate us for letting them down. We had to be fast but careful that we were neither scalded by the hot water nor scolded by the lady's maids. I was often feeling faint with hunger by this stage and, if hurrying extra fast, I sometimes had to cling to the banister at the top of the stairs to hold myself steady before regaining my equilibrium. We were completely at the whim of the family; we could prepare a beautifully warm, full bath for one of the daughters, who might then decide she needed an extra hour of beauty sleep, thus creating more work for us.

After a welcome breakfast of creamy porridge and cups of tea, Emma, Sarah, and I cleaned the vacated bedchambers and dressing rooms. Eliza and Jane did some of the lighter cleaning, but we did the fires, emptied the chamber pots, and made the beds. The heavy feather mattresses needed beating, turning, and shaking into place until the feathers were well spread and even. I thought that if I was ever given the opportunity to lie on one of those soft beds, I would sleep for a week. Sarah and I did the mattresses together, while Emma arranged the bed linen required. Mrs. Milton kept a tally of all the linen in use, and Emma would ask for more from the locked linen cupboard if needed.

I had hardly been at the manor a week when, one morning, all the housemaids were summoned to Mrs. Milton's parlour.

"We're in for it now," muttered Emma as we stood nervously outside, straightening our aprons and caps before finding the courage to knock on the door and learn of our transgression.

The cause of angry alarm was an audacious bed-bug biting Miss Davenport. The bug's actions had been reported to Mrs. Davenport, who immediately called for Mrs. Milton and berated her for allowing sloppy bed-airing to take place. We were then of course summoned to be severely admonished for this poor work. We all stood in a line looking contrite, but inside I was boiling with anger. The young ladies often lay in bed far longer than was planned, not realising or caring that their lie-in upset our routine. Beds had to be made before midday, so sometimes we could not air the beds for as long as was ideal. I wanted to open my mouth and explain fully, but Emma kicked my foot to shut me up, and Mrs. Milton made it abundantly obvious that our only reply was to be an apology, which we duly muttered and escaped.

"If ya wanna keep ya job, ya need to keep ya mouth shut, and preferably ya brain too," warned Emma, but the wink that accompanied her words revealed that she felt as infuriated as I did.

Although the footmen were responsible for most of the lamps in the house, we had to clean and trim the ones in the ladies' bedchambers. When our morning routine was completed, Mrs. Milton would allocate us a number of rooms that needed a clean-through. In this way all the rooms in the house had a good clean at least once a week. In the summer, our routine work was somewhat reduced as we did not have to light and maintain fires in each room, and did not have to contend with the huge amounts of dust that open fires produce.

However, there was no time for taking it easy, for Mrs. Milton filled our time with spring cleaning and mending.

Any spare time of an evening was spent in the servants' hall. A piano and old armchairs were provided for our entertainment and comfort. Some of us knitted or sewed, others read the newspaper or a book, and often there was a buzz of conversation. At any time our relaxation could be disturbed by a bell signalling some large or trivial task awaiting upstairs. We would groan and, depending which bell was swinging, the appropriate servant would attend.

The Matrimonial Causes Act had been passed the previous year, and the Divorce Court had been set up, so every day the newspapers were full of the lurid and lascivious details of the strange matrimonial goings on of the elite. Mr. Davenport's newspaper found its way to the servants' hall every evening and became the highlight of the footmen's evenings as they read out these smutty reports. The daily diet of these stories did nothing to recommend our superiors—rather, we realised they were superior to us only in secrecy, hypocrisy, and deceit. It was especially horrifying, yet gratifying to read of well-known persons who had dismissed servants with pharisaical sternness for some minor moral misdeed, only to be publicly exposed for their own longstanding and complex extra-marital liaisons. Often the conversation in the hall became crude and raucous, and although I admit to finding it amusing, I also felt uncomfortable and preferred to retire. I knew this made me seem prim and humourless, and at times like that I longed for the congenial company I once knew—especially dear Pa and Ma.

After a hard day's work when I was feeling stiff and sore, it was not unusual for me to lie in bed sobbing for my parents and my old life, with a heart full to bursting point with longing and sadness. As the breeze of the evening wafted into my attic room I remembered the companionable evenings at the vicarage. While Ma pottered about the garden dead-heading her roses in the cool of the day and Pa tended his vegetable patch, whistling a hymn tune to himself as he worked, I would sit on the wide sitting room window ledge reading a book, absorbed in the story, but ever conscious of the scene outside the window, the scent of roses and cut grass and hope that Ma would not notice the lateness of the hour and send me to bed. Other times, as I lay on my saggy servant's bed, I remembered Ma and Pa's loving embrace as they tucked me up in bed and then sang an evening hymn with me. It was easy to delay proceedings by asking Pa difficult questions just as he was saying goodnight. As my mind filled with these beautiful memories and my eyes filled with tears, only stubborn pride kept me from rushing back to Pemfield and admitting that I had made a mistake.

Day in, day out, from dawn to dusk, I swept and scrubbed, brushed and polished. My body ached all over, and my hands dried, cracked, bled, and chapped. I learned to sprinkle fresh tea leaves on carpets before brushing them to help pick up the dust and give off a pleasant aroma. I learned how to make furniture polish from turpentine, vinegar, linseed oil, and spirits of wine, and the correct use of emery powder, common asphaltum, and muriatic antimony in cleaning and polishing. None of these substances were designed to relieve my sore hands. My knees became dry and hardened from washing the vast entrance hall and brushing the long staircases, so parts of me began to look and feel a decade older than my real age.

The more I learnt about the internal life of the manor, the more I was surprised and perplexed at the way two groups of people could live in the same house, both mutually dependent on each other, yet hold one another in contempt. The servants were quick to secretly mock their employers, and the family viewed their servants as a necessary evil. The rules about our conduct in front of them seemed designed to reinforce the idea that we were beneath them. When I was sweaty from hard work and had permanently black nails from soot and I met a well-groomed, beautifully dressed, and sweet-smelling lady, I began to feel worthy of their disdain. I had to check these thoughts by reminding myself that my physical appearance only reflected on the honest, hard work I was doing and was nothing to be ashamed of.

During that first month, I had vast amounts to learn and get used to—I was so exhausted that I just worked, ate, and slept. At the end of the month, Mrs. Milton called me aside and said she was satisfied with my standard of work and that I pulled my weight; therefore, I could remain in the establishment as a permanent second housemaid. I thanked her profusely, but she brushed my gratitude aside, ordering me to quickly change my attire and have a half day holiday. I ran to tell Emma.

"I've proved you wrong. I have not only stayed a week, I have stayed a month and have been told I can stay permanently!"

"Well, I never," Emma said with an easy laugh. "Standards 'ave slipped, but I must admit, I 'ave never been so 'appy to be proved wrong. Now get along with ya before ya 'alf day disappears before ya very eyes."

CHAPTER 5

AS I BECAME MORE CONFIDENT in my work, I had time to notice the people around me and how they interacted. My master, Mr. Davenport, was part of the landed gentry, living solely off the rents he received from the tenant farmers on his large estate. He did not waste his time or talent on the practical details of managing and maintaining his vast acreage but left this entirely to his estate manager. With no business cares to trouble him, he was able to devote his time and energy to his great passions of shooting, hunting, and fishing. I learned from a stable lad that his horses were kept in better housing than his staff; they had brand new stables with modern under floor heating. Mr. Davenport was under the illusion that bursts of outrage and fits of temper were signs of power and manliness, while attributes like forbearance, patience, and forgiveness were for lesser men and the weaker sex. His love of fine food and wine had left him with a portly figure, but he walked with a strut of self-importance, reminding me of a robin red-breast.

Mrs. Davenport was chosen by her husband in the similar way he might choose a new mare. She came from good stock and had fine looks, a mild temperament, and hopefully could produce an heir. She had indeed fulfilled her obligations and provided her husband with two sons, an heir and "a spare," as well as two daughters. As a great lover of peace, much of her time and energy was given to keeping each family member happy, but she had neither the wit nor wisdom to negotiate lasting peace treaties. As the mistress of the house, her incompetence and neediness could be exasperating, but it also inspired our pity and loyalty.

When I joined the household, Miss Davenport and Miss Annabel were aged seventeen and fifteen respectively. They were still being tutored by a governess, but lessons were held only when nothing more important was taking place. The harassed governess had been given responsibility but no authority and was often frustrated by her impossible role. The young ladies had no natural thirst for knowledge, and the governess lacked the imagination to make lessons exciting; this combination resulted in their education being very superficial. Indeed, their father discouraged too much "book knowledge" but was anxious that his girls be accomplished in all "ladylike" skills such as needlework, music, and dance. The girls were brought up to please and captivate men but were not equipped to make sound moral judgments, and no one seemed to notice that this was a recipe for disaster. Emma accurately but rather cruelly pointed out that their greatest protection from men's unwanted attention was their unfortunate looks. Indeed, their lady's maids had the huge task of finding ways of creating beauty where nature had not. They used elaborate lotions to tame their hair and tried many modern beauty concoctions to enhance their eyes, cheeks, or lips. We benefited from this, as any rejected or old lotions were passed on to us.

Miss Davenport and Miss Annabel had spent more time in the company of hired servants than their own parents. From infancy, I was told, they were in the care of a nanny and nursery nurse, seeing their mother only when she visited the nursery or sent for them. An official daily viewing of the infants took place after dinner, with the girls dressed in their prettiest clothes, but at that late hour the poor girls were usually tired and did not always comply with their father's wishes, so he often sent them back to the nursery in disgrace. Mrs. Davenport was not without natural motherly affections, but this is how she had been brought up and to her it was the "right thing to do." Her loving but inept attempts at dressing, soothing, and feeding her offspring were greeted with sighs and tuts from the experienced nanny; Ma'am soon realised her presence was not welcome in the nursery, so in order to keep the peace, she reluctantly retreated. The girls had spent many happy hours in the kitchen, playing in the sinks or licking bowls or in the servants' hall playing games with the houseboy, who was only a few years older. But as they grew older, they "put away childish things." The very people who had often given them piggy-back rides or kissed their grazed knees were now treated with disdain and aloofness.

I did not meet the two sons until the summer vacation, as they were termly boarders at a respectable and costly private school. Master Charles and Master Bernard were lively lads who shared their father's love of outdoor pursuits. They had more of their mother's mild temperament than their father would have liked, but he did his best to toughen them up. At the ages of twelve and ten, they were still not above visiting us below stairs and would proudly bring pheasants they had shot or fish they had caught for our inspection and admiration. In return, they were rewarded with freshly baked biscuits or treats.

The Davenports were also wards of an orphan son of Ma'am's late sister. For the last eight years, Mr. Davenport had been the reluctant guardian of this unfortunate boy who had lost his mother to consumption and his father in a railroad disaster. Master Edward Thorpe had been given the same opportunities as the other children in the household, but he was taught that he was slightly below them in rank. He was always to show gratitude and humility for being allowed the honour of living in their house. Mrs. Davenport was incapable of expressing her love, even to her own offspring, so she was unable to comfort the grieving boy she hardly knew. Master Edward found a mother figure in the governess and was the darling of all the staff. Master Edward was now at Oxford University studying law, being of the lower ranks that have to live by the sweat of their brow. Once again, I did not meet Master Edward until his vacation.

The whole Davenport family was privileged with all that wealth and influence could provide, but the head of the house did nothing for their spiritual well-being, apart from insisting all attend the Sunday morning service at the local church. From one Sunday morning to another, not a word or deed would indicate that the family had any concern for their eternal welfare or that of their staff. In many big houses, there would be a time of daily prayers that all the household would be expected to attend, but nothing like that occurred at Barton Manor. I enjoyed the company of my fellow servants and, on the whole, they were a decent and honest team, but I lacked true Christian companionship. No one else seemed to understand that Christianity was a living, personal relationship with the Saviour rather than a vague assent to the Apostles' Creed.

This lack of understanding was surprising, as the preaching of the vicar, Reverend Penfold, was clear and biblical. He did not hesitate to preach "the whole council of God," warning of sin, judgment, and eternal damnation and then recommending Christ, His work, and perfect sacrifice. He presented Christ as a most suitable and willing Saviour, one who was truly God and truly man. He showed believers their security in Christ, based on His great promises, faithful love, and limitless power. He encouraged believers to look to Christ for assurance rather than for certain emotions in their own fickle hearts.

I found Reverend Penfold's sermons of great comfort and encouragement. When I considered the privilege of being in Christ, I would not swap my place with the richest person in England. I was sad to see my fellow servants and the family sit through powerful sermon after powerful sermon, week after week, with no apparent impression being made.

Homesickness often wafted over me on Sundays. There was no one to discuss the service with, no sense of the day being special and holy or a day for God-given relaxation. My mind often went to the companionable evenings snuggled up with a religious book by a roaring fire eating toasted tea cakes, or the first Sundays of every month, when after the evening service, all were invited to our house for hymn singing and supper. Many people came, young and old. Miss Miller played the piano in our parlour and anyone could choose a hymn. We usually had soprano, alto, tenor, and bass singers present and the harmonised singing was beautiful; so beautiful that old Mrs. Grey always nodded off, until the clatter of tea cups woke her and her appetite. I am sure a musician would have found many a fault with our amateur rendition of the hymns, but I had never heard such lovely, heart-warming singing, and I longed to hear it again. After about eight hymns, or when our throats were too dry, Ma and I would make the tea and bring in the scones and cakes. The older people tended to stay in the parlour, but the younger ones often drifted into the kitchen and we would sit around the large table chatting and laughing. Sometimes the parlour crowd was noisier than the kitchen group, but it was often the other way around. The parlour people had more of a sense of what were suitable "Sunday subjects" than the youngsters, so became less exuberant. But all that now seemed a million miles away and a different life altogether.

Mrs. Milton was kind enough to allow me time off to attend the Sunday evening service most weeks. I knew this would give extra work to Emma and Sarah, so I tried to do more chores other evenings. The congregation in the evening was very small, and soon I began to recognise people and be recognised. In the morning I was there as a housemaid of the Davenports, but in the evening I was there as Rebecca Stubbs. Before long I was invited to various older parishioners' homes for cups of tea on my half day. These little social events were enjoyable, reminding me of the village life I had left behind in Kent. I felt valued once more for the person I was rather than for the tasks I could perform. The work at the manor was absorbing, taking up so much of my time, energy, and thoughts that it was refreshing to remember that there was a life beyond its ornate walls.

I particularly enjoyed the hospitality of Mr. and Mrs. Crookshank, the local butcher and his wife. They were a middle-aged couple, and their children had all left home. Mrs. Crookshank would sit and listen to my stories of life at the manor and tell me her family news. Their little home was always calm and inviting, and I felt that here was a place where I could relax and be myself; indeed, during my first few months at the manor, when I was tired all the time, I sometimes had a nap in an armchair by the stove as Mrs. Crookshank prepared the evening meal. Other times I would help her in their small kitchen garden, enjoying the fresh air and genial company. I spent the afternoon of my eighteenth birthday with the Crookshanks, having been given a half day off, but I felt so disinclined to celebrate the day and so loath to lumber anyone with the responsibility of making it special for me, that I did not inform them of the day's significance. On the way home I popped to the baker and bought myself an iced bun. This was a mistake, for as I sat on the grass verge to eat it, I remembered Ma baking me birthday cakes and letting me lick out the bowl. My eyes filled with tears and the bun turned to sawdust in my mouth.

My role of housemaid seemed repetitive and mundane, but I soon realised that further down the servant ladder was a far less enviable role—that of the scullery maid, Nancy. She worked from dawn to dusk in the hot, steamy scullery, enduring the wrath of the kitchen maids and the explosive nature of the cook. All the glass and silverware was cleaned and cared for by the footmen, but all the dirtiest, greasiest pots and pans were scrubbed and rescrubbed day by day by poor Nancy. She was also responsible for keeping the various ranges burning and so had to start her day early to ensure the fire was well established and the kettle boiling before the cook entered her domain. The kitchen maids delegated most of the scrubbing of vegetables and plucking of fowls to the hapless girl, ensuring that she didn't stop from morning to night. I soon learned that Nancy was from the workhouse and did not know her exact age but was told by the workhouse superintendent that she was about fourteen.

Nancy knew nothing about her family. Her whole life had been dominated by hard labour and an indoctrination of her worthlessness. She could not read or write and had no ambition beyond keeping out of trouble. The workload at Barton Manor was no worse than what she had been used to all her life since she could walk, and the living conditions, especially the meals, were far superior, so she was content in her own pathetic way. She worked with neither enthusiasm nor resentment, but plodded through her tasks like a pony plodding in a treadmill. She had learned to expect harsh words and never kindness. Her loveless life had made her incapable of feeling—or at least showing—any emotion.

My parents had spent much of their time helping people in need and had instilled this principle in me, so I was naturally moved by Nancy's plight and desperately wanted to help her. The whole pecking order of the staff made it almost impossible to show concern and offer help, as it would be seen as neglecting my own chores and position. Even the staff's attitude indicated their belief that Nancy should be grateful for the opportunity to work in such a great house, as if her low start to life was of her own making.

One night after a particularly elaborate dinner party that had created a huge burden of extra work on all the staff, I was finally free to climb the stairs to bed at one o'clock in the morning, but just then I saw Nancy alone in the scullery with piles of pots to scrub. I knew she had risen at five o'clock that morning to light the stoves, and I felt for her. I fought my overwhelming tiredness, rolled up my sleeves, and started washing up alongside her. Her incredulous look either expressed gratitude or the belief that I was deranged. We quickly finished off the washing up and headed wearily for bed.

Mrs. Milton seemed all-knowing at times, and this was one of them; the next day I was called into her room and told in no uncertain terms not to interfere with other people's work, as it would leave me less able to perform my own tasks and would undermine the structure of the household. The vicarage at Pemfield seemed so far away from Barton Manor, not only in miles, but also in attitudes, principles, and priorities. Without the plumb-line of the Bible to guide me, I would have been reeling in confusion. Even with the teaching of Scripture in mind, I felt confused and at a lost to know how I was to act out my Christian faith in a house full of manmade rules, where I was paid to work and not to think.

## CHAPTER 6

ONE OF THE FEW PERKS of the job was the freedom to borrow books from the family's large library. The library was my favourite place to work. It was on the first floor, and its windows overlooked the extensive gardens. A huge fireplace dominated one wall, but on either side were dark wooden bookshelves. The opposite wall had three large windows with dark red velvet curtains. The other two walls were covered in bookshelves from floor to ceiling. The floor was of highly polished wood, with a large red rug in the middle; there were various little tables with chairs for reading and two comfortable chairs by the fire. The bookshelves were full of beautifully bound books, most of them old, but a few were from recent years.

Mr. Davenport's grandfather had been a keen reader and had set up the library, which reflected his wide and varied interests. All books were meticulously set out in subject groups, the obscurer the subject, the higher the bookshelf. Servants could avail themselves of any of the books, but we had to sign them out using a register and, of course, all books had to be kept in pristine condition. If a member of the family wanted a book that was being read by a servant, they could identify who had the book from the register and immediately ask for it to be returned. This had been the system in the household for two generations and no one could fault it—mainly because no one used the library now.

Every Tuesday, one of my afternoon tasks was to clean the library, while Emma cleaned the silver and Sarah the billiard room. I carefully dusted the long, wooden shelves of the library, and as I did so, I got to know the books on them. During any rare, quiet intervals of the day, I would rush to the library, borrow a book, and take it to my room for perusal at my leisure. I became rather embarrassed at the long list of "Rebecca Stubbs" in the register, but not embarrassed enough to stop borrowing. I read books on natural history, the kings and queens of England, and many of the (rather heavy going) Puritan writers. Each book took me a long time to read, as I managed to read only a few paragraphs every night before sleep overtook me. As our supply of candles was strictly rationed, I bought my own, and while Emma was applying her nightly face cream and putting rags in her hair, I would curl up in bed and read. Emma warned this was bad for my sight and would give me wrinkles around my eyes, but she did not complain about the extra candlelight.

One June evening, as I walked into the room to return a book, I realised one of the family was in the library. I hastened toward the door, but a voice I had not heard before said, "Stop." Looking around, I saw a blond young man coming toward me with a grin.

"Aha, I have caught the bookworm red-handed, coming to devour yet another tome," he said.

"No, sir, I have come to return one," I replied.

"Then I'd better not continue my bookworm metaphor, as to regurgitate a book sounds rather crude, doesn't it?"

I nodded and smiled, and then he went on. "So you must be the Rebecca Stubbs who has an uninterrupted line of signatures in the register book."

I said "Yes, sir" as he walked up to take the book out of my hand.

"*Expository Thoughts on the Gospel of Matthew* by J. C. Ryle? Why, that is one of my books!" the young man exclaimed.

"Oh, I apologise," I said quickly.

"No need for that. On the contrary, I am delighted the books I left here have, much to my surprise, been read."

"And heartily enjoyed, sir," I replied with more freedom than before. "I am much indebted to you."

Once again, he waved my comment away. "Not in the least. I am delighted that you have read and enjoyed them, just as I did."

The incident gave me something new to think about, and I went to bed lighter-hearted, knowing there was another person under the roof who was interested in the writings of a Church of England vicar. The next Sunday evening in church, I noticed that the young man, whom I had learned was Master Edward, not only sat in the congregation but was treated as an expected attendant of this service. He was welcomed back with warmth and affection rather than deference and awe.

By now I had been able to do a quick study of his features and noticed that he was of average build, had blond hair, blue eyes, and a ready smile. He had youthful looks but could look much more mature when deep in thought. That night I questioned Emma a little about Master Edward. She had heard that his parents had been "religious" and his bereavement had made him "very serious."

The next Tuesday when I arrived at the library to clean, Master Edward was sitting there reading. I apologised for disturbing him and was about to withdraw, but he beckoned me in.

"I was pleased to see you at the Sunday evening service," he said.

"Yes, I try and attend as often as work permits, sir," I replied.

"How long have you been working here?" he asked.

"Since April, sir."

"Have any of the church members befriended you?"

The congregation's freeness with him gave me courage to treat him in a less stilted manner, and we were soon talking about the church and the congregation. As the minutes passed I began to get restless and finally said, "Excuse me, sir, but if I tarry any longer talking, I will get into trouble with Mrs. Milton."

"Of course, how silly of me!"

"But I could dust and talk at the same time, sir."

"What an excellent idea, then I will continue to tell you all I know about the Crookshanks."

This brief exchange of observations was enjoyable and gave me something to think about for the rest of the day.

I hoped that we would get another opportunity to talk. I was annoyed with myself that an insignificant conversation, which he had probably forgotten by now, could be mulled over so much by me. I clearly lacked interests and excitement in my restricted, monotonous life.

Sunday evenings now gave me a two-fold pleasure: First, I enjoyed attending the church service, and second, afterwards Master Edward would often catch me up as I walked back to the manor and we would have about twenty minutes to chat. The footpath from the village to the manor was secluded, leaving the village at a stile and then crossing a small wood that was carpeted with bluebells in spring. The path then crossed a corner of the estate's park before climbing steeply up to the gardens. The hedge that surrounded the garden gave privacy to the path, so we could walk with very little fear of being seen. Walking seemed to make us feel freer to talk, and it was not long before we were sharing with each other stories from our childhood.

We had both known what it was to love and lose both our parents and could sympathise with each other in a way very few people can. Master Edward's mother had been weak with consumption as long as he could remember. She had been a God-fearing woman, and her religious persuasions caused friction between her and her family. They were further alienated from her when she met Master Edward's father, who was a highly skilled engineer working for the railways. His Christianity and station in life made him a very poor choice of partner in her parents' sight, and she married without their blessing or money. Master Edward's parents (Mr. and Mrs. Thorpe) lived happily and comfortably in Hampshire and were delighted when young Edward was born. From very early on in life, Master Edward was taught Bible knowledge and doctrine, and this was matched with the consistent lives of his parents. When Edward was ten, his mother finally succumbed to the illness that had beset her all her adult life. When Edward was twelve, he embraced Christianity for himself. Mr. Thorpe and Edward muddled together the best they could without Mrs. Thorpe, but tragically Mr. Thorpe was killed by an explosion at the railway, along with five other men. Master Edward had previously had very little to do with his mother's sister's family, apart from the occasional visit at Michaelmas, but within days of hearing of his double loss, they came to fulfil their guardianship duties toward him, and thus he had come to live at Barton Manor.

The walk from the church to the manor now seemed far too short, and we sometimes lingered along the way, but I was always very conscious of needing to be back in time to fulfil my evening duties.

Our "accidental" meetings in the library on Tuesdays also became a regular occurrence and one that filled me with great pleasure. Master Edward often had an amusing cartoon from *Punch* or an interesting article ready to show me. One Tuesday, Emma decided that she needed to help me in the library, and I could hardly conceal my disappointment. Was I flattering myself, or did Master Edward look disappointed too? Whatever his feelings, he soon left the library.

Now thoughts of Master Edward filled my waking moments, and his name entered into my every prayer. Had our stations in life not fixed such a gulf between us, I was sure I would have fallen in love with him. It seemed to me that the summer was progressing with undignified haste, and I dreaded the day that Master Edward would return to Oxford to start a new university term. Any interruption to our Tuesday meeting in the library was frustrating, as was the knowledge that Mrs. Milton or Emma could inadvertently stop them at will. Master Edward and I soon found that we shared the same interest in watching people and spotting their oddities; his impressions of his cousins left us weak with laughter. But we could also have good conversations about spiritual matters or concerns and seemed to be in agreement on most matters of a theological nature. During August, by agreement, we both read the same book by a Puritan writer and spent some time each Tuesday afternoon or Sunday evening discussing the

THE VICAR'S DAUGHTER    61

content. He teased me about my being the widest-read housemaid in the country, and I retorted that I could limit my conversation to mixtures for various polish recipes if he preferred.

This friendship of laughter and discussion meant a great deal to me, but I still did not know whether he valued it as highly as I did. He was the only one I could confide in so freely, but I did not know if I was just one of a number to him. These questions went around and around my mind as I worked. In normal circumstances, I would have confided in Emma and asked her opinion, but as Master Edward was one of the family that employed me, I felt my familiarity with him may be deemed inappropriate and presumptuous. I also knew that if I tried to explain about our friendship, she might belittle or sully it.

The inevitable final Sunday evening walk came all too quickly, and we ambled as slowly as possible along the pathway, knowing that the next morning, before dawn, Master Edward was to leave for Oxford. I tried to sound cheerful and interested in his studies, but my heart was heavy, and I had a lump in my throat. I was pleased that the gathering dusk hid some of the emotion written on my face. As we said farewell, Master Edward grasped both my hands and said he would remember me and pray for me. He went on to say that he was grateful we had met each other, as I was the easiest person to talk to he had ever known. I wished him every blessing for the new term, and we parted company. As soon as I possibly could, I rushed to my bed and cried into my pillow. My heart was full of sadness at his departure and the warmth of his kind words. I had never felt so close to him or so far away.

## CHAPTER 7

I AWOKE THE NEXT MORNING with swollen eyes and a dull headache. I had never felt so reluctant about going to work; brushing and dusting all day with no prospect of an unexpected sighting of Master Edward seemed tedious and futile. I dragged myself through my duties with my overactive mind mulling over last night's parting. I wished I had a reliable friend who could interpret men for me. Even having a brother might have helped. Was Master Edward's warm farewell merely brotherly? If it was, was it appropriate for a man to be brotherly to someone who is not his sister? As I scrubbed the stairs, my thoughts on the matter changed with every step I cleaned, and I left the task no more decided on the subject than when I began.

My other hope was that Master Edward might write to me. Half of me dismissed this idea as ludicrous. How many Oxford scholars write to housemaids? But how many Oxford scholars leave housemaids in such a friendly manner? I hoped against hope, but the days passed and no communication came for me—just as I had expected, but I was sorely disappointed. I realised Master Edward met and socialised with many interesting people, and a housemaid who may have seemed vaguely interesting in the surrounding intellectual wilderness of his aunt's home would soon pale into insignificance compared with the brilliant minds of Oxford. Yet, I argued with myself, had we met in another situation, for example in Pemfield, we would have not been so very different in estate. This drew my thoughts on to think about one's class and position in life. Was it based on our parents' lot in life, or money, family name, education, or purely one's present circumstances? Was it right or biblical to question one's place in society, or should we always "be content with such things as ye have"?

As I got more accustomed to my work, it seemed laughable that at one time I didn't know a banister broom from a staircase broom, or the recipe for furniture paste. I was less exhausted at the end of the day, and although the job occupied me physically, my mind was free to wander and ponder. I watched the daily lives of Miss Davenport and Miss Annabelle, and I began to wonder who really led the most restricted life: the servants or the served? Their lives were dictated by tradition and family expectations from birth. Unless they married "well," they would be social failures and nobodies. To marry well often meant suspending one's own dreams of Mr. Right and marrying a man of wealth whose family reflected the values and interests of your own, no matter how ugly, old, obnoxious, or incompatible he might be.

It had been decided that Miss Davenport should have her coming out at the next London season. The family would arrive in London during May for the opening of the exhibition at the Royal Academy of Arts and would spend two months in the capital, socialising in a far larger and "more suitable" circle than their country life at Barton Manor allowed. Mrs. Davenport had been complaining for years, or so I was told, that there was such a limited selection of notable families in their part of Sussex to invite to dinner, and the locals were more likely to talk about turnips and cabbages than Turner and

Constable. Now, at last, they were going to immerse themselves in a society worthy of them.

Although it was only October, the young ladies were already full of dreams of concerts, balls, dinners, visits, exhibitions, and strolls in parks. They would meet other lively girls—so unlike their parents' normal visitors—and be introduced to handsome and admiring men. Society would be amazed that two of its most sparkling treasures had remained hidden in the provinces for so long.

Their excitement was infectious, causing Eliza and Jane to talk about nothing else as they helped to plan wardrobes, try out new hairstyles, and mix up new beauty treatments. The weekly *Home Notes* magazine was studied with great enthusiasm, especially the "Fashions from Paris" page, where the latest patterns were discussed and recommended. Paper patterns were now also available to reproduce Paris fashions accurately—even in remote, rural Barton.

It made us smile that more material was used for the elaborate sleeves than for the narrow waists. But secretly we all longed to try them on and look glamorous for once. The fashionable dresses were clearly not made for women who had to do anything more than look decorative. Suddenly, the normal frocks of the two girls seemed most outdated and provincial, so they were discarded, much to the delight of the lady's maids who acquired them. Eliza and Jane were to accompany the ladies to the great metropolis, and as neither had been there before, they were looking forward to their own adventures. Emma, Sarah, and I were willing volunteers for any new hairstyle that needed to be practised, but Mrs. Milton made it clear that no such elaborate style should be worn by us "above stairs," as it was not befitting of our rank. Laughter rang from our rooms as styles were attempted and aborted.

We housemaids had more mundane matters to attend to—all the light muslin curtains had to be taken down and replaced by heavy velvet ones for the winter. The weight of yards of velvet made our arms ache as we stood on wobbly ladders. The only people who hated this change of curtains more were the poor laundry girls who had to carefully wash and store them.

The colder weather also hailed the return of the open fires and hauling coal and logs from room to room, with all the extra cleaning involved. The daily chore of blacking the grates was back, along with the vexation of fires that failed to light or smoke that blew into the room. I liked to consider myself an expert at efficient fire lighting, but a cold chimney and an unfavourable wind could cause hours of extra work. Indeed, my precious half day off was sometimes eaten into as I became late in doing the prescribed duties, due to a difficult fire. Sometimes I secretly resorted to the forbidden trick of soaking paper with turpentine to get a reluctant fire going, but Mrs. Milton considered this wasteful and dangerous.

The excitement of the proposed London visit and the daily grind of work did little to erase thoughts of Master Edward from my mind. I was sometimes annoyed with him and felt that he had trifled with my feelings, but then I would blame myself for exaggerating a normal friendship into a romance in my fanciful imagination. I could not talk to Emma about Master Edward, but we could discuss men in general. She had strong views on their behaviour and said that their brain was wired differently from a women's and that we would never be quite able to understand them. The type of women men like as friends are rarely the type that they eventually marry, she propounded, and all logic and sense seems to desert them as they choose their life-partner. I wondered aloud if Christian men were the same, but Emma retorted that the best of men are men at best.

Some winter evenings, Sarah would visit our bedroom and would curl up at the bottom of my bed; then she, Emma, and I would talk about our dreams for the future. The flickering candlelight would produce a cosy and intimate atmosphere, and we would open our hearts to each other.

"Of course, what I want is an 'andsome man," Emma said with a sigh.

"Don't we all?" I replied, laughing.

"A young vicar would suit our Rebecca well, wouldn't 'e?" suggested Emma.

"I could do a lot worse," I reasoned.

"Well, we all know what Sarah wants, don't we?" teased Emma, winking.

The colour rose in Sarah's cheeks. "What do you know?"

"Everyone knows," we teased her.

She sat up. "Knows what?"

"About your little soft spot for the under-gard'ner," Emma said, watching Sarah's reaction intensely.

"Oh, you mustn't!" Sarah pressed her palms to her reddened face.

"Don't be alarmed. We've known for a long time, and we honestly wish you well and hope you get him," I said, feeling for her distress and knowing that I had a bigger secret to hide.

"But what if we don't get married?" I asked, trying to change the subject.

"I'd be a real lady's maid," replied Emma. "Not a lady like one of ours 'ere, but a real one—a proper titled one who travels abroad and takes me with 'er. I would see all the sights, then meet me an 'and-some, rich man and abandon the 'elpless lady for wedded bliss!"

We hugged our knees under the covers and laughed at this idea.

"And what about you, Sarah?" I asked.

"I would become a nursery nurse for a good family," she said, looking into the far distance.

Emma and I exchanged a knowing look – a person who cannot be trusted to dust a precious ornament without dropping it was highly unlikely to be trusted with holding an upper-class heir.

Emma turned to me. "What if ya parson don't turn up?"

"Then he'll have to mourn his loss!" I answered and immediately ducked to avoid a flying pillow.

"You, not 'im," Emma said with a chuckle.

"Oh, me?" I replied in mock surprise. "Well, I would become a housekeeper in a big establishment. I would buy turpentine by the gallon for lighting fires and provide hand salve for the housemaids, who would, of course, love me and realise their good fortune in working for me."

"And ya'd give them good quality candles," added Emma.

"And allow them followers," Sarah chipped in, showing where her mind was.

"And more half days," I suggested.

"All very nice I am sure, girls, but look at ya candle, Sarah. Unless ya 'op it quick, ya won't get ta ya room before it dies out!" declared Emma, thus ending our enjoyable conversation and ensuring we got to sleep before midnight.

I was keenly aware of the wide difference in circumstances be-tween Emma and Sarah, and myself. Their wages were sent, almost intact, back to their families, who relied heavily on their contributions, whereas I was able to use my money (after buying hairpins) as I wished. I tried not to flaunt my comparative wealth and was always pleased when I could buy them a small luxury or when they could enjoy my candlelight.

Sarah's home was only about two miles from the manor, and she sometimes went there on her half days off. When she came back full of stories of her mother's baking, father's news, and younger siblings' latest achievements, Emma always looked anxiously at me, as if afraid it would rub salt into my wound of being without family. I loved her for her awareness and sensitivity. She had received very little schooling, but she was an excellent observer and learned much through watching others. As the middle child in a large family, she had learned to fight her corner and get herself heard.

My friends at Pemfield were in no wise forgotten, and I often wrote to Miss Miller and Mrs. Brown. Mrs. Brown was not good at "words on paper," but Miss Miller kept me up to date regularly with the village news. I was always delighted to see a letter waiting for me in the servants' hall to inform me of recent births, deaths, or romances in the village. I was also told about which vegetables had done well in the schoolhouse garden this year, how many bushels of apples were stored in the loft for winter, and even how many piglets Mr. Hicks' sow had reared.

My half days were spent either at Mrs. Crookshank's home or, if the weather was favourable, with a long walk, armed with something tasty from the village bakery, a good book, and writing paper. As the weather became colder, it was hard to know where to go for a quiet read, so I sometimes retreated to a hay barn or the church. I felt robbed of my brief and fleeting liberty if the cold, wet weather forced me to stay at the manor.

The winter crept on with all the disadvantages that I was used to, but few of its previous pleasures. Our room was cold and dark, the work was heavy with endless fires to keep fed, and there was very little respite to enjoy the beauty of the morning frosts or to anticipate cosy evenings around the family fireside. The only thing I seemed to have to look forward to was the prospect of Master Edward coming to the manor for the Christmas vacation. Even that hope was tinged with doubts about how much he valued our friendship and my own stupidity for over-estimating it.

At last the happy day arrived when I heard that Master Edward was expected to return by luncheon and that Sarah was to light a fire in his room. When I happened to meet him in a corridor that afternoon, he gleefully and quickly ushered me into the library for a catch-up chat. I stayed as long as I thought prudent, hearing about his university work, his lodgings, and his late nights of study. His enthusiasm at seeing me banished all my doubts about our friendship, and I left the library with a lighter heart than I had known for the last three months. Rushing through the rest of my afternoon chores was no problem as my heart was singing and my feet barely touched the ground.

As in many rural parishes during the dark winter months, the second Sunday service was conducted in the afternoon rather than in the evening, giving parishioners time to get home and tend to their animals before nightfall. This also suited me well as my solitary walk home from church was undertaken as dusk fell, rather than in total darkness. Now, once again, I had my companion back and as if he had never been away, we recommenced our rendezvous on Sundays and Tuesdays. No explanation was offered to explain his lack of communication, but as he told me more about the difficulty of his studies and of the long hours of "grind" he had to put in to keep up with the class as he headed toward his final examinations, I could understand that he had no time for trivial correspondence. I also reassured myself that he had little time for socialising and meeting the beautiful, cultured women of Oxford. As opposed to being forgotten by him, I found that during the term, he had collected various snippets from magazines and newspapers to give to me, either for my amusement or instruction.

Not only did Master Edward find the study hard, but to make matters worse, his heart was not in it. He had never wanted to study law, but it was inflicted upon him by Mr. Davenport, who saw it as a suitable subject for a member of his household. As the domineering Mr. Davenport had shown Master Edward such benevolence in allowing him to live in Barton Manor and also firmly held the purse-strings, he was not to be argued with. Master Edward had received a good and sufficient education, but now, compared with his peers, he realised how limited and superficial it was. Master Edward gave vent to his frustrations and vexations to my willing and sympathetic ear.

Much of Master Edward's leave was spent in the library studying. Never had a fire been so well attended and stoked as the library fire that winter! We both knew that Master Edward was quite capable of throwing a log on the fire himself, but either by a selfless desire not to disturb his study with mundane fire stoking or a selfish desire to see him, I made it my task. I was always rewarded with a witty comment or a "come and look at this nonsense" invitation to see his work.

In mid-December the whole Davenport family, Master Edward included, went away for a few days for an annual trip to visit relatives in Surrey. The valet and lady's maids escorted the family and always looked forward to catching up with gossip in the host's servants' hall. Seasonal festivities kicked off in Surrey with games, charades, and dances. We humbler servants were left at Barton Manor, but our pleasure was no less than theirs as we relaxed from our normal duties and routine and spent our time festooning the house with decorations. The gardeners collected barrow after barrow of holly, mistletoe, laurel, and ivy, and we arranged them with ribbons and lace throughout the living rooms and hall. Our voices no longer had to be moderated, so our laughter could ring out, filling the manor with an air of joy it so frequently lacked. With no bells disturbing our evenings, we felt free to play games and charades, which probably produced more fun and excitement than the more refined entertainment the family was enjoying. The various habits and mannerisms of the family became a central and hilarious theme of our acting and mimicry.

Every day our evergreen decorations became more elaborate and beautiful. We added bows and frills to our hearts' content. The hall was the focal point of our labours, as we wanted all visitors to be enchanted and impressed. Mrs. Milton had a cupboard full of glistening Christmas decorations that she rummaged through with sparkling eyes as she enthusiastically led our festive project. Years ago the ladies of the house helped with the decorating, but they soon tired of the fun and risk of being scratched by the holly and so were happy to leave it in the capable and imaginative hands of their housekeeper. Compliments on the decorations were often paid to them, which they graciously accepted, never acknowledging who had been the real artists. Yet the fun of decorating and the satisfaction of the result far outweighed the minor irritation of the ladies' deception.

The Christmas week was a whirlwind of visitors and entertaining. Not only did we have more bedrooms to clean and keep warm, but there was more food to prepare, more dishes to wash, more silver to clean, and more bells to answer. The food was more elaborate than normal, and the mood in the kitchen was tense with the occasional explosion. We all had extra duties to attend to and worked far into the small hours, tidying up and preparing for the next day.

All time off for staff was suspended due to the workload. I wondered what would wilt first, the evergreen decorations or the overworked staff. The only time during daylight hours that I had time to sit and reflect was in church, and then, as I relaxed, tiredness almost overcame me and I struggled to stay awake. I felt rebuked for failing to rejoice in the good news of the birth of Christ, my Saviour. I was also grieved that the family used the Christian feast days for such excess that their staff were too shattered to reflect on the real meaning of Christmas.

Before I went to sleep, my mind often went back to the wonderful Christmases at Pemfield.

On the first Sunday in Advent, Pa always dug out the ancient carol sheets for the evening singing, thus marking the start of the delightful season of anticipation and rejoicing in the amazing gift of Emmanuel: God with us. Throughout Advent we would gather every Sunday evening and practise the carols, almost raising the vicarage roof as we sang well-known Christmas hymns with enthusiasm and festive cheer. The grand finale took place on Christmas Eve when, bearing lanterns and muffled up in warm clothes, all the singers gathered at the vicarage. A few older folks stayed behind to prepare the supper and stir the soup, while the rest of us, with high spirits, laughter, and "goodwill toward men" traipsed around the lanes, singing out the carols to all. The sidesman gave us the note on his pitch whistle and immediately the trebles, altos, tenors, and basses began weaving their melodies together. Fearing that our singing would sound feeble outside, most of us belted out the carols with more gusto than finesse, thus producing a rather nasal roar, more reminiscent of the donkeys than of the angels in the nativity story. But our undiscerning audience approved of our hearty renditions and many a window was thrown open for the inhabitants to express their gratitude, wish us a happy Christmas, or pass out mince-pies.

Once we had toured the village and local farmsteads, we wandered back home to warm up, eat supper, and (for the sake of the soup-stirrers) hoarsely sing a few more carols for good measure. This annual festive activity was the perfect beginning of many happy Christmases, full of church services, rich food, and visiting. Now looking back longingly, I could almost smell soup, and I was left feeling empty, not longing for soup, but for my darling parents and their love.

Moreover my meetings and discussions with Edward were few and far between as he had to fulfil his duties in entertaining guests and I was far too busy to loiter. I had to be satisfied with a smile or nod as we passed each other on the stairs or corridor. I flopped into bed every night, exhausted with the work and disappointed that Edward's university vacation was slipping away rapidly with so little opportunity to enjoy his company.

## CHAPTER 8

AT NEW YEAR, LORD AND Lady Bertram and their offspring arrived to stay for a week. We busied ourselves preparing the guest rooms, which had only recently been vacated. These new guests were rather more distinguished than the Christmas visitors, and Mrs. Davenport made it clear to Mrs. Milton that we were to give an impeccable impression. Apparently the eldest son, Gerald, was "still available" and would be a good catch for Miss Davenport.

We were keen to meet our new guests, but quickly realised that they had little to recommend themselves to us beside a large bank balance and impressive genealogy. As servants are not impressed by either of these, we all took an instant dislike to the visitors but wanted to show them that we were able to give as good a service as anything they would be used to in superior Hampshire. Lady and Miss Bertram were accompanied by their maids, and once they had ensured the ladies were comfortable and suitably attired, they joined us for a cup of tea and regaled us with stories of the ill-treatment they received at their gentle-ladies' hands.

The Bertrams' thin veneer of gentility could impress the Davenports, but the constant ringing of bells for our attention to relieve petty inconveniences soon informed us of the visitors' true natures. All the maids quickly became aware of Lord Bertram's groping hands, and we nicknamed him the octopus. He particularly targeted

Emma, being the prettiest of us all, who was so troubled by his pestering that we had to ensure she was never alone in a room. It was sad to see her looking so worried and vulnerable, so at night we pushed the chest of drawers in front of the bedroom door. It seemed a bit dramatic, but that was how the octopus made her feel. She did not feel entirely safe until he had left.

Regular bulletins from the footmen and lady's maids were sent to the servants' hall on how the plan to capture the future Lord Bertram's affections was going. A sweepstake was taken among some of the staff as to the possible success or failure of the ambitious project. The poor Miss Davenport's future happiness seemed to be trifled with by her scheming parents and made a thing of careless speculation by the servants. But we soon realised she was not such a hapless pawn in the proceedings when she revealed to Jane that she had no intention of getting "hitched up" before the London season, as "being shackled to a man" would spoil her fun.

Meanwhile, I could not help noticing the attention Miss Felicity Bertram was paying to Master Edward. She seemed to be set on capturing his admiration and had many schemes to do so. She was not without the blessing of average good looks, and to enhance these she spent many hours closeted in her room with her longsuffering maid, applying beauty treatments. She had an amazing selection of beautiful gowns that showed off her figure to the very best advantage. Her maid informed us that she rarely opened a book at home, but on finding out that Master Edward was something of a bookworm, she became a frequent visitor to the library.

Much to my rather unchristian annoyance, Miss Felicity also became a devout churchgoer and attended the Sunday afternoon service. Such a fine lady was not to be expected to walk to and from church, so a carriage was provided. By the time the service had finished, it had begun to sleet, so Master Edward also took the carriage and, much to Miss Felicity's annoyance, he asked me to join them. She did her best to ignore my presence, but when Master Edward asked my opinion on the meaning of the parable of the talents (the subject of the sermon) and I had the audacity not only to have an opinion but also to voice it, she looked most annoyed. When she offered her opinion that the Apostle Paul was to be admired for writing such useful parables, we could scarcely conceal our amusement; she quickly detected this and shot me a daggered look.

There was an awkward moment when the footmen dropped us off at the front door. Not only did Master Edward help me down from the carriage, but he unthinkingly assumed I would enter the same door as they did. The look of triumph on Miss Felicity's face as I quickly excused myself and made my way through the biting sleet to the servant's entrance was insufferable.

On Monday I was busy brushing the main staircase when Miss Felicity passed me. I made way for her and tried to look invisible, as the rules direct. As she sailed past, her foot deftly kicked my full dustpan, scattering its contents down the stairs. I looked up at her in amazement.

"Oh, do be careful, you clumsy fool," she snarled and continued her ladylike descent of the stairs.

I felt like grabbing one of her elegant little ankles, causing her to follow my dustpan nose first; instead, the staircase carpet got a battering as I angrily brushed up the mess and rued my lot in life.

The next day I was doing my normal Tuesday duties in the library, and as usual Master Edward made time to come and have a chat. We were close together, leaning over an amusing Punch cartoon on his desk and giggling, when the door opened, and in walked Miss Felicity. In an instant I knew that she, with the quick comprehension of a rival, understood the extent of our friendship, or at least my regard for Master Edward. To make matters worse and to my great annoyance, I blushed. Master Edward seemed not to realise, or chose to ignore, the awkwardness of the situation and invited Miss Felicity to look at the cartoon. I picked up my cleaning basket and hastily retreated.

That evening I smelt trouble when Miss Felicity rang her bedroom bell and then sent a message down saying that she had given her maid the evening off and therefore required me to help her undress. With all the reluctance of a fly being driven into a spider's web, I obeyed the orders and went to her room. Miss Felicity was standing by the fireside, her eyes full of malice. Her first order was to untie her elegant shoes. As I knelt down to undo the laces, she kicked me, with surprising speed, strength, and accuracy on the nose. The impact knocked me off balance, and I fell on my side to the floor, crashing into the fire guard. Miss Felicity took advantage of my fall and kicked me repeatedly in the ribs. I got up as fast as I could and staggered to the door, catching the blood from my dripping nose. My heart was pounding, and I could hardly hear Miss Felicity's venomous voice hissing, "Leave him alone."

I stumbled toward my bedroom, praying I would not meet anyone, and lay shivering on my bed, wondering what to do next. I did not have to wonder for long, as Mrs. Milton soon appeared. Apparently she had been summoned by Miss Felicity, who informed her that I had been unsteady and tumbled in her room, sustaining an injury. She "kindly" suggested to Mrs. Milton that maybe I needed help with a drinking problem. Mrs. Milton, who had seem many things in her time, brushed such a suggestion aside, sensed trouble, and sought me out. She was alarmed to see me in such a state and immediately went about to alleviate my discomfort with a cold compress, leaving questions until later.

My face was swollen and red, but my side hurt the most, making it painful to breathe. Mrs. Milton feared I had broken some ribs and sent for the family physician. He raised an eyebrow when he heard about the incident, and after some painful poking and prodding, announced that he believed my ribs were still intact, but that I had sustained serious bruising. He prescribed pitch plasters, bran tea, and strong analgesia, instructing me to take deep breaths regularly to prevent a chest infection developing. I was unable to stop myself shivering, probably due to the pain and the shock of being attacked in such a vicious manner; I had never in my life seen such hatred directed at me and was aghast.

The kind physician seemed to understand this and administered a sleeping draught to relax my frayed nerves. I soon fell into a fitful sleep, waking every time I moved due the pain in my side and the difficulty breathing through my swollen nose. By the morning I had two black eyes, and my ribs felt as if a bull had trampled over me. Emma was horrified when she saw my face and offered to cut up all Miss Felicity's gowns. It was an interesting idea, but with a weak smile we rejected it, as Emma needed to keep her job.

Mrs. Milton and Emma insisted that I stayed in bed for the next three days, much to my relief, as any exertion left me tired and aching. Between them, they made sure I was comfortable and well looked after. Of course, they wanted an explanation for the incident, and I gave a mumbled answer that Miss Felicity seemed to be jealous of a perceived friendship between Master Edward and myself. Mrs. Milton looked pitying at me, obviously understanding more than I had hoped about my feelings for Master Edward, and gently told me to be very, very careful, as any friendship like that "can only end in tears." Indeed, in my battered, bruised, and vulnerable state, her well-meaning words released a torrent of fresh tears, which I shed freely once I was left alone.

If Miss Felicity had planned to make me indisposed and unable to see Master Edward before his return to Oxford, her scheme worked remarkably well. As I lay in my cold attic room, it dawned on me that I would now not see his face or hear his voice until his spring vacation. This restarted the tears that fell all too easily.

I wondered why he sent me no message via Emma, until she explained that Miss Felicity had told him that I had gone on leave for a few days, strongly hinting that I was planning to meet an old sweetheart, and apparently Master Edward had no idea of the real reason for my absence. The only silver lining to my dark clouds was that the Bertrams had also come to the end of their visit and were about to return to Hampshire, much to the secret (or not so secret) relief of everyone. Emma and I plotted our revenge on Miss Felicity, but most of our ideas were wildly unrealistic. At last I remembered a powerful laxative syrup that Mrs. Milton kept in her store room, "just in case." Somehow Emma managed to "borrow" it and ensure that the laxative was plentifully added to Miss Felicity's last cup of tea at Barton

Manor. We had cruel delight in imagining her uncomfortable and embarrassing journey back to Hampshire.

After tasting the sweetness of revenge, Emma and I were reluctant to leave it there. In the cosy candlelight of our bedroom, we formulated an official-looking letter to Miss Felicity. Anyone with any knowledge of the ways of the judicial system would immediately have identified it as a hoax, but we hoped she regularly filled her pretty little head with fashionable murder novels so would readily swallow the message hook, line, and sinker.

The letter went something like this:

Dear Miss Felicity Bertram,

An act of violent assault was performed at Barton Manor, Sussex on 3rd January, resulting in a domestic servant being gravely injured. Should these injuries lead to her untimely death, we would be forced to open a murder inquiry. At present you are the chief and only suspect. I hereby give notice of your possible pending summons.

Yours sincerely,

PC Fleetfoot

We toyed with the idea of trying to obtain headed note paper from the local constabulary, but on failing to come up with a good plan, I wrote the letter out in my best copper plate handwriting and marked the envelope as *Strictly Private and Confidential.* We never heard about the letter again, but we giggled as much as my sore sides would allow as we imagined her agitation every time the front doorbell rang.

Mrs. Milton suggested I should make a brief visit to Pemfield as I was unfit to work, but I knew that if I arrived there with two black eyes, Mrs. Brown would never let me out of her sight again. I was thankful when snowy weather quickly put travelling out of the question. I felt guilty about not working, as Emma and Sarah had to work even harder, but I also enjoyed the time that I had to read, write, and relax. At last I had time to read my Bible slowly and at leisure. My prayer time was no longer a hurried and sleepy few minutes in the morning, a few request prayers "on the hoof" through the day, and then a tired and sleepy few minutes in the late evening, often (to my shame) falling asleep before the amen. I now had time to focus more on God and His attributes rather than on my requests and needs. My quiet times once again became a source of spiritual enrichment, rather than a routine duty, and I felt grateful that the Lord had given me this unlikely time off to appreciate my Saviour anew.

After a week Mrs. Milton deemed me presentable enough to recommence my duties. With the aid of a little face powder, my appearance would not alarm any of the family or raise any questions. The first week back at work was agony, as my corset pressed tightly on my bruised ribs, causing continuous pain when I moved. Emma helped me to loosen the corset as much as I could within the constraints of my uniform, thus making movement a little more bearable. I am indebted to Emma and Sarah for their kindness to me during the time I struggled to fulfil my duties, as they insisted in giving me the lighter, easier tasks and worked harder themselves. They swept aside my appreciation by joking that I had learned my lesson not to cross a refined gentlelady.

Sarah was in the frame of mind to bestow benevolence on all she met with, as her gardener had become amorous when passing under the mistletoe at Christmas, and their courtship had flourished like a greenhouse flower ever since.

## CHAPTER 9

THE SNOW AT THE BEGINNING of the year lingered long and was followed by a frosty and foggy February. Emma and I were so cold in our drafty attic room that we used our rag rugs as an extra layer on our beds. The glass of water by my bed was frequently frozen in the morning.

Keeping the house warm for the family seemed to be a constant task that we barely succeeded in. The damp air created drafts throughout the house, making the more sedentary members of the household chilly and quarrelsome. A brisk walk in the park might have made the daughters a little warmer and brighter, but it would also have involved getting their boots and hems soiled, so such an idea was unthinkable. Instead they paced around the parlour and drawing room like lions in a cage.

"Dash this hideous weather!" moaned Miss Davenport.

"Moderate your language, my dear," chided her mother.

"But this miserable weather is making us prisoners in our own home."

"And no one visits us; even the dressmaker cried off her visit due to the weather. I am annoyed at her lack of commitment," added Miss Annabel.

"Apply yourself to some cultivating pursuits, my girls. We have a library full of books to read."

"How utterly boring!" said Miss Annabel's sister.

"Father forbids us to become bookish," added Miss Annabel triumphantly.

"Then find your needlework," suggested their longsuffering mother, only to be greeted with deep sighs.

"What about playing the pianoforte or painting?"

"You and Father hired such incompetent governesses to teach us, that we were never properly instructed in these arts."

Miss Annabel's lie stirred my indignation on behalf of the governesses.

"Then try to teach yourself and strive for improvement."

"And what may I ask, is the point of that?" spat out the elder Miss Davenport. "We never have visitors or anyone to impress with your so-called 'cultivating pursuits.' If I had an admiring audience, I may endeavour to shine, but I certainly won't put myself to that effort for my mother and grumpy sister."

"May I remind you, young lady, that had you been more obedient and obliging about Gerald Bertram, you could even now be planning your wedding trousseaux and escape to sociable Hampshire," said Mrs. Davenport, bringing up a sore subject.

"Oh, mother, you are so unreasonable," huffed her eldest daughter, and she stomped out the room.

Such were the snippets of conversation Sarah and I heard as we stoked the hungry fires, and as we compared notes, it was apparent that the same arguments and subjects were gone over time and time again, with no satisfactory conclusion or reconciliation.

The same could almost be said for the conversations that Emma and I had as we got ready for bed. Her kindness to me after my battering and her pertinent questions forced me to confide in her about my feelings for Master Edward. It was a great relief to have a sympathetic ear to listen to my bottled-up emotions, and they came spilling out like fermented drink when the cork is released. Together we analysed his attitude toward me, our conversations, and his actions. Emma was romantic enough to believe cross-class relationships possible, but realistic enough to know they do not happen very often. We both concluded that Miss Felicity must have seen an amount of interest in me on Master Edward's part to stir up such vehement jealousy. In her analysis, Emma failed to take into account the one great fact that kept me hoping and praying, that is: "with God all things are possible." I believed that Master Edward and I could do each other so much spiritual good, and as this would be God-glorifying, it could not be wrong to want such a union.

Emma wanted to stretch her wings and began looking at adverts for lady's maids. We poured over the Situations Vacant columns of *The Morning Post*, trying to read between the lines to ascertain the type of lady advertising. Emma decided she needed to practise on a kind, respectable, and sociable lady for a few years before launching herself on real aristocracy. She wanted a young and beautiful woman to work for, so that when she had dressed her ladyship and arranged her hair, Emma could feel real pride and satisfaction in her work. She wanted a mistress with original thoughts and an easy manner so that they could discuss the day's events together and share opinions. All these characteristics could only be observed when meeting the employer face to face, so Emma resigned herself to the idea of wasting many of her precious days off attending interviews. For her, the concept of an interview was that it enabled her to choose the right lady as much as they were choosing the right maid. I helped Emma formulate letters in response to various adverts, and then we waited expectantly for replies.

I was dreading the idea of Emma leaving Barton Manor, as we had become close friends and worked well together. Her laughter and astute observations made her delightful company and often lifted my spirits. She could spark my humour in a way that no other member of staff could. Sarah was also due to leave work soon, as she was marrying her gardener and they were to set up home in one of the estate's tied cottages. Married women were not permitted to continue their employment, so although Sarah's wages would have been useful for the newlyweds, she was forced to give notice. Mrs. Milton was dismayed to hear of Emma's plans and complained that as soon as she had a good working team, someone "goes and leaves, and I am back to square one."

Mrs. Milton could vaguely understand why Emma wanted to better herself and advance up the domestic service ranks, but she failed to see why Sarah would "chuck in a good job to marry a man, least of all a gardener, of all people." Despite her disappointment at the breaking up of her housemaid team, she busied herself and us in turning old, rejected sheets into beautiful, embroidered tablecloths and napkins for Sarah. If people had to marry, they might as well do it properly.

Emma was looking for change, and Sarah was getting married, but my life seemed destined to remain the same—but if my future seemed bleak, Nancy's appeared hopeless. As I contrasted her with my excited fellow housemaids, I once again pitied her lot and wished I could in some way help her.

Nancy never had any time or inclination to take care of her appearance, and although the staff rules stipulated that we should be clean and presentable at all times, in a scullery it is hard to stay in such a condition for long. One quiet evening I tentatively suggested to Nancy that I help her wash her hair with some Castile soap I had recently purchased. She readily agreed and within half an hour, her long brown locks were cleaner and more fragrant than they had been for years. She was obviously pleased with the result; indeed with clean, brushed hair and a smile, she almost looked pretty.

I decided to offer her the use of my Castile soap on a frequent basis, but before I could execute my plan, I found the soap had disappeared from my room, only to reappear the next day. This coincided with Nancy appearing with well-groomed, clean hair. I had grave suspicions, but when it happened again a fortnight later, I was sure that Nancy had been into my bedroom and borrowed my soap bar. This seemed a trivial transgression, but to enter unauthorised into someone else's bedroom and to take their possessions was against any rules of decency. I was worried that this might lead to further theft.

It was hard to know how to deal with the situation: I did not want Nancy dismissed for a few bubbles of my Castile soap, but she had to know that such behaviour was not to be tolerated. I told no one of the incident but prayed for wisdom. In the end, I decided to speak to Nancy and tell her that my soap bar seemed to disappear frequently from my room, and whoever was doing it risked instant dismissal for theft. I then gave her half a bar of soap to keep for herself. Nancy looked very embarrassed but rapidly pocketed the soap, and nothing else ever disappeared from my room again.

As March roared in upon us like a lion, with more freezing and blustery weather, I counted off the days to the end of the university term and Master Edward's return. I was bitterly disappointed when I heard Mrs. Milton tell Emma that he was not coming to the manor this holiday due to his heavy workload and examinations, so she need not get his rooms ready.

Now that I had no idea when I would see him again, I could only commit him and his studies into the Lord's hands and pray that we would soon meet. By April, when the atmosphere at the manor was full of excitement due to the forthcoming London trip, I received an even bigger blow when I heard it casually mentioned in the servants' hall that Master Edward had accepted a junior position in a law firm in Oxford and would be starting immediately. Now he would be permanently based in Oxford and have very little leave to visit Barton Manor. I should have been thankful that he had found employment, but I was heartbroken that the chances of our friendship being rekindled had been dashed. Life, as it stretched ahead of me, now looked bleak and grey. I felt as if the Lord had dangled a treat in front of me and then snatched it away. I felt out of sorts with the Lord for treating me thus, but then cross with myself for questioning an all-wise God.

Satan, the great enemy of souls, suggested to me that if God did not care for me enough to give me my heart's desire, how did I know that He had really answered my prayers for salvation? Surely all the hopes and spiritual experience I knew could turn out to be false and futile on the last great day? Christ's promise is that "whosoever cometh I will in no wise cast out," and I believed that I had come, but was my understanding of coming the same as God's? I never doubted Christ's power to save, but I started to doubt His willingness. Verses like "Many are called, but few are chosen" and "strait is the gate and narrow is the way that leadeth unto life and few there be that find it" haunted my thoughts and stifled my prayers. If God's plans were already set and our lives ordered by Him from beginning to end, then what was the point of praying for things to happen? Why not just be a passive puppet and wait for Him to pull our strings and make things happen? How could we be responsible and answerable for our actions while all is predestinated for us? These thoughts spoiled any pleasure I had in feeling that God was my Father and Christ my Saviour, or that I could leave all my cares for time and eternity in His loving arms.

I hated being in this state of mind and prayed that the questioning thoughts that haunted me might be removed. After a few weeks, this prayer was answered. It was a Sunday evening and the sermon was from Jeremiah 18, where God likens himself to a potter and Israel to clay and asks, "O house of Israel, cannot I do with you as this potter?" During the sermon, the vicar showed us how God was our Creator, creating us and giving us all our reasoning ability; therefore, how futile and sinful it was to use this God-given ability to question Him or think in our arrogance that we know better. He went on to state that it is only due to God's mercy that we are not cast aside. He concluded by showing us that we are in God's hands, but they are the best hands to be in, and our prayer should be "Oh God, forsake not the work of Thy hands." His words melted my hard heart, and as I walked back to the manor, I thanked God for taking me in hand and prayed that I would be submissive to the moulding influence of His Spirit.

But with no visits from Edward to look forward to, the daily grind of everyday life seemed endless, and as the other housemaids discussed their anticipated changes, I grew restless. Maybe it was time for me to seek a new situation too. I wanted to be submissive to the Lord, but also I needed guidance as to how to spend my Edward-less life. I dearly longed to visit Pemfield and once again be within the safe and loving embrace of my old friends who had known my parents and could reminisce with me. I broached the subject with Mrs. Milton. She kindly agreed that I should have an unpaid week off when the family had gone to London and the house had been thoroughly cleaned. I scribbled a letter to Mrs. Brown with such excitement and enthusiasm that I'm afraid that I told her that I was coming, rather than asking if it were possible, but she obviously didn't mind, as a reply came shortly afterwards expressing her delight.

## CHAPTER 10

AS SOON AS WE HAD bundled the family off to the metropolis with their trunks, hat boxes, glove boxes, shoe boxes, and the mountain of other paraphernalia which seemed vital for months of social gaiety, we set to work cleaning the quiet house. The noise levels had reached a crescendo during the last few days as each family member demanded the immediate attention of the servants to help with preparations, all of them believing that their particular wants were the most important. The ladies drove their maids near to distraction as they constantly changed their minds about the clothes they wanted to take and the accessories needed for each outfit. Eliza and Jane packed and repacked their ladies' trunks until they could hardly remember what was in each trunk or if indeed certain items were packed at all. But now, finally, peace prevailed, and room after room was attacked with mops, dusters, brushes, polishes, and soaps until they sparkled with cleanliness and our hands bled from the various potions used.

Although we worked hard, there was still a noticeably more relaxed atmosphere. We no longer had to moderate our voices, and meals were timed to suit our work, rather than the family's whim. With no family to get to bed, we could call the evenings our own and enjoy free time after supper.

The sound of the messenger boy's bike on the long gravel drive became a frequent noise, as the family regularly sent a telegram down from London, asking for this broach or that gown to be sent up post haste. Just as these telegrams were becoming a predictable joke with the staff, one of a rather different nature landed in Mrs. Milton's hands. The message informed her that Eliza had been taken ill and that a replacement was urgently needed. Please could she send one of the housemaids to "act up" until further notice?

I held my breath and tried to look invisible as Mrs. Milton explained the situation, but Emma almost danced around with child-like exuberance, begging Mrs. Milton to send her and promising she would "be good and work 'ard." It was difficult to know which of us was the more relieved when Mrs. Milton dismissed Emma with a curt "Stop dancing and get packed up as quickly as you can, but don't get ideas above your station." Emma winked at me and skipped out of the room, leaving me to hear Mrs. Milton's grumbles about staffing levels and work load. At least, she conceded, most of the cleaning had been done.

Now my time off seemed to hang in the balance. Would Mrs. Milton consider us too short staffed to let me go? Sarah had only two more weeks to work before her wedding, and Mrs. Milton had the extra burden of interviewing potential replacements. Once the house was spotless and we were merely mending laundry, I tentatively asked Mrs. Milton if I could still visit my friends and she replied, "Of course: a promise is a promise," and then told me I could leave in 48 hours' time and have five days off. I thanked her warmly and returned to my work with renewed enthusiasm (as far as one can be enthusiastic about mending pillowcases), my mind full of memories of characters and scenes from dear old Pemfield.

As I waved good-bye to the staff, I felt sorry for Mrs. Milton that she never had time off or any kind of interest outside her work. This wondering about her and her solitary life—stuck in between the underservants and the family, and her lack of blood relatives who cared for her—occupied my thoughts as I walked down the drive to catch the stagecoach. But soon the delights of travelling and the beauty of the countryside around me blotted out all thoughts, and a feeling of anticipation and excitement grew within me as we neared the Kent border.

After eavesdropping a while on the rather repetitive conversation of two lady passengers on my left about the shocking high price and the equally shocking low quality of groceries available these days, I turned my attention to the middle-aged couple on my right. They seemed well matched in their pettiness and their need to have the last word, so their bickering over trivia continued throughout their journey . . . and probably throughout their married life.

Once I had gained all the private amusement I could from the conversations left and right, I turned myself and my full attention to the passing landscape through the window. The sun shone as white fluffy clouds swept rainless across the blue sky. The windows of the stagecoach protected us from the sharp, chilly wind outside, but let us enjoy the warmth of the May sunshine. The blossoms had recently disappeared from apple orchards, leaving just the fresh green of the spring leaves. The lambs were confident and playful in the meadows, while their mothers grazed contentedly in the thick grass. Fields of crops looked green and lush with many a trespassing rabbit eating to the full. Coarse and strong bines were beginning once again to creep clockwise up the hop poles.

Trees waved and bowed as we sped through woodland, and beneath the swaying bows some late bluebells nestled among primroses and buttercups. We passed through villages alive with daily life and toil. Washing flapped on lines, boys rolled marbles, dogs chased our wheels, and people hurried about the streets or stood to chat. Passengers joined and left the stagecoach, always causing it to rock and sway and us to shuffle and fidget until all was arranged and settled. At last it was my turn to disembark, and after stepping on as few toes as possible and avoiding landing on a fellow traveller's lap, I extracted myself from the coach, paid the fee, and stepped into the fresh air. Once again, Mr. Hicks would provide the next means of conveyance, so I went to find him and his cart at the market square. He was deeply engaged in farming conversation, so I stood and watched the charismatic auctioneer in action until my driver and his mare were ready.

Mr. Hicks greeted me with slight indifference, as if he saw me on a daily basis. This attitude suited me well, and to humour him I asked after his livestock, thus beginning a conversation that would last our entire journey to Pemfield.

Mr. Hicks dropped me off outside Mrs. Brown's cottage and before I knew it, I was wrapped in her warm embrace. In my arms she felt smaller and frailer than eighteen months ago, and when I looked at her face, I saw hollow eyes and tight pale skin. Her legs were swollen and pitted, indicating immediately to me that she was suffering from dropsy.

My heart smote me that I had been neglectful of my dear, kind friend. But as soon as she spoke, I knew that Mrs. Brown was still the same calm, happy person, despite her failing body. How we chatted and enjoyed each other's company that evening! It was lovely to be back in her homely cottage, eating her delicious food, far away from the tyranny of call bells. As we caught up on each other's news, I was delighted to hear that her daughter was coming to stay the following week and was considering making this a permanent arrangement.

Of course, I was interested to hear all the village news and especially how the replacement vicar was.

"I declare I've never seen such a minister in all my days," Mrs. Brown began.

"Why?" I asked. "Is he good?"

"Good? Oh yes, 'e's good all right, at dressing up all posh like and being all theatrical, oh 'e's good at that, all right."

"But what about his preaching? Is the content good?"

"Well ta be 'onest with you, I don't 'ear a great deal. Me pew is right near the back."

That seemed strange. "Can you not move forward?"

"No, them seats are taken by some more wealthy folks who pay their seat rent but 'ardly ever come along."

"How annoying!" I said, grieved at this injustice.

"But from what I 'ear, I ain't missing much. 'E don't preach like your good old pa used to—nothing solid like."

I was unsure whether this harsh assessment by Mrs. Brown was the result of her loyalty to my father or a true depiction of the man, but by Sunday evening I realised she was totally correct. After hearing an appallingly vague sermon with no mention of sin, redemption, or the preciousness of Christ, I had to agree that Mrs. Brown was not missing much and had "meat to eat" that the vicar knew naught of.

The vicar seemed to assume that all who lived in a Christian country were Christians and the chief end of man was to be nice to others. I was disappointed and annoyed with the vicar, but even more so with Pa's former church members, who seemed to drink in the syrupy sermon without a splutter. The sidesman made a point of speaking to me after the sermon and expressing how delighted they were with their new vicar "who has none of your poor father's uncomfortably narrow views" and "respected people's privacy enough not to visit their homes without being invited." Maybe I was too thin-skinned, but I felt as if my father's diligence, both spiritually and practically, had been either forgotten or despised in the village and that his legacy was eclipsed by the new "enlightened" preacher.

When busy working at the manor, I had often thought with longing of Pemfield as my place of belonging and my home, but now I could see this concept starting to crumble. The Pemfield I knew and stored up in my memory was disappearing. When I went for a walk around the village and fields, retracing my steps, I found that the meadow where Bessie and I used to lie in the hay and chat was now an orchard, trees that we climbed had been chopped down, and as for our lovely old vicarage garden—all my mother's favourite roses had been grubbed to make a croquet lawn!

As I knelt to weed my parents' grave, I was thankful that they were far above these earthly mutations and in the happy realm where there is neither change nor decay. My feelings of no longer belonging were also increased by visiting Bessie, my old best friend and companion in crime, who was now a busy mother of twins. Our day-to-day lives were so different that we had little more to say to each other. My time with her was mainly spent holding crying, regurgitating babies, so any conversation was limited anyway. Bessie seemed rather disappointed that I didn't regard her squealing offspring with the same adoration as she did, although I did my best to look enchanted.

The highlight of my stay at Pemfield was the cosy evenings around Mrs. Brown's warm range with her and Miss Miller. We reminisced about the "good old times" and heard stories about Miss Miller's pupils. They were genuinely interested in hearing about my work and my fellow servants. In her daily conversation, Mrs. Brown dropped comments that indicated that her thoughts were already in heavenly places. She was like a full ear of corn, bowed down with weight, ripe and ready for harvesting. It began to dawn on me that I would probably not meet her again on this side of the grave. I could not really be sad at this realisation, as she was such a testimony to the Lord's faithfulness "even to grey hairs," and her various aches and pains made her long for release.

How quickly my five days' leave sped past! Before I knew it, I was back in the stagecoach, bouncing my way back to Barton Manor and the endless round of work. I watched the scenery pass with feelings very different from those on my outward journey. There was no excited anticipation, just a sinking feeling of realising that a monotonous daily grind awaited me.

My visit to Pemfield had unsettled me, as I had always seen the village as home and had expected this to remain so, but after the changes that had taken place, I felt like a stranger there and wondered what and where home was for me now, or if indeed I even had one. I mused over the elements that make up the concept of home— companionship, love, memories, warmth, family, mutual concerns, and a base to sleep and be accepted exactly as one is. How many of these components can disappear before a home ceases to be home?

I never considered Barton Manor anything more than a place of work. If it were to become the nearest thing to home for me, I feared I would become as desolate and friendless as Mrs. Milton. Such were my rather despondent musings as I was reluctantly propelled back toward normal, daily life.

# CHAPTER 11

I ARRIVED BACK AT BARTON Manor just in time for the evening meal. After taking my luggage to my room and neatening myself up, I went straight into the servants' hall and greeted all the staff. As I was taking the first mouthful of steaming steak and kidney pudding, Mrs. Milton asked if I had heard the latest news. I had not and expected to hear about the latest escapade in London, but what I heard was most unexpected.

Master Edward had been left a manor and estate by Sir Richard Tenson, an old friend of his father. The deceased gentleman had been involved in the faulty decision-making that eventually contributed to the explosion that killed Master Edward's father. The guilt of his inaccurate calculations dogged Sir Richard Tenson's life. He immediately gave up any involvement with the railroads and retreated to his country estate, living there almost hermit style, brooding on his mistake and exaggerating his contribution. He knew of Master Edward's existence but could not face meeting his friend's offspring or explaining the fatal incident. With no family or close friends, Sir Richard Tenson had decided to leave all his worldly goods to Edward, and that was no mean amount.

The news had come via London in a long telegram yesterday, causing much discussion and speculation among the servants. I would have liked to have heard more, but obviously it had been chewed over sufficiently already to satisfy most of the staff and they were not going to repeat it all. I longed for solitude so I could digest this stunning information in peace. I was already sure of two things—that Edward would make a wise and discerning landlord, but also that the gulf between our stations in life was such that it could not be bridged.

When I went to bed that night, I thanked the Lord for blessing Edward in such an abundant way and prayed that he might be given all the wisdom and skill he needed in this new sphere. I also felt need of sustaining in my dreary, lowly lot, which seemed to stretch endlessly in front of me. I missed Emma's lively, observant presence and longed to have a good chat with her. I even missed Sarah's predictable comments on life, now that she had gone off to prepare for her forthcoming marriage. Everyone seemed to have an exciting future ahead of them except for me. Alone and with a heavy, empty heart, I fell asleep in my attic room, ready to begin duty at the crack of dawn.

The Davenport family extended their stay in London for several more weeks. Apparently, a certain young, firstborn son was beginning to take a marked interest in Miss Davenport, and a few more weeks might just secure the match. Even Mr. Davenport felt that the further expense in London was worth the gamble if his eldest daughter would catch a wealthy man from good breeding stock.

We did not object to having the house to ourselves for a while longer and used any spare time helping Sarah prepare for the marriage to her gardener. With or without the Davenport's blessing (I could not discover which), the kitchen staff raided the pantry to produce an extensive and delicious wedding breakfast for the couple. The gardeners made it their task to supply casks of ale and cider for the event, and they did this with great liberality. We all abandoned the house to attend the marriage service in the village church, after which friends and relatives came to the servants' hall for refreshments and to dance a few reels. A band of local musicians played most enthusiastically for us, their only reward being a regular supply of food, ale, and cider throughout the evening. As the evening progressed, their playing became less and less accurate, but more and more enthusiastic until at last it was impossible to dance to their endeavours, and it was time to wave the happy couple off. We'd all had a thoroughly enjoyable time, and never was it better illustrated that "when the cat's away, the mice will play"!

The next morning it was all hands on deck to clear up all traces of the previous day's events and return the servants' hall to its normal austere tidiness. That afternoon, as I was busy sweeping the floor, Mrs. Milton came in with the post and handed me a letter. I recognised the handwriting immediately—it was from Master Edward!

I slipped the envelope into my pocket and longed for an opportunity to read its content. My thoughts were in a whirl, my heart was pounding, and I knew I could be fit for nothing until I knew what was contained in the letter. As soon as I had finished sweeping I hurried to the broom cupboard, sat on an upturned bucket, and opened the envelope. My hands shook as I read the words. Edward wrote about his unexpected good fortune and how he had immediately given up his post to take on his new estate and responsibilities, and then he continued, "The weight of my new situation presses heavily on my shoulders and I need much wisdom from the Lord to be a good landlord and employer. I also feel the need of a wise and sensible friend by my side, one I can trust, who holds values similar to my own, and therefore ask if you would consider becoming my . . ."

I felt faint and shook as I hastily turned the page.

". . . housekeeper."

Housekeeper! My heart sank. *Housekeeper.* How foolish and romantic I had been to imagine he wanted me as his wife. I read on, realising that he wanted me to help him run his home, manage the redecorating required, and organise a team of servants. While I should have been flattered by the proposal, I was feeling disappointed as a result of my dreamy, unrealistic, and mistaken imagination.

I folded the letter and sat with my head in my hands, trying to grasp the implications of the message. But this indolence would not do, and I steeled myself to get up and get going with the next task, which was to polish the huge floorboards of the servants' hall, before my short absence was noticed and questioned. With no Emma or Sarah to work with, I had to complete this large chore all alone, but this perfectly suited my present state of mind.

I was very annoyed with myself for being so disappointed at receiving a proposal so much less than a marriage one. The suggestion clearly showed that he would never see beyond my servant status. This, I told myself severely, was something I had to take on board and never forget. I was not in some romantic "lived happily ever after" novel, but in the gritty, real world of social class and prejudice. I had thought that Edward was above this narrow mindset, or that I could charm him out of it, but I had only been deceiving myself. On the other hand, I told myself, if I was more sensible and realistic, the offer of a role as his housekeeper was very flattering. He clearly thought I was capable of running his house for him and that he could trust me to make good decisions. To see him every day and to help him would be delightful—but only if I stayed sensible and remembered my place, I added.

My romantic and my realistic selves argued and chewed over the proposition as I slowly polished and prayed my way across the room. By the time I had reached the door, the floor was gleaming and I had decided to accept the position and keep any romantic fancies in close check.

Breaking the news to Mrs. Milton was difficult, but after her initial moans and groans at losing yet another of her team, she became surprisingly supportive and was full of tips about various aspects of housekeeping.

"Organisation is the key," she instructed. "And make it your business to know everyone's business. Get to know the butcher, the baker, and all your suppliers. If you are loyal to them, they will be loyal to you and give you decent discounts."

I nodded, feeling slightly overwhelmed.

"And keep good accounts. Enter every expenditure and keep all receipts."

She showed me her book of accounts. Every now and again, Lady Davenport would request to see the accounts, and Mrs. Milton prided herself in the fact that she could account for every penny entrusted to her. The inspection was on the whole ceremonial and rather cursory, due to Lady Davenport's poor mathematical skills and lack of understanding of basic economy.

"But that," said Mrs. Milton, "is no reason to keep shoddy records. A housekeeper," she added, "should be beyond reproach."

I nodded again, now feeling totally overwhelmed.

"And you will need new uniforms. Now let me find my tape-measure and get you measured up. Then we can order some nice material. I know just the right supplier."

I was excited by the thought of wearing a housekeeper's uniform of neat, patterned blouse and long black skirt. It seemed much more becoming and authoritative than the dresses and aprons I was accustomed to, and they allowed more scope for personal taste and style. I would also wear my hair in a less severe style, maybe letting a ringlet slip out . . . but I checked myself! Of course, I would no longer be addressed as Stubbs but as Mrs. Stubbs (for all housekeepers were known as Mrs.). This concept had struck me as a very strange, and it would make me sound like a plump, middle-aged matron.

It took me a few attempts before I was satisfied with the acceptance letter I wrote to Edward.

## CHAPTER 12

IN LONDON, THINGS WERE GOING decidedly well for Miss
Davenport. The young man of good pedigree had become a regular
caller at the Davenport's London residence, and he frequently escorted her to Hyde Park for strolls or rides. The respective families
had dined together on a number of occasions and seemed satisfied
with the unfolding of events.

Emma sent long and lively letters to me, sharing her delight in
exploring London during her free time. She enjoyed the challenge
of public transport and had ventured into more places and museums
than had the Davenports themselves. Through the servant grapevine,
Emma had discovered that a duchess was looking for a replacement
lady's maid for her daughter. Emma had observed the daughter whilst
escorting her ladies and was impressed by her vivacious and witty
character. When Emma also learned that the family often travelled
to Europe, she lost no time in applying for the post. Emma was to
have an interview with the duchess the following week and was busy
practising her most cultivated articulation and manners. I wished I
could be there to witness her endeavours and act out the interview
with her in her attic bedroom. All business in London needed to be
wound up by 12th August, when all families of influence would disperse to their Scottish estates to begin the grouse shooting season, so

both Miss Davenport and Emma were under some pressure to reach their intended goals.

Mrs. Milton lost no time in recruiting two new housemaids. They were both keen and willing to learn but had very little experience of working in a big house. As they had looked with bemusement at the various brushes, potions and polishes, started work and retired, shattered and homesick at the end of a long working day, I was reminded of my early days at Barton Manor and did my best to make them feel welcome. Mrs. Milton and I had only a few weeks to lick them into shape before I left and the family returned. I taught them all the tricks I had learned for making work easier and recommended high doses of hand salve.

A great deal of my scarce spare time was taken up with making farewell visits. As I contemplated my departure from Benton, it dawned on me how much I would miss the good preaching of the Reverend Penfold. Pa always said that hearers are quick to complain and slow to congratulate, and taking this to heart, I wanted to visit the vicarage. I was given a warm and courteous welcome, which, as an example of not showing partiality according to rank, would have pleased the Apostle James. I was invited to join Rev. Penfold and his wife for their afternoon cup of tea and scones. Rev. Penfold was pleased and touched by my expression of appreciation, and the conversation flowed easily as we discussed life in a vicarage, their grown-up children, and my plans. I had visited the vicarage with the fear that it would take up too much valuable time, but left two hours later wishing I had visited more often.

I spent a pleasant evening with Mr. and Mrs. Crookshanks in their familiar, homely kitchen, enjoying some of Mr. Crookshanks' delicious sausages. I would also miss this godly, wise couple and their hospitality.

Another afternoon I walked across the estate to visit Sarah in her new little tied cottage. Sarah looked as pleased as a queen as she busied herself in her tiny kitchen, making tea for us both. She proudly showed me around her domain, and I had to peek up her chimney to see the large joint of bacon received from her father-in-law. Sarah spoke excitedly of the thrill of doing domestic chores and shopping for one's own home, of planning and organising one's own time, and of her plans to keep hens and sell eggs, all the time fiddling unconsciously with her new, shiny wedding ring, which gave an air of maturity to her hand.

She was interested to hear about my new position, but as she herself enjoyed the freedom of being newly released from domestic service, she seemed to pity all those who were still under that yoke, whatever their job title may be. I shared the letter I had received from Emma with Sarah, and we chatted about the exciting news. Of course, Emma had landed on her feet and charmed her way into getting the lady's maid position, and because her new employers were planning to travel to the continent in the near future and were determined to have Emma with them, they had arranged an immediate discharge from the Davenports' service and for her few possessions to be collected from Barton Manor. Sarah and I smiled over the hastily written letter describing such dramatic events and concluded that "it could only happen to Emma."

I felt the greatest sadness at the thought of leaving Mrs. Milton. Her demanding job would continue as ever, with very little support from staff or family. Throughout my time at Barton Manor, I had never felt close to her, but she had always shown fairness and kindness as far as her superior rank would allow. I knew we could have been good friends had we met in a different situation. I couldn't decide whether she was content with her isolated position or whether she secretly craved companionship. She was upright and good, always respecting Christian values but never embracing the salvation offered in the gospel. She seemed to keep everyone at arm's length, including the Saviour.

I longed for her to come to know Christ's love and to belong to His family. I wished I had been a better witness to her. I thought hard and long about an appropriate leaving gift to give to her and finally ordered a book of *Expository Thoughts on the Gospel of Mark* by J.C. Ryle. It felt like a coward's way of evangelism, but I prayed that it would be a blessing to her. I hastily finished embroidering a bookmark (originally intended for Miss Miller) and placed it in the book to add a more personal touch.

On my final day at Barton Manor, I visited the library for one last time to return a book and sign my name in the borrowers' book. I smiled as I saw the long, uninterrupted list of *Rebecca Stubbs* signatures and spent a few moments perusing the pages to see what I had borrowed. My romantic self got the better of me as my fingers traced the signature of Edward Thorpe. As I gazed around the beautiful, panelled room, I remembered all the secret meetings we had enjoyed together. These conversations had been most satisfying and agreeable times of true mutual understanding, something I had rarely found at Barton Manor—moments I had felt truly understood and valued as a person rather than as a useful cleaning machine. All my other friendships made among the inhabitants of Barton Manor lacked a spiritual dimension, and without that, they seemed hollow and temporary.

As I took off my housemaid uniform for the last time, I was surprised at the pang of sadness I felt that this part of my life was over. How the next chapter would unfold, I had no idea.

## CHAPTER 13

THE NEW MASTER OF BIGGENDEN Manor and estate had kindly arranged for a private carriage to convey the new housekeeper to his residence; thus, I departed Barton Manor in style. At first I enjoyed the luxury of my solitude, but the anticipation of actually seeing Mr. Thorpe again (I kept reminding myself to address him as such, rather than with the somewhat juvenile title of Master Edward) soon created butterflies in my stomach. This was exacerbated by a feeling of nausea due to the motion of the carriage along the roads. The driver seemed to be an excitable type who was either urging the horse to gallop or halt suddenly, causing me to be flung hither and thither.

I discovered that the only way to cope with this was to adopt the unconventional position of sitting on the floor and pushing my feet hard against the opposite seat, thus anchoring myself against some of the extremes of motion. I had to keep my eyes tightly shut, which was a great pity, as normally I enjoyed watching the activities of daily life of villages I passed through. I had left Barton Manor in my smart new clothes and was travelling for the first time in a privately owned cab, but now I was feeling wretched, green, and unsightly. The Lord had effectively cut me down to size, and as my stomach churned and my head reeled, I prayed for help and support to survive the journey and meeting with Mr. Thorpe.

At first the journey took the same route as to Pemfield, but after Tunbridge Wells, instead of travelling north toward the Greensand Ridge, we turned eastward along the Medway Valley. That area was all new to me. I had no idea how near or far we were from Biggenden Estate. This was vexing, as I wanted to smarten up my appearance before arrival. A very bumpy peer into my small looking glass reassured me that my outward appearance was not as dishevelled as my inward feelings were; a multitude of hairpins and a hat had more control over my hair than I had over my emotions. My palms were so clammy with anticipatory nervousness that I decided to keep my gloves on until any handshaking was over.

My first impression of Biggenden Manor was that it looked like a small monastery. A thick hedge surrounded a garden of overgrown shrubs with not a flower in sight. The house was Jacobean in style, built of Wealden sandstone, with gabled façades. Mullioned arched windows gave it a somewhat ecclesiastical appearance. I had never seen such a masculine looking house and felt disappointed by its severe, unwelcoming appearance.

Much to my joy and relief, the manor's new master gave me an altogether different welcome, rushing up to the vehicle before it had barely stopped to release me from the carriage and set me down on solid ground.

I had never before seen Edward as animated and excited as when he opened the front door and showed me into his kingdom. He was no longer the misfit family member at Barton Manor but the proud owner of his own house and estate.

My eyes took a while to adjust to the darkness of the entrance hall, but as soon as they had, I inspected the interior with great interest. The hallway was spacious but not expansive, and everything to behold was of timber. The wide staircase that ascended up three walls of the room was uncarpeted oak, and the hall floor was bare oak boards except for one Turkish-style mat in the centre. The walls were covered with elaborately carved oak panelling.

Edward started to explain what the carvings represented, but instead of concentrating on the panelling, my eyes wandered and I studied him. He looked so well, happy, and handsome; I felt a wave of joy at being in his presence again. His eyes met mine and before he moved on to show me more of the house, he gave my arm a squeeze and said, "It's so lovely to have you here." That was enough to crown my day.

Had a female greeted me from my coach, no doubt I would have been given an opportunity to retire, straighten my clothing, and tidy my hair. A polite question about my journey would have been asked, and a refreshing cup of tea offered. Such pleasantries were ignored by Edward, and I was not offered any refreshment until the whole house had been explored from top to bottom.

The manor was modest in size, having only six bedrooms and two attic rooms, one of which was mine. The downstairs consisted of the hallway at the centre with a dining room, sitting room, study, and library coming off the hall. Beyond and behind the dining room was a comfortable small room that was to be my sitting room. It faced westward, catching the afternoon and evening sunshine. Large sash windows overlooked the back garden and meadows beyond. The room was well furnished with a chest of drawers, bookshelves, a desk, a pair of armchairs, and my own stove; I was delighted. Next to my room were the kitchen, pantry, and scullery. The back door of the kitchen opened onto a backyard where hens were scratching the ground. A house of this size did not have a servants' hall, so the kitchen was used for eating as well as preparing food.

It was in the kitchen that I was introduced to the other members of staff—all two of them! Mr. and Mrs. Kemp had been Sir Richard Tenson's faithful servants during his latter years, providing him with all the nursing care he required. The two were well past their prime and seemed worn out by the constant attention their former employer, who had been bed-bound for almost a year, had needed. Mr. Kemp was slim, slightly stooped, and almost completely deaf. Mrs. Kemp was square in size and her walking was severely limited due to arthritic knees. This faithful couple had kept the manor running, with the occasional help from Agnes Brookes, the shepherd's daughter.

When I heard the story of the Kemps' loyal devotion to Sir Richard Tenson, I feared that they might resent Edward's—and more especially, my—presence. But the opposite was true: the honest couple seemed pleased that someone was coming to take control of the house they loved but could not manage. The long months of Sir Richard Tenson's decline and the increased infirmity of the couple had brought about some unconventional arrangements in the house. Mr. and Mrs. Kemp more or less lived in the kitchen, and their two old armchairs stood companionably at each side of the kitchen range. In the evening the quaint couple could be found sitting in silence together, Mr. Kemp dozing quietly with his feet on the fender and Mrs. Kemp knitting, counting stitches under her breath. They struggled to manage the stairs to the attic bedrooms after a tiring day and had turned a storeroom near the kitchen into a makeshift bedroom.

Every evening at nine o'clock, they had a cup of milky tea, filled their hot-water bottle, and shuffled off to bed.

After our introductions, I finally got my longed for cup of tea. Mrs. Kemp was all for serving Edward's tea on a silver tray in the study, but he brushed the suggestion away and sat with us at the kitchen table. I suspected that this went against the Kemps' sense of decorum. They were very stilted and reserved at first, but as Edward probed more into their life with Sir Richard Tenson, they seemed to forget the rules and answered with animation and warmth. Mrs. Kemp often finished her husband's sentences for him.

As I watched Edward listen intently to the elderly couple with tender respect, my heart filled with all the emotions I had strictly forbidden myself to feel. When the teapot had been drunk dry, Mrs. Kemp eased herself off her chair and was about to struggle up the two flights of back stairs to show me my quarters. I quickly assured her that I knew the way and that she need not trouble herself.

When I had unpacked my trunks and organised my belongings in the bedroom, I shut the door and knelt by my new bed to thank the Lord for journeying mercies and for making things so well here. I prayed for wisdom to settle into the household and especially in how to handle myself with Edward. After surveying my pleasant room with the evening sun streaming through the window, I washed my face and hands with water from the jug provided and straightened my hair, then left the room to inspect my sitting room downstairs.

I suddenly realised there was no one else to empty my bowl of washing water, so I returned to dispose of it myself. I opened my bedroom window and looked down to see what was directly below. When I found it was a small border of overgrown roses, I quickly threw my washing water to them. I stilled my troubled conscience by saying to myself that the soapy water would help prevent green-fly. This became my daily routine, and the roses flourished.

I descended into the kitchen via the narrow servants' staircase and found Mrs. Kemp busy preparing the evening meal, but only for three of us as Mr. Thorpe was spending the evening with the headmaster of the local school and his wife. I felt a pang of disappointment but soon got busy in my sitting room, arranging my desk, exploring the drawers and cupboards and finally, writing of my travels to Miss Miller and Mrs. Brown.

The evening meal was a quiet and quick affair around the kitchen table. Mrs. Kemp's cooking was plain but substantial. Everything was well cooked, but nothing was added to enhance the natural taste or the enjoyment. The whole aim of the meal seemed to be to ingest nourishment in a business-like fashion, and talking was not deemed necessary or appropriate. I spent a solitary but contented evening in my sitting room before retiring early to bed after my busy and exciting day. As I knelt by my new bed, my heart filled with gratitude to the Lord for the comforts and kindness that surrounded me. I had feared that the many impressions of the day would whirl around in my mind, driving away sleep, but as I snuggled under the soft, clean bedding, I soon found myself drifting and then falling deeply into a welcome sleep.

## CHAPTER 14

THE HOME FARM COCKEREL WOKE me the next morning, but as I sat up in bed, I felt far from a confident housekeeper. I realised I knew nothing about the household routine, not even the normal working hours. I chided myself for neglecting to find out such vital matters from the Kemps the previous evening. As I sat in bed deliberating as to whether I should dress before going to the kitchen for warm washing water or go in my nightie, my quandary was answered when I heard heavy footsteps slowly coming toward my door, followed by a thud on the floorboards. I peeped out into the passage and saw a jug of hot water and a cup of tea by my door and the figure of Mr. Kemp ponderously heading for the stairs. At half past six every day, as regular as clockwork, this would be my gentle wake-up call.

After breakfast, I revisited all the downstairs rooms, planning my cleaning campaign. The rooms had hardly been used for months and smelt stuffy with a hint of stale tobacco smoke. I flung open every window that had a working latch, and fresh air wafted in. The morning sunlight revealed the enormity of my task as it shined on grimy windows, ledges of dust, and yards of cobwebs. Agnes had cleaned the study and master bedchamber to an adequate standard for Edward's arrival, but all other rooms had been neglected by both the previous owner and his overstretched staff.

The dining room was decorated with plain wallpaper, which had been hand stencilled with a pattern of exotic birds sitting in oriental-looking trees. This sort of wallpaper had been popular as it bypassed the wallpaper tax introduced during the reign of Queen Anne, a tax that was not abolished until 1836; plain paper was untaxed, so hand stencilling became the vogue. Now the wallpaper looked tired and grubby, but when washing the walls, I soon discovered to my horror that the pictures were more easily removed than the grime.

The other reception rooms were all painted with what I assumed was a cream paint, but as soon as I started scrubbing, I realised that the original colour was bright white. The yellow tint was the result of years of tobacco smoke. The cream walls had looked respectable, but as soon as a patch was cleaned white, the rest looked awful, so I knew I had once again totally underestimated the size of the spring-cleaning project.

As I was perched up a ladder, Mr. Thorpe entered the room. He was surprised to see the original colour of the paintwork and seemed to realise the enormity of the task I had taken on. I decided to strike while the iron was hot and suggested that we go from room to room, discussing the interiors. I was reluctant to suggest new wallpaper and repainting and so was delighted when he decided for himself that several rooms needed redecorating completely. The remaining rooms would receive a thorough spring clean, and my tentative suggestion that Agnes be employed for extra hours to assist was endorsed.

By the end of my first day at Biggenden Manor, I felt satisfied that the old building was being overhauled and that I had an important role in the task. I had worked hard, but no harder than I would have done in my former job. The luxury of planning my own working day gave me great delight.

That evening Mr. Thorpe remained at home and enjoyed his evening meal alone in the dining room, waited on by Mr. Kemp. We then gobbled up ours in silence around the kitchen table. At nine o'clock on the dot, the Kemps shuffled off to bed, and I was left to serve Mr. Thorpe his evening drink and slice of cake at ten.

On entering his study, I found him relaxed in an armchair next to the open fire, reading a farming periodical. A friendly black Labrador lay at his feet, basking in the warmth of the fire and looking decidedly contented. It was Sir Richard Tenson's old gun-dog called Rex, and he had clearly taken a shine to his new master. As I poured his tea, Edward invited me to fetch an extra cup and join him. I hurried to the kitchen for a cup and saucer, thoroughly pleased that he had asked me, but wondering what the Kemps would think if they were to hear about it.

Meanwhile, Edward had drawn another armchair near to the fire in a companionable manner opposite his. Whilst sipping tea, Edward told me all about the home farm, its acreage, crops, livestock, and coppicing woods. For someone who had lived a rather urban existence, I was surprised how much knowledge he had already acquired about milking and mangel-wurzels (a kind of beet plant, used as animal feed).

Sir Richard Tenson had let his house go to wrack and ruin, but his land had been well managed by a very capable steward and a team comprised of a herdsman, a shepherd, and a loyal workforce of farm labourers and woodsmen. Most of the staff lived in tied cottages on the estate.

Soon after arriving at Biggenden Manor, Edward had toured his new estate with Mr. Hull, the steward, meeting all the employees, their wives, and families, and inspected the cottages and farm buildings. Edward confessed that he was embarrassed by the respect and deference shown to him by his workforce and how humbling he found the whole experience. He was forcefully hit by the fact that about twenty families were relying on him to keep them employed and housed.

As the last log in the hearth gradually burnt to glowing embers and Rex snored gently on the mat, I reminded myself that another busy day lay ahead tomorrow and reluctantly bade Edward good night.

Cleaning, washing, and polishing occupied my time for the next fortnight. The thirsty wooden panelling and floor drank in any polish I applied and still asked for more. It was satisfying to watch dull wood gradually yielding a beautiful shine and to notice the odour of tobacco smoke and old dust being replaced by the clean smell of polish and soap suds.

During the rigorous process of being washed and squeezed through the rolls of the finger-biting mangle, some of the older curtains gave up the ghost and disintegrated. Once I had got over the shame of admitting another cleaning casualty to Edward and being asked if I was gentle enough with the fragile fabric, I had the great pleasure of choosing and ordering new material from a London catalogue. Agnes and I were rather cautious with beating the ancient rugs and runners after our curtain experience, so after beating out about a decade's worth of dust, we left the rest to hold the warp and weave together.

Whilst working, I often wondered what Edward's plans would be for the evening and fervently hoped that he would not be invited to dine out. By nine o'clock my back and limbs would be ready for bed, but whenever invited to join him, my aches and tiredness would vanish. I gladly fetched another cup and stayed up for another hour or more, drinking in the joy of having time alone with Edward and his devoted dog. I often wondered who enjoyed those evenings the most, me or Rex.

The recent arrival of a bachelor with a modest estate proved to be an interesting development in the locality, and Edward received many invitations from the scattering of upper-class families in the area. My private and cynical observation was that families with unmarried daughters seemed more tenacious at pressing an invitation than those without. Edward often moaned to me about the dreariness of these visits, the predictability of the shallow conversations, the length and richness of the meals, and the overbearing, inquisitive mothers.

He was always looking for new reasons to decline an invitation, but when none could be found, he took a rather unchristian pleasure in remembering the most ridiculous or uninformed comments uttered and recounting them to me verbatim the following evening. When the women had eventually retired, the men's conversation became solely shooting and hunting related. Having no experience with either sport, Edward could not contribute but was the captive audience to tales of sporting events "shot by boring shot, told with much enthusiasm of their own prowess." He could think of nothing more ridiculous than spending money on raising hundreds of pheasants, paying a gamekeeper to keep them safe, for the sole purpose of inviting friends to shoot the birds as quickly as possible and then "talking about it ad infinitum."

When not supervising and assisting Agnes with the cleaning, I was busy in the kitchen helping Mrs. Kemp deal with all the autumn fruit that came in abundance to us from the farm and garden. The local children knew that picking a basket of blackberries and handing them in at the kitchen door was rewarded by some sort of tidbit from Mrs. Kemp's pantry, so we were almost swamped by blackberries. Every day there were pounds more to boil, strain, jell, and jar. Apples arrived by the bushel, and these had to be grouped according to condition and purpose: for immediate use, storage, or bottling. Strictly speaking, bottling and preserve-making was the job of the housekeeper, not the cook, and I hoped that the following year, with less cleaning work to do and providing Mrs. Kemp could be gently persuaded to relinquish her role, I could take it over altogether, but for the time being, I was happy to learn all I could from Mrs. Kemp's years of experience.

Before the end of September, Edward received an invitation from Mr. and Mrs. Davenport to the wedding of their eldest daughter. Even the letter font seemed to ooze smug satisfaction as it proclaimed to friends and family that they had succeeded in getting a daughter financially secure for life and off their hands. Edward was reluctant to attend the ceremony but went out of a sense of obligation.

Two days at Barton Manor, being wooed by various distant relatives who until then had hardly acknowledged his existence, was "too nauseating to stomach," and Edward escaped to Biggenden as soon as the bridal pair had left for their continental tour. I had anticipated hearing lots of interesting news about the wedding, the flowers, and the bridal gown, but Edward had noticed only the carriages and food. He also failed to pick up any news from the servants, so his cursory description of the whole trip was wholly unsatisfactory.

With my days full of interesting work and my evenings of interesting company, I felt I had really fallen on my feet in coming to Biggenden and was very grateful to the Lord for this turn of events. The cloud to my silver lining was the preaching at the local church. Biggenden Estate was in the parish of Capford, and this parish was served by a vicar called Rev. Brinkhill. The first Lord's Day I attended Capford church, I excused the man's poor performance, putting it down to him having an attack of dyspepsia or the like, but I soon found that his deliverance never varied.

He looked a striking picture with his balding head, white beard, and flowing robes in the high pulpit, and one expected the liveliness of an ancient prophet, but he addressed his congregation in a slow monotone. His sermon structure never varied: he announced his text, explained the key Greek or Hebrew words, and then listed where they were also used in Scripture. His concordance seemed to be his greatest delight in life. The warmest of Bible verses he could reduce to mere technical words and meanings. The glorious invitations and promises of the gospel he narrowed down, sapping them of their fullness and freeness, always encouraging self-examination but discouraging a simple faith in Christ, thus leaving believers questioning their own salvation. Unbelievers became hardened in fatalism as he emphasised election and the sovereignty of God, neglecting man's responsibility and the reality of gospel invitations.

His eyes were either focused on the lectern before him, the right hand wall between the clock and a memorial tablet, or the point where the back wall and ceiling met. I was used to looking intently at the preacher, but soon I started to follow the example of most of the congregation and became very familiar with the flag stone floor and the knots in the wood of the pew in front.

I was amused and intrigued to find that the church still boasted a gallery band. A small group of ageing men sat in the west gallery with their fiddles and accompanied the singing. All other churches I had attended had long ago replaced their bands with a pipe organ or harmonium. The church was cold and damp, thus making it difficult for the fiddles to hold their pitch.

Every sermon, at the moment the vicar uttered "and in conclusion," an unholy screeching and scratching of flat, clashing notes emanated from above as the band limbered up for the final hymn. The unharmonious noises drowned out the final utterances—maybe even an application—of the minister for anyone more than halfway back in the church, but neither the minister or the congregation seemed to mind this intrusion. To make the situation even more amusing, the ancient fiddlers were hard of hearing, so their "whispers" of advice to each other were audible to all. In the coming months, I took delight in seeing the startled expressions of visiting clergy as the cacophony of fiddles drowned their concluding remarks.

At first I was amazed at the size of the congregation. Despite the dry preaching, the whole parish attended twice on the Lord's Day, come wind or rain, but I was soon enlightened to the fact many were there due to a fear of their landlord, rather than the fear of God. The expansive neighbouring estate, including most of the village, was owned by a certain Lord Wilson, who employed most of the villagers and insisted on their regular attendance at the church. He was not a religious man, often failing to attend church himself, but he thought that the teachings of the church would help keep his workers submissive and continually aware of their God-given station in life.

Shortly after my arrival at Biggenden Manor a skilled woodcutter from Lord Wilson's estate had become greatly exercised about his spiritual condition, and in finding no help from the local vicar, he started attending a Strict Baptist Chapel. The preaching there greatly helped him, and he soon became an assured believer, speaking to his fellow woodcutters of eternal matters. He was convinced that only believer's baptism by immersion was scriptural and became a member of the chapel. Lord Wilson was so incensed by this behaviour that he dismissed the woodcutter, making him and his family homeless.

Such news travels fast in a small community, so the shocking tale was relayed to us at the kitchen door before Lord Wilson's horse had been brushed and given water after his hard-driven gallop from the woodcutter's cottage. I thought I was imparting news when that evening I told Edward of the terrible treatment, but he had already heard the story from his estate manager and was so angered by the lack of religious tolerance shown that he had immediately offered the woodcutter employment and accommodation. I was delighted that Edward had shown such Christian integrity and compassion at the expense of his good relationship with a fellow landowner, but my admiration of him was somewhat dented when he went on to comment "anything to avoid another dinner invitation from Lord and Lady Wilson."

## CHAPTER 15

AS AUTUMN TURNED TO WINTER, Biggenden Manor became more shipshape and my workload lessened. Painters had been in to redecorate some of the reception rooms. I kept out of their way as much as possible, but painting seemed to produce an unquenchable thirst, requiring cups of tea on an hourly basis. Every time I entered the room with a tray of cups, I was subjected to some lewd but witty comment that would invariably make me blush and become clumsy, so I made my entries and exits as quickly as possible. I suggested that Mr. Kemp deal with the workmen, but apparently the paint vapours set off his lung complaint, so I just had to grit my teeth until the redecorating was finally completed. To give them their due, the painters did an excellent job. It was wonderful to see the manor restored to a well-polished and lived-in home, and I felt proud and privileged to be part of the team that ran it.

As the cold wind and pelting rain lashed against the lattice windows, it felt snug and cosy to draw the heavy curtains, light the lamps, stoke the fire, and settle down to an evening in the study. Edward would often sit in his armchair, put his stockinged feet on the back of his sleeping hound and read the newspaper or discuss the day's events. I would draw a lamp close to sew the seam of a curtain or work on whatever project I had in hand. The lamps and log fire cast a warm glow on the homely scene, excluding the wider room and the rest of the world from its embrace. The crackling and hissing of the burning logs and the dog's gentle snoring contrasted sharply with the wild weather outside.

Mrs. Kemp rarely baked cakes, so I often took it upon myself to make something to supplement our cups of tea. The results were always warmly received by Edward. We enjoyed toasting crumpets on long forks and spreading them with honey, allowing it to run into all the holes before eating them as warm as possible. Rex was rather partial to my crumpets too.

If Edward disliked evening invitations, I hated them even more. Instead of sitting in the study, I would either retire early or sit in my housekeeper's parlour, working on the household accounts (never my favourite chore), reading, or writing letters. My room was much smaller than the study and had a good fireplace, so it actually was warmer, but the lack of companionship made this of little comfort.

Rex often sought me out on these evenings, and I appreciated his presence. On rare occasions we would have a pleasant surprise, which began with Rex rising from his dreams and cocking his ears as he heard his master return early. Edward would then join us in my parlour, dispelling all despondency or tiredness and I would put the kettle on my small range for more tea.

Once or twice I went out for an evening, but it was a fairly rare occurrence, mainly due to the fact that I had neither the time nor the inclination to make many new friends. Mrs. Brooke, Agnes's mother, was a warm-hearted individual, and I sometimes had afternoon tea at her cottage on my half day off. The churchwarden's wife invited me to the charity knitting evenings in aid of the London Society for

Promoting Christianity Amongst the Jews. The industrious ladies of the church would knit or crochet blankets and clothes throughout the winter months and then have a stall at the May Fair, when the same women would buy each other's products and give the proceeds to the mission, which worked among Jews in the East End of London and ran a hospital in Jerusalem. Many hours were spent knitting and fussing over arrangement and prices for the fair, and I secretly thought that more money could be raised simply by having a yearly collection in the village for the mission.

My already meagre enthusiasm for the knitting evenings was further damped when the churchwarden's wife expressed loud and disapproving surprise at how little progress I had made with my knitting since we last met. All conversation seemed to stop, all eyes fastened on my rather halfhearted attempts, and I distinctly heard, from the far corner, a plump lady mutter, "No wonder she ain't got a man."

My one consolation was to go home and argue with Edward that knitting evenings were even more ridiculous than his friends keeping pheasants to shoot. This led to a hot debate on the subject and finally having to agree to disagree.

But life isn't all evenings. During the days, I kept busy and occupied. I encouraged the Kemps to take every Thursday off, and after some initial reluctance, they agreed and soon fell into a routine of visiting their married daughter in the village for the day and returning in time for the evening meal.

On their day off I assumed the role of chief cook and thoroughly enjoyed it. I made some subtle changes to the menu, hoping to influence Mrs. Kemp's repertoire, but to no avail. Instead of boiled potatoes, I did roast. Instead of white sauce, I made cheese. I never included cabbage in the meal. I preferred to make lighter desserts like mousse and trifle rather than jam roly-poly and suet pudding.

Every Thursday the Kemps returned to the kitchen at five o'clock and sat down to eat the meal I had prepared. The food went down in the same speedy, silent manner that all meals were consumed, and I never could discern their opinion, only that it was never imitated.

Once the house was in order, I developed an enjoyable habit of going for a walk after lunch. For the first few weeks, these walks were merely for exercise and entertainment, but it was not long before Edward thought it would be useful if I did some of his charitable visits to ailing or elderly tenants. He was regularly informed by an estate worker of some need or problem and would visit with a basket of provisions. Any female in need he began to pass over to me as "my department," excusing himself by saying it was "awkward, and anyway, you have the knack for knowing what to say."

I often wondered if he begrudged me my afternoons of freedom, but whatever his motivation, after initially feeling awkward at acting as Miss Bountiful at someone else's expense, I soon began to enjoy my visits and build up valuable friendships with many cottagers. I would go with a basket of groceries and receive a warm welcome, a seat, and cup of tea by the fire, and became a confidant of family stories and woes.

One of the saddest situations was that of an elderly widow of a woodcutter by the name of Mrs. Bridges. I had been informed that she was ill and in pain, but for several visits I could not make out what was wrong with her. After I had been to see her regularly with provisions for a few weeks, I noticed a strange, unpleasant smell and a fixed stain of discharge on her bust. With some tactful prompting she admitted to having a large, oozing tumour on her breast, which she had concealed for as long as possible, but which was causing her severe pain. She insisted that no doctor should be called, as she wanted no male "prodding me about," but I organised a regular supply of clean dressings and Laudanum to be ordered to ease her discomfort. We both knew her end was near, but she was ready for the great change, having fixed her hope on Christ many years ago and proved His faithfulness. She had lived a difficult and tough life, but had no complaints. Instead, she was full of thankfulness to the Lord for all the good she had received and much more she could look forward to in glory. She enjoyed me reading the Bible to her and I enjoyed her wise observations, always leaving her small cottage feeling richer for the experience.

One cold February afternoon, as she prepared vegetables for her supper and I worked my way through her darning pile, she told me about her children. Her first three babies had all died soon after birth, but eventually she was blessed with a healthy little baby girl called Elizabeth, who was "bonny and bright" and who grew up to be beautiful in looks and character. She was her father's pride and joy. A few years later a darling son, Simon, was born. He was also a great delight to them. He had thick, curly brown hair and trusting brown eyes; when he smiled dimples appeared in his cheeks, and a spark twinkled in his eyes.

The two small children filled their small cottage with happiness and joy as they played around the house and later explored the woodlands together. They were not without sibling squabbles, but on the whole played well together, making up fine adventures and exploring the village. Mrs. Bridges often took the two children into the woods to have lunch with their father and she glowed with pleasure as she recalled the happy times they had, sitting on logs, making tea in a can over the woodsmen's fire, the children chatting happily as they told their father of the day's activities.

At this point Mrs. Bridges heaved herself out of the chair and shuffled away to a wooden chest under her bed. With love and tears in her eyes, she carefully lifted out some beautiful little dresses she had made for Elizabeth and a pair of well-worn little boots Simon had taken his first steps in. As she sat and continued her story, Mrs. Bridges' rheumatic fingers gently caressed the items.

All too soon it was time for the children to attend school. Elizabeth settled in well, was popular with the pupils, and found learning easy, but Simon struggled. He struggled to differentiate between a *b* and a *d*, a *p* and a *q*, and he found it almost impossible to write with his right hand. He wanted to use his left hand, but the schoolmaster caned his hand and tied it behind his back. The young lad, who used to be happy and confident, soon became fearful and suspicious, hating school and anything new. The schoolmaster became frustrated at Simon's lack of attainment and would often make him wear the dunce hat and stand in the corner for hours, subjecting him to humiliation and mockery. Mr. and Mrs. Bridges watched helplessly as their son developed nervous twitches and became increasingly sad and solitary. Mr. Bridges once confronted the teacher, only to be told that he had no knowledge of modern teaching methods and should not interfere but should be grateful for the free schooling his unworthy son was receiving. As Mr. Bridges' boss and landowner had selected the schoolmaster and paid his salary, there was little that could be done.

The school years dragged on, and at last Simon was free from the tyranny of the schoolmaster, but not from his fears and nervous habits. The twinkle had disappeared from his eyes, never to return. Not only did he fear other humans, but he also feared the voices in his head that frequently told him of his uselessness. Sometimes these voices would exasperate him so much he would scream out in desperation, and Mrs. Bridges would have to soothe his head in her lap and stroke his hair whilst praying aloud for her agitated son. Simon had committed his soul to Christ but was frequently tormented with doubts and misgivings. Mr. Bridges arranged for Simon to work with him in the woods, but sometimes the sound of the falling trees or the crackling of the fire was too much for him, and he was soon dismissed as an unreliable worker.

By this time Elizabeth was happily married to an ambitious solicitor's clerk and had moved away to Canterbury when he received promotion.

One fateful day Simon heard a neighbour suggesting that "the lunatic should be shut away in Barming Heath Asylum." Fearful of being imprisoned in a "mad house," Simon disappeared. After he failed to return home that night, Mr. and Mrs. Bridges rose early the next day to search for Simon, looking in all his favourite haunts in the woodland. But a fellow woodsman found him first, hanging from a tree, dead.

I looked into Mrs. Bridges' eyes and saw fresh grief and anguish as she related the tragic story of her son. Her fingers busily traced the stitching on the leather boots. I put down my sewing and put my arms around her and she sobbed into my breast.

When she had sufficiently composed herself, she went on to explain how shunned the family was for her son's death. Even the vicar visited only once—to express his view that their son was now in hell as a punishment for taking his own life and that the family should not grieve so much as it showed lack of submission to God's judgments. Of course, he added, Simon could not be buried in the consecrated ground of the church yard.

Elizabeth's husband wrote, explaining that as an up-and-coming clerk with prospects, he felt unable to continue associating with a family so shamed, and from hence forth he and his good wife would have no further dealings with them. Mr. and Mrs. Bridges found themselves forsaken by all and lived with the burden of constant grief for a dead son and estranged daughter. Their one consolation was the love and power of Christ, even to those tormented in their minds, and the fact that He is the same forever. But even this consolation could not be shared with others, as all around them, people were indoctrinated with the dogma of the church that those who commit suicide were outside the scope of Christ's love and salvation.

I trudged home at twilight, distressed and musing on the tragic story I had heard, feeling intense love and pain for dear Mrs. Bridges. As I stepped into the kitchen, I was immediately confronted with a message that Mr. Thorpe had needed my help for at least an hour and was "put out" at hearing of my truancy. I hastened to the study only to find him pouring over a shooting catalogue, unable to decide what kind of riding boots to order.

"Ah, you've arrived at last! I desperately need your help."

"How can I assist, sir?"

He passed me the catalogue. "Which of these riding boots should I go for?"

"Well, it is hardly my area of expertise, sir."

"But it would be nice if you showed an interest."

I tried to apply my mind to riding boots and with a rather absent air helped him choose a pair.

"Good, I'll order them first thing tomorrow," said Edward. "Anyway, what makes you so tardy tonight?"

"I was assisting Mrs. Bridges with her chores."

"You are becoming too involved with the villagers. Remember you are paid to run my household and not to help every Tom, Dick, and Harry in the village."

I bit my lip hard to prevent an unguarded reply and after giving a most servile "and will that be all, sir?" I exited the room. That evening he drank his tea and ate his extra thin slice of cake alone; I feigned tiredness and retired early.

## CHAPTER 16

THAT NIGHT I TOSSED AND turned in bed, unable to forget Mrs. Bridges' heart-rending story and her enduring pain of being estranged from the only living member of her family and of the church's reaction to Simon taking his own life. I was also troubled by Edward's reaction and it began to dawn on me that he had feet of clay. This then led to the realisation that if I perceived him to have feet of clay, he was obviously an idol to me—and I was an idolater. But, I reasoned to myself, I am not worshipping him or praying to him; yes, I admitted, he does fill much of my waking thoughts, but as I am in his employment and he is a friend, surely this is permitted. Thus I accused and excused myself into the small hours when sleep finally overtook me.

The next morning I was again summoned to Edward's study. He invited me to sit down as he had an important matter to discuss. My mind raced as I wondered whatever the matter would be that demanded such a formal and urgent meeting.

"Over the past few months, I have been subjected to the hospitality of many families in the vicinity, and I feel socially indebted to them," Edward explained.

I waited for him to elaborate.

"As you clearly have a reduced workload, it is high time I reciprocated the kindness of these families and start inviting them here for evening meals."

"I see."

"Obviously you will need more staff, so I would like you to advertise for whomever you feel you require."

"I will attempt that, sir." He cleared his throat and studied his hands. "And I would prefer it if you cooked the meals rather than Mrs. Kemp producing bland, heavy stodge for my genteel guests. I will leave it in your capable hands to arrange this tactfully and discreetly."

I mentally raised my eyebrows at this last request but agreed to carry out his orders.

My immediate response to the need of more staff was to consider Nancy, the poor scullery maid from Barton Manor. What an opportunity it would provide for her to better herself! But to my shame and eternal regret, I rejected this charitable idea because she would need to live-in. I preferred to employ local girls so that our evening arrangements would not be discovered or discussed. I silenced my conscience by arguing that it would not be right to rob Mrs. Milton of a dutiful member of staff.

Finding suitable staff was easier than anticipated: I simply asked Agnes if she knew of any young, industrious girls in the neighbourhood, and she soon came up with some suggestions. There was a great lack of employment for young women in the area, and many of them followed their mothers by taking up seasonal agricultural work, which was poorly paid, unpredictable in availability, and back-breaking.

Mrs. Kemp and I interviewed four girls and selected the two who seemed the most willing and quick of mind: Molly and Clara. Agnes had the task of instructing them in all cleaning matters, and I provided instruction on waiting at the table—after consulting a few books on the subject.

Mrs. Kemp was pleased with extra help in the kitchen, but this was slightly overshadowed by the fact that she now had two more mouths to feed. We agreed that they should learn all-around tasks and not become either a housemaid or kitchen maid so that we would have greater flexibility.

As we were busy training the new maids, Edward was becoming more and more absorbed in his new hobby of shooting game. At social functions the conversations of the males predominantly centred on the latest shoot, the quality of their guns, and the amount of game bagged. Each, praising up his fellow marksmen, felt secretly assured that none was as accurate a shot as himself.

While at first Edward privately scorned the fashion, as he was invited to more and more shoots, he found it necessary to purchase a good gun. Before long he became known for his shooting prowess. He soon could regale the events of an afternoon's shoot, shot by shot, as well as any man.

I was amused to learn all the reasons (or rather, *excuses*) for a poor performance, including rough terrain, unhelpful beaters, wrong wind direction, and even uncooperative birds.

Edward began hosting shoots on his own land, and the need to invite these gentlemen and their wives for a meal became pressing. Once the new maids were reasonably competent in their new roles, I let Edward know that we were ready to attempt entertaining, and he promptly sent out invitations. I dreaded speaking to Mrs. Kemp about the cooking arrangements, but that too was easier than I had feared. Mrs. Kemp reacted with such alarm at the thought of entertaining the gentry that I immediately had to reassure her I would be willing to do the task, if she would be so good as to guide me. She readily agreed, offering to cook for the servants on the days that the master entertained. I did not feel it necessary to inform Edward of how easily Mrs. Kemp had been persuaded to relinquish her role, and he seemed in awe of my diplomatic skills and extremely grateful.

My triumph felt hollow as I sat in my room, pouring over *The Art of Cookery, Made Plain and Easy*, trying to produce a menu that was both easy and impressive. The art of cookery seemed far removed from plain and easy to me! I finally settled on leek soup, followed by *filet de bœuf en croûte*, with roast potatoes, vegetables, and thickened gravy laced with port. The dessert needed to be light, so I chose apple trifle.

Edward decreed that three courses was sufficient and gave a cursory glance and nod to my carefully constructed menu. I ordered double the amount required of all the ingredients and practised the meal on the staff, learning by it that the beef took far longer to cook than I had anticipated. The appointed day of the dreaded meal arrived and saw me frantically darting between kitchen and the reception rooms, rolling pastry that refused to roll, blowing a stove that was reluctant to roar, and checking the flower arrangements. My cooking apron soon had the marks of every ingredient in the recipes.

A meal that would take the maximum of one hour to eat took me all day to prepare, but at last it was ready. I wished I could present the food better and in a more decorative manner, but all I could manage was for it to look edible. Mrs. Kemp fussed and bossed around her husband, helping him into his best suit (normally reserved for weddings and funerals), and he was sent to the hall to answer the door and greet the guests. Agnes and the girls looked neat and tidy in their clean black dresses with lacey caps and aprons, while I had traces of pastry through my hair, and sweat stuck my clothes to me. We were all nervous but also exhilarated by the challenge of succeeding.

Mr. Kemp served the wine, while Agnes and Clara served the food. Molly transported the food from the kitchen to the dining room, bringing back used crockery and reports of how the meal was progressing. She had never in her whole life been so close to the gentry and was totally star-struck by the *"an'some men 'n bootiful ladies."* The empty platters that kept appearing in the scullery were the only indication I received that the food was acceptable.

When the ladies had retired to the living room and had been served coffee, Clara returned to the kitchen, exclaiming her amazement at the appetites of the ladies *"wiv them tight corsets, I dunno where they put it awl,"* which made us all double up with laughter harder and longer than the comment deserved, probably out of relief and exhaustion, although the work was by no means over.

As the guests relaxed by the log fire, we rolled up our sleeves and started the washing up. While we tidied up, we picked at the leftover food and agreed we were too tired to eat the supper Mrs. Kemp had prepared, because, as Agnes rightly pointed out, "eating supper will only make more washing up." So, saving it for the next day, we filled up with chunks of bread and cheese, eating as we worked.

Finally, when Mr. Kemp shuffled in, having closed the door on the last lingering guests, we all collapsed into chairs around the kitchen table, and Mrs. Kemp boiled up some milk for us all, as if we were her young family, "to relax the mind." We sat nursing our warm cups, longing for bed, but too tired to move. The maids stayed the night as it was too late to walk home. After a while of girlish giggling, Clara and Molly settled in their beds, and we all slept like logs.

The following morning we reassembled, blurry-eyed, at the breakfast table and ate in a sleepy silence. The maids then set about the task of cleaning the dining and sitting room, expressing surprise at the amount of mess the genteel guests had generated. Crumbs were trodden into the dining room mat, coffee and port had been spilt, chair backs were stained with gentlemen's Makassar oil, and cigar ash dusted the tables. Even the flowers looked wilted after an evening of glory.

Mid-morning Edward invited me into his study to "dissect" the previous evening. From his point of view, the evening had gone very well, better than expected: the conversation flowed, the guests were agreeable, the staff did him proud, and (finally he said it) the food was superb.

I flushed with joy at his assessment. Forgetting the hours of toil in the kitchen, I said that it was my pleasure. After telling me more about his guests and their conversations, he ended our discussion by saying, "We must entertain again, but, as for tonight, I can't think of anything I would like more than a quiet evening by the fire with you and a slice of your cake." This, of course, sent me flying back to the kitchen to bake, with a spring in my step and a smile on my face. The cake would not only be for Edward, but for all the staff, to express my gratitude for making our first dinner party at Biggenden a success.

The next day, as soon as I had organised the maids, I escaped the manor to visit Mrs. Bridges. There was still some leek soup left, and I took a jug of that, along with a loaf of Mrs. Kemp's freshly baked bread. Since I knew that Mrs. Bridges enjoyed hearing about life at Biggenden, I gave her a full report of the dinner party.

As she sat in her armchair by the stove, sipping her soup, her face looked strained with pain and weakness. She was wearing a woolen shawl and had a blanket over her knees, but to me she looked smaller and frailer than just a few days ago. Whilst our guests had been dining on their copious meal, it was doubtful that Mrs. Bridges had summoned up either the strength or inclination to prepare herself anything. I was resolved that from now on I would bring her food every day. Her good neighbour ensured that her log basket was always full and her stove alight, but she had a large family of her own to care for and could not do much more.

I stayed with Mrs. Bridges until twilight, helped her into bed (which was now downstairs), and sat with her until she fell asleep. As soon as she was soundly asleep, I did something slightly dubious. I went to her small desk and looked through her papers until I found what I was looking for: the address of her daughter. I quickly wrote it down, returned the paper, threw a log on the fire, and crept out of the house.

Late that night, in the privacy of my parlour, I wrote to Elisabeth, explaining that her mother was gravely ill and unlikely to survive a month. I informed her of her mother's weak, pitiful condition and how she spent most of her solitary time remembering the happier years of her life when her two dear children brightened up the cottage. I begged Elisabeth to hasten a visit to her mother before death would separate them forever.

I wrestled with and prayed over the phrases and wording of my letter, endeavouring to pull on the daughter's heart strings as much as possible. Many attempts at the letter were aborted and thrown in the fire, but finally, in the small hours, when I admitted that I could not improve the wording, I sealed the envelope and put it out for posting the next day.

After obtaining Edward's consent, I visited Mrs. Bridges twice a day to ensure she had food and drink. There was a local woman who could be called upon to help with births, deaths, and laying out, but her reputation was somewhat dubious, some even saying that dying patients gave up the ghost early rather than be subjected to her rough nursing. Through the grapevine this same woman had heard of Mrs. Bridges' condition and came to offer her assistance, but, in unison, the kind neighbour and I dismissed her and said that we would cope, thank you very much. One overpowering waft of her breath convinced us she wasn't even sober enough to care for our dear friend.

At first I was so convinced that my letter would bring Elisabeth running to her mother's bedside that I almost told Mrs. Bridges of my actions, but as the days went by, each sapping more and more life from her weak body, I started to run out of hope. As so many things might have gone wrong: the family could have moved, the son-in-law remain unmoved, the post be delayed, and the letter lost, any chance of a happy reunion seemed smaller and smaller.

Each morning Mrs. Bridges' eyes sank deeper into her face, and her skin stretched tightly over her cheek bones. High doses of opium were necessary to ease her pain. Instead of speaking or at least acknowledging my conversation, she spent most of the time asleep. I sometimes sat reading the Bible to her or singing softly, but most of the time she seemed unaware of my presence. The cord that held her body and soul together grew weaker every hour, and often I had to look hard to detect any sign of life in her as her strength ebbed away.

Then, during one afternoon visit, I found her lifeless body tucked up in bed, her waxen face now free from the careworn wrinkles, her soul released from her pain-torn body to the place where her heart had been for a long time. As I gazed through my tears at her lifeless but beautiful face, the truth that "blessed are they that die in the Lord" hit me with great power. Mrs. Bridges' sorrows and struggles were over, she was forever reunited to her husband and son, but even more amazingly, she was in the presence of her Saviour, gazing upon His beauty.

As I looked around her poor, damp, sparsely furnished room and thought on her mansion in heaven, I could only rejoice for her but cry for myself, being once again bereft of one I loved. The old grief of losing my parents swept over me anew, and I sat down by the unlit stove, weeping uncontrollably. But the human mind is a strange thing, for as I lifted my head from my hands, it struck me that a painting on the wall was skew-whiff, and it suddenly became important to straighten it.

In times of great sorrow or shock, I have found that I seem to have a strangely heightened awareness of the trivial details, for example, that the hat worn by a bearer of bad news is at a strange angle or the individual's coat is missing a button! Maybe I am alone in this or maybe it is a thing common to man. These trivial thoughts at a time of great seriousness have annoyed me as inappropriate and distracting follies, but over the years I've begun to wonder if they are the mind's way of gradually processing and coping with shocking news—and somehow actually helpful!

So I straightened said painting, and this trivial action awoke my senses, lifting me from inertia, and I went to tell the neighbours.

## CHAPTER 17

AS I TRIED TO CONTAIN my grief, wanting to help with sorting out Mrs. Bridges' cottage and the funeral arrangements, Edward was absorbed with preparations for a trip to Scotland with a shooting friend to enjoy the grouse season. A tailor was urgently instructed to produce a tweed shooting outfit, and a number of cases were packed, full of suitable clothes. His excitement infected the whole household, and everyone happily busied themselves on his behalf—the whole household, that is, except me: his enthusiasm could not penetrate my sadness.

During our evening meetings he had genuinely sympathised with the loss of Mrs. Bridges, but I did not want to burden him with the cloud of bereavement pain for my dear parents that descended upon me. After all, he himself was an orphan, and to be drawn into my grief might have caused him to feel bereft once again. My duty as a housekeeper was to run the household efficiently, and I tried to put on a brave face, only to break down in the privacy of my bedroom. I was aware of looking pale and sombre. Of course, the prospect of a fortnight without Edward did little to lift my mood.

I had long since given up hope of gaining encouragement and comfort from the vicar's sermons. Instead of finding peace as I listened to his monotone, I became increasingly annoyed that his God-given opportunities of speaking to the parish about the Saviour's worth were invariably wasted. I also became more and more aware of the disapproving faces of Mrs. Brinkhill, his sour wife, and their anaemic, unmarried daughter, but not without feelings of guilt for remaining unmoved by the church services.

Edward explained that he tried to supplement this meagre diet by preaching a sermon to himself in his head from the vicar's text. I tried this idea, and sometimes it worked, but more often than not, my mind just wandered.

Preaching your own sermon has its advantages, as one knows what train of thought is most likely to warm one's heart. For instance, I think of the Lord as the Creator of trees, the One who supplies the sun and rain they need, and the One who makes them grow. I follow that with thinking of Jesus as a young man working as a carpenter, making everyday objects with wood, and then those same skilful hands healing the sick, and later those same hands nailed to the very wood He created. Finally, my thoughts will move to those same hands wiping away all the tears of the redeemed in glory. As I say, this sometimes works, but often thoughts of the coming week's chores or how to handle the maids filled my mind.

What I have always enjoyed, though, is the beautiful liturgy found in *The Book of Common Prayer*. The rich and beautiful phrases chosen by Cranmer in the 1550s express so eloquently the confession, contrition, and praises of the human heart and extoll the holiness and majesty of God. I realised that my reasons for loving the liturgy were a mixture of spiritual resonance, as well as nostalgic reminiscence of people and places where I had first used these words before, chiefly, my father's old church in our family pew, snuggled up to Ma in her best Sunday dress. I mused on the idea that for three hundred years Christians throughout the land, in humble rural parishes and in splendid cathedrals, had by wonderful language been united in their offering of petition and praise.

Rev. Brinkhill was rather selective in when and how to use the Prayer Book, but generally included just enough to satisfy my taste. Thankfully, at Mrs. Bridges' burial, the vicar saw fit to use the whole of the set liturgy, so the confident language of precious promises of the resurrection of the dead sounded forth over her open grave, putting life's little day into perspective.

Ma always maintained that work is a great healer, and with this in mind I galvanised my team of maids to do a thorough clean of Biggenden in the absence of the master. This cleaning task illustrated how far we had progressed at Biggenden: instead of carrying out most of the task myself, I now had a team of three capable girls to do the work as I supervised and cleaned only the most delicate objects like lace and precious china—not that there was an abundance of either in the bachelor establishment.

We all worked hard, but, following Mrs. Milton's example, I tried to relax the normal daily timetable . . . until I found Molly taking advantage of my leniency and slipping off work early. This was a perpetual problem with the two new maids: if I was relaxed and friendly, they thought they could cut corners and take advantage, but if I was strict and demanding, I detected a subtle rebellion. Agnes seemed to be loyal, but soon I discovered that she also tried to "run with the hare and hunt with the hounds" to remain on good terms with both the girls and me, by agreeing with both parties. I missed the camaraderie of being a housemaid and began to realise what an isolated position housekeepers up and down the country were in as they walked the tightrope of friendliness and authority.

Another growing concern was what to do with Mr. and Mrs. Kemp. Mr. Kemp had aged rapidly during the time I had known him: he was becoming increasingly stooped and was almost completely deaf. He seemed to assume the rest of us suffered with the same affliction and muttered to himself, often uncomplimentary comments. This was proving to be an embarrassment when he greeted guests. Sometimes he completely forgot to do the small routine tasks allocated to him. One's nose also got the distinct impression that his personal cleanliness was not as good as it could be. He continued to shave daily, but missed some areas, resulting in various tufts of whiskers at different stages of growth around his mouth and jaw line.

Mrs. Kemp gradually did less and less in the kitchen but was as helpful as possible. She seemed well aware of her husband's dotage and tried to cover up for him, but her arthritic joints prevented her from venturing farther than the kitchen. Sometimes she appeared troubled and distressed by their declining power and usefulness.

Edward had mentioned that he wanted to stop employing the elderly couple before any further social function, but we were at pains to know of a diplomatic and sympathetic way to carry out this plan. Their daughter and son-in-law lived in the village, but their little cottage was already overflowing with children, and they hardly had a penny to rub between them. Then, one morning as I helped to clean up Mrs. Bridges' house, I had an idea: here was one of Edward's cottages standing empty, and who were more deserving of filling it than the Kemps? If a few roof tiles were replaced and some white-wash painted on the grimy walls, it would be a decent place to live.

Moreover, it was only a field away from their daughter, too far for Mrs. Kemp to walk but not too far for the young legs of grandchildren to run errands or call in after school. I was bursting with enthusiasm for my idea, but I had to keep it under my hat until Edward returned.

Back at Biggenden Manor, the cleaning was completed and I allowed the maids a day off. The Kemps, of course, stayed in the kitchen but enjoyed the luxury of having it all to themselves and were soon dozing contentedly before the range. I packed a picnic, found my stoutest boots and straw hat, and set off on a long walk to enjoy the late August sun. The neighbourhood was full of activity as the farm labourers and casual workers made the most of the sunny weather and were harvesting the wheat.

I stopped to watch the rhythmic movements of the cutters as they worked together in a line, cutting the stalks with their sharp scythes. Women, girls, and boys followed, rapidly but carefully, gathering the wheat stalks into sheaves and taking them to be stood for drying in skilfully crafted stooks. Between the workers, toddlers crawled through the stubble or sat with chubby fingers in dribbling mouths, taking in the scene. Edward's trusted foreman was overseeing the events and tapping a barrel of Biggenden cider to relieve the thirst of his sweating workforce.

Among the women I noticed Molly's mother and sisters. It then dawned on me that Molly probably had to do extra chores at home this time of year and that I should not have been so quick to judge her. As I walked on, feeling somewhat guilty that I did not stay to lend a hand, I passed orchards full of ripening apples, hop gardens dark with fully laden bines, and small cottages occupied by only the old, left to keep house and prepare a meal for the hungry labourers.

It seemed strange to me that Edward had seen fit to leave his estate at such a busy and important time of year. His decision, to pursue his beloved pastime when all his employees were working every daylight hour to line his purse, troubled me and seemed out of character. I held out hope that he would come to his senses and return to the manor.

Before long I came to the River Medway. Sitting down on the river bank, I ate my sandwiches and then reclined to enjoy the sunshine on my face. My eyelids grew heavy, and soon the gentle noise of the flowing river and the chirping of crickets sent me to sleep.

It was after six o'clock before I was woken by ant bites. Wandering home leisurely, I passed the wheat field, now peacefully deserted of human life, with neat stooks standing upright testifying to the day's labours. A few rabbits and crows supping on fallen grain disappeared when I clapped my hands. The sun was low in the blue sky, and the whole scene was a perfect illustration of the reality that "The Lord is good to man and beast."

The next morning I rose early with enthusiasm and determination. The master of Biggenden might not be present, but I was sure I knew him well enough to issue some benevolence on his behalf. I lit the kitchen range early and got to work baking bread. As soon as the maids arrived they began kneading the dough. We left it to rise on a sunny window ledge whilst we had breakfast before kneading it again. By lunch time we had produced a dozen crusty loaves, which we cut into thick doorsteps, liberally spread with butter and made into cheese and pickle sandwiches. We dusted off some old wicker baskets, lined them with cloths, and packed them full.

The maids enjoyed themselves as much as I did, as we put on our bonnets and tripped off down the lane to the next wheat field. We were given a warm and hearty welcome by the workers, who invited us to join the impromptu picnic. Our prim, high-necked uniforms contrasted sharply with the unbuttoned necks and rolled up sleeves of the other women, but as I sat eating the fresh sandwiches and sharing a flagon of cider, I felt happy and content, remembering the wonderful days of my childhood spent helping on Bessie's farm.

The food disappeared at an alarming rate, as did the cider. The amount some labourers ate and drank would have put me into a stupor, but they were soon back on their feet, ready for the afternoon's work. We indoor girls reluctantly got up, dusted ourselves down and, empty baskets in hand, returned to more sedate duties. With the bright sunshine outside and the knowledge of the activity less than a field away, the manor felt as restrictive as a prison. I dismissed Clara and Molly early that day, knowing full well that they would be down in the harvest field before you could say "Jack Robinson." Whether they were propelled by a sense of duty or the wish to admire and flirt with the young, muscular reapers was anyone's guess!

I could not sneer at their enthusiasm for male company, as I longed for the evening when we were expecting Edward to arrive home. He arrived after sundown, due to delays on the railway. I quickly prepared a tray of supper for him and was invited to join him in the study. Though tired from travelling, he was full of enthusiasm about his holiday, the shooting, his new boots and outfit, and the Scottish scenery and steam trains.

I sipped my tea and listened to his lively descriptions. He had been hunting, shooting, fishing, riding, and dancing; he had met many interesting men and stunning ladies. During his time away, he had also come up with a new plan: he would rear pheasants in his woods, employ a gamekeeper, and have high quality game to offer his newfound friends. His woods were most suitable for bird rearing, and he was surprised it had never occurred to him before. This is what Biggenden had been waiting for. The Bridges' old cottage could be modernised for the new gamekeeper, he added.

I continued to sip tea and eat cake, deciding to take time to formulate persuasive arguments before sharing my alternative idea for the cottage. He asked me how things had gone at home, and I described the harvest scene and our picnic. He was interested to hear about it and pleased with what we had done, but he seemed somewhat distracted, his mind still somewhere in Scotland.

As I lay in bed later, my worry was "had he also left his heart there, and with which stunning lady?" Our spheres of life were moving farther and farther apart as he made new friends and explored more of the opportunities that had opened up for him in his new position, whilst I remained not much more than a dependable domestic servant with the willingness to lend a listening ear. Was I supposed to stand forever on the sideline of his life, ready to offer him the applause and encouragement he wanted?

## CHAPTER 18

THAT NIGHT WE HAD A severe thunderstorm. The oppressive heat of the previous days made it no surprise. Not being of farming stock, I had never personally witnessed the damage a summer storm can do to a crop in harvest time. At first I enjoyed watching the lightning eerily illuminate the whole landscape and feeling the refreshingly cool air as it blew through my chamber window, heralding the rain, but as my mind became more alert and awake, the danger the farm was in dawned on me, and I prayed earnestly for its safety.

The storm soon passed and I returned to bed and dozed, but from the pale and drawn face of Edward the next morning, I gathered that he had not slept. He and his foreman had already travelled around the estate to assess storm damage. The hay-ricks had taken a beating but remained intact, thanks to the skilful way they had been constructed. The main damage was to the wheat that remained uncollected in the fields, which the rain and hail had beaten into the muddy soil. It was difficult to assess how much was wasted, since it was impossible to guess the yield of any field accurately until threshing had taken place. Many apples had fallen, but once again the damage was hard to assess. The bruising of the apples remaining on the trees would come out over the next few days.

Other farmers who still had wheat to harvest had fared far worse: their crops had been partially knocked to the ground and lay like sodden matting. A whole hop garden, heavy with flowers and foliage, had crashed to the ground at a nearby farm. The hops were not yet ready to be picked and would probably just rot in the mud.

As a point of encouragement, the experienced foreman told Edward, "'Tis the thing with farming. Ya can always find a farm better off and a farm worse off than ya own." Farmers develop their own stoic philosophy to cope with the many knocks from the weather, the markets, or the diseases that batter them.

When I went to bring Edward his coffee, I found him sitting with his head in his hands. He ran his fingers through his hair and without looking up said, "I don't think I can cope with this farming malarkey."

I felt like embracing him, but instead I just patted his shoulder and offered a few rather pathetic but sincerely meant words of encouragement. He obviously appreciated my feeble efforts of comfort, as he squeezed my hand that lay on his shoulder, raised his downcast eyes to mine, gave a weak smile, and said, "Thanks, old friend."

Despite the reduced yield from the harvest, the labourers deserved a reward for their hard work, and the harvest supper needed to be planned. The housework was neglected as we all bustled around the kitchen making pies, puddings, and pastries for this much anticipated evening. Any villager with a connection to the harvest work, however tenuous, would find their way to the great barn to enjoy an evening of fine fare and cider at the landlord's expense.

We served a hearty supper, and Edward gave a short speech of thanks for the hard work given during the harvest. This was acknowledged by loud clapping, table banging, and cheering. Then the church

gallery band struck up, and the dancing began. As the cider reached
the bloodstream, more and more people got up from the benches to
dance the night away. My team of housemaids was quickly depleted
as they joined in the merrymaking, leaving only Agnes and me to
clear the tables and feed the latecomers.

The cidery breath of the panting dancers, their sweaty bodies,
and the dust disturbed by their pounding feet combined to create a
heady and intoxicating atmosphere. The daylight dwindled to dusk,
and the oil lamps were lit, adding to the cosiness of the now warm
barn. Agnes and I looked on longingly as the dancers lined up for
various reels, until finally more women were needed to make up a set,
and we eagerly took off our aprons and volunteered.

Many of the dances were new to me, some in circles and some
in lines, but I soon got the idea on the movements, and besides, no
one seemed to mind mistakes or collisions, rather seeing it as yet another reason to laugh and crack a joke. I was guided through the steps
by various villagers; some of the men grasped me in a vice-like grip
and dragged me across the barn like a sack of potatoes, while others
offered a limp hand and danced with awkward caution, as if I was
breakable. We weaved between couples, making different formations,
stepping forwards, backwards, left or right, first clapping, then holding hands and sometimes linking arms. All of this was performed
with great enthusiasm, tempo, and merriment. Each dance would in-
volve swapping partners, linking arms as a foursome, as a couple, or
as the sexes, creating different circles.

Every now and again, I was Edward's partner, and my feet hardly
touched the floor as he swung me firmly down the avenue of clapping dancers.

"This easily beats the staid dancing of Barton Manor," he said and laughed as, hand in hand, we danced the length of the barn.

I longed for the moments to go on forever, but all too soon another girl was his partner, and I found myself with a man with two left feet and hobnail boots.

Soon after midnight Edward bade the gathering goodnight and made a decorous exit. The dancing produced a thirst and appetite, so the cider jugs and food tables were revisited again and again. Once Edward had departed, much of the allure of the event disappeared, and I became aware of how tired I was. While the fiddlers were pausing for another drink, I slipped out of the barn and made my way to bed.

The days whirled by, and soon there was a chill in the air, but as the year progressed, so did Edward's plans for the farm. An experienced gamekeeper was employed (and given Mrs. Bridges' newly restored cottage, as I had been unable to convince Edward to let the Kemps have it), and a semi mature flock of pheasants was brought in for winter shooting parties. I looked pityingly at the beautiful birds as they walked proudly through the woods or, when startled, sounded a guttural alarm call and took off with a great flutter of their colourful wings, knowing that before long I would be asked to pluck, gut, and roast them.

Edward's favourite occupation of an evening became cleaning, oiling, and caressing his guns or looking through shooting catalogues. I listened with mixed emotions to his reports on the progress of the pheasant project, knowing full well that soon I would be instructed to prepare for an invasion of his friends for a shooting party. Indeed, this duly happened and early November found my team and me busying ourselves around the house, airing beds, planning menus, and cleaning the spare rooms.

Edward's guests were to be two married couples: Mr. and Mrs. Thomas, and Mr. and Mrs. Harrington accompanied by their youngest daughter, Miss Sophia. These visitors would be joined by Edward's local shooting companions for one big day of shooting and then enjoy unlimited opportunities for shooting pheasants during their stay.

Clara, Molly, and Agnes were to sleep at Biggenden so that they could take on any lady's maid duties required. Mr. Kemp did very little besides polishing the silver, and we fervently hoped that no valeting duties would be required—surely grown-up men could dress themselves for a few days? Edward was keen to employ a handsome young lad from the village, but I persuaded him that we had neither the time nor expertise to train him.

The day of our guests' arrival dawned, and I looked around the house with pride. Every polish-able surface shone, each fire was roaring, each lamp trimmed, each bed looked inviting, and appetising aromas emanated from the kitchen (mainly thanks to Agnes). Edward, dressed in a new outfit and smelling of a strong eau de cologne, seemed less satisfied and fussed about like an old mother hen. Was the house too sparse or shabby for his awaited guests, he wondered?

I was surprised at his lack of composure, but when the guests arrived, things became clearer. I had imagined the young daughter to be a sweet, chubby twelve-year-old girl, but as I saw her emerge from the carriage, I realised my huge mistake. She was a stunningly beautiful young lady with great presence and poise. Miss Sophia wore a beautiful sky blue dress with white lace trimmings, perfectly complementing the blueness of her eyes. Her blonde hair was rolled almost carelessly into a bun, with a few curly strands escaping to give her a soft and carefree look.

I watched from an upstairs window as she alighted, and I saw Edward, full of smiles, hurrying to meet her and lend a hand. Even from my distant viewpoint, I could glean all I needed to know: Edward was in love, and it was not with me.

With this new insight, I hurried downstairs to ensure the kettles were boiling for the guests' afternoon tea. Animated conversation and laughing drifted into the kitchen from the hall and then the sound receded as the guests entered the parlour. I served tea and cake, while Molly and Clara started to unpack the visitors' trunks. Agnes was busy preparing an elaborate evening meal.

The conversation in the parlour was centred round the journey and the guests' first impressions of Biggenden. Miss Sophia found it "quaintly rustic," and the men were delighted by the number of pheasants they had seen already from the carriage. I silently entered the room, placed the laden tea tray on the table and slipped out again, leaving the ladies to decide for themselves who would preside over the pot.

The day of the great shoot arrived, and a vast crowd of tweed-clad men bearing guns and capacious game bags gathered enthusiastically at the front door. I led the maids in supplying them with port and rich fruit cake as Edward organised them into groups. All the farm labourers had been enrolled as beaters and were given frantic, last-minute tuition on their role by the gamekeeper. Then, with much noise, pounding of feet, and shouting at dogs, the throng marched down the drive toward the unsuspecting pheasants. All day, as we went about our domestic chores, we could hear the guns. Every minute I expected someone to be accidently shot and brought bleeding to the back door, but nothing untoward happened and by the evening, the cold room was filled with hanging pheasants, the hall with muddy boots and the laundry baskets with sweaty clothes.

For the duration of the guests' visit, we servants worked hard, from dawn to dusk and beyond, to ensure everyone was comfortable, well fed, and watered, and that the rooms were clean and pleasant with the fires stoked. Every whim of the guests was met. Breakfasts were delayed for sleepers, and suppers brought forward for hungry shooters.

We watched with interest as Edward's guests strolled through the garden, went shooting, paid visits to neighbours, and lounged the evenings away. The upper class fascinated us, as we observed their lives, so very different from our own, but the person we were most captivated by was Miss Sophia. She seemed utterly impeccable in taste and deportment. She had a suitable and beautiful outfit to fit every occasion: for a horse ride, she had a neatly tailored habit; for country strolls, she had a practical but feminine tweed suit. As for day dresses, she had demure but fetching frocks with intricate tucks and folds, beautifully complementing her lovely figure; but in the evening, she outdid all her other outfits with delicate, flowing, almost ethereal white silk dresses. She often had a flower in her hair, which seemed to emphasise how natural her beauty was. It was clear that Edward found her as enchanting as we did, as his adoring eyes followed her around the room.

So far the only fault we humble servants had found with this goddess was her attitude toward us. She was by no means rude or demanding, but she seemed to view us as a bunch of dated rustic peasants, always finding our ways "quaint" or "homely." Her harmless observations were given in such a light-hearted, even teasing tone that it was impossible to take offence. Her mother was less reserved in her comments: in her *refined* opinion, our uniforms were out of date, our meals too substantial to be elegant, and she found it strange to be served at dinner by maids rather than footmen.

Edward looked uncomfortable when such remarks were made in front of us but made no effort to defend his household. Miss Sophia seemed to sense his discomfort and often managed to playfully change the subject to something more pleasing to Edward. Indeed, throughout her stay, she seemed determined to please her host and to make herself as agreeable as possible—and she most definitely succeeded.

In everything the house party did, they seemed to naturally evolve into three couples: the two husbands, the two wives (who often stayed indoors, doing fancy work), and Edward and Miss Sophia, and it looked no hardship on their part. During the long evenings, the older men snoozed by the fireside and the wives chatted, but Miss Sophia entertained them all on the pianoforte.

The instrument had seemed almost redundant for a long time. I was the only one who played it, occasionally thumping out "Old Hundredth" or some other easy hymn tune, but under Miss Sophia's elegant fingers, the keys and strings seemed to come alive and sing, and beautiful music flowed out. It was a pleasure to stand outside the door and listen. Edward had enough musical knowledge to appoint himself to page-turning duties, thus ensuring close proximity to Miss Sophia.

For us, the visit was taking its toll. We were working long hours, trying to be as un-quaint and un-homely as possible, whilst getting all the jobs done and ensuring everyone was happy. I was also low in spirits due to the shattering of my long-held romantic dream. In some ways the heavy workload was a blessing, as it meant I could not wallow in my emotions but had to just get on with organising deliveries, meals, and household chores.

But one time my thin veneer of normality cracked. Molly and Clara were serving lunch, and they came laughing into the kitchen, declaring that "Mr. Thorpe was positively flirting with Miss Sophie" and speculating when the wedding would be. I swung around from my position at the range and flew at them for gossiping about their superiors. They looked shocked and muttered apologies, but later that afternoon when I was in the scullery, they entered the kitchen and, unaware that I was within ear-shot, started talking about me, calling me an old maid and wondering if "Spinster Stubbs" had ever had a sweetheart. Clara thought it unlikely before adding "and she is too old now." I did not know what to do. I could not leave the scullery and face them, so I sat behind the door on a milk churn until they had vacated the kitchen, and then I hurried to my room and cried. I was only twenty years old. Was that really too old for romance?

Now I had seen myself as they saw me, and it all seemed so horribly true. I studied myself in the looking glass and saw the grim-lined face of an ageing spinster with a shrivelled heart. I had bags under my red eyes from a week of short nights, and my hair was brushed back far too severely in order to fit under my unflattering cap. I couldn't help thinking of the beautiful face of Miss Sophia, fresh, wholesome, and playful. How naive and foolish I had been to imagine that Edward would ever see me as a suitable wife—Edward or, for that matter, any man. My future was staring me in the face: one of servitude and of a bystander, watching other people's lives unfold and flourish while mine stayed monotonously static.

After a quick weep, I forced myself to regain composure and get back to work. It was Clara's turn to serve the evening drinks, so I was able to retire early and benefit from a good night's sleep. Our guests had been with us for seven days and were due to go on the tenth; I longed for their departure.

I was saddened that on Sunday the company decided to remain at home rather than attend the evening service. I understood the reluctance to leave a warm living room and instead sit in a cold church, listening to a dry and lifeless sermon, but I wished Edward had shown his Christian colours more openly.

On Monday evening, Miss Sophia retired early due to a headache. She called me to her room and requested a cold compress, and I stayed to help her undress and recline on her bed. Afterwards, I went down to my sitting room to write an order for the butcher, make a pot of tea, and toast some bread on my little stove. As I sat mindlessly watching the flames, I burnt the toast so had to open the window to disperse the smoke.

I was just about to pour the tea when Edward knocked on the door and walked straight in. I was very surprised to see him. He flung himself into his normal chair and asked if there was enough tea for two. He explained that he had escaped from his visitors, as he was sick of playing bridge yet again. I was delighted to have his company but also realised that it was mainly due to the absence of Miss Sophia rather than his boredom with bridge or the desire for my company.

We had just started sipping our tea, when there was another knock at the door and the voice of Miss Sophia softly calling, "Mrs. Stubbs." In one neat movement Edward jumped out of his chair, dashed to the window, and leapt out into the garden (into a rhododendron bush, to be precise). With the same haste, I hid the second cup behind my chair and answered the door. Miss Sophia wanted to see if I happened to know the whereabouts of Mr. Thorpe, but I (ignoring the sound of breaking twigs outside the window) feigned ignorance and suggested he may have taken Rex for an evening stroll. Miss Sophia apologised for disturbing my evening, and I graciously accepted her apologies, wished her goodnight, and closed the door. I heard a faint chuckle of laughter as I closed the window and drew the curtains.

Normally I would have found such an incident amusing, but now I just felt annoyed. It seemed to sum up Edward's whole attitude toward me: I was useful when there was not a better option but, being a mere servant, I was without feelings so could easily be dispensed with when more worthy company was available. As I looked back on our friendship I realise how little he had ever enquired about my comfort or well-being. He moaned if I was not available in the evenings when he wanted company, thus never encouraging me to have a life outside Biggenden Manor. He never seemed to mind that I often sat alone of an evening because I thought he would be around and would require my company, not knowing that he had suddenly changed his plans and gone out. It was clear that over the years I had known him, Edward had never quite forgotten that I was a hired servant, making me something less than a proper woman.

Once again, I was angry with myself for being so foolish as to imagine that such a gap in status could be bridged—or that there was any willingness on Edward's part to even consider trying. I was annoyed with Edward for his insensitivity and selfishness, and I'm afraid I was also annoyed with God for allowing me to dream and pray fervently for such an unlikely outcome. It seemed as if He allowed me tantalizing tastes of happiness with Edward, which boosted my hope, only to have them all crushed. I could almost imagine God sneering at my foolishness.

In flooded the voice of the evil one with his insidious lies, suggesting that God does not hear prayer, and that if He couldn't be trusted with my future happiness, how could I trust Him to care for me and preserve my soul? My resistance to this barrage of untruths was weak, and I soon lost all joy in spiritual things. My spiritual diet had been very meagre due to the poor preaching, and so my sickly soul crumbled at this onslaught.

## CHAPTER 19

AT LAST THE SHOOTING PARTY disbanded, and our guests went home. As we stripped the beds and dismantled the drooping flower arrangements, everyone gave a sigh of relief. We had all foregone our half days to cover the extra work, and now we were keen to get out of the house. But there was still plenty of work to be done so, much to Molly and Clara's disappointment, although they were able to sleep at home again, they were unable to take an afternoon off until the end of the week.

I praised the team for their hard work during the past fortnight and hoped that Edward would do the same, but no such recognition was forthcoming. In fact, Edward hardly seemed to realise our existence: he wandered around the house in a daydream, only becoming animated when he heard the post-boy's footsteps. After days of disappointment the desired letter arrived and almost having hugged the post-boy, Edward rushed into his study, fondly fingering the precious envelope. It did not take much deduction to realise this was not an agricultural invoice, but a letter from the beautiful Miss Sophia.

That evening, for the first time since the visitors' departure, Edward invited me to join him for evening drinks. I joined him with a mixture of reluctance and curiosity as to how much information he would divulge to me. I did not have to wait long. Edward was like an agitated champagne bottle, ready to burst. Before we had even sunk our teeth into coffee cake, Edward introduced his theme.

"What an agreeable bunch of people my guests were!"

"Yes, indeed," I agreed.

"What an honour to enjoy their company for so long!"

"Hmm."

"But how quickly the time has gone!"

I could not agree less, so kept quiet.

"But did you notice how wonderful Miss Sophia is? Why, you could not have helped noticing!"

"Yes, I noticed."

Edward failed to note my lack of enthusiasm and continued to gush as he gazed into the distance.

"And so utterly enchanting and beautiful. She is such delightful company, so refined and cultured, yet natural and free. Indeed, I have never met a person with so many fine attributes all wrapped together and adorned with such beauty!"

Even in my pain I had to smile to myself at the eloquence of the besotted man in front of me—but a shadow soon passed over his glowing face as he wondered aloud of her feelings toward him. He recounted some of her actions and words to him.

"What did they mean? Can you, as a fellow woman, explain her motives or design?"

I was unable and entirely disinclined to offer such an interpretation and pleaded my ignorance on all things related to love. Much to my annoyance, he muttered, "Yes, I suppose so."

He revealed that he had received a thank-you letter from Miss Sophia today in which she expressed her sincere appreciation of her visit, the time they spent together, and getting acquainted with his lovely house. But, he mused, was this just a standard response she would have sent to any host? He plagued himself with the thought that she would return to her sophisticated Surrey life and soon be swept up with more dazzling and cultured circles of society than his. She would meet richer men and soon forget about Edward and his rustic abode.

I commented that surely she wasn't so mercenary, which made Edward sit up and retort, "That is not mercenary, but sensible!"

"Oh, *sensible*," I responded vehemently. "If I was in love with the poorest labourer on your estate and he with me, I would marry him despite his poverty."

"What a lot of sentimental codswallop," answered Edward. "Money and influence are essential cogs in romantic alliances."

"Maybe they are in the high circles you now move in, but love, friendship, and mutual Christian convictions are good enough for my humble class."

"Well, naturally," said the ruffled Edward. "But there are considerations that have to be taken into account."

"Bank account, you mean," I joked bitterly, provoking a slight smile. "Anyway, sir, to save more arguing on a subject we clearly view very differently, I think I will retire to bed. Good night." With that, I swept out the room with all the haughtiness of one who knows she is in the right.

That evening marked a change in my relationship with my employer: freed from the desire to impress and please him, I was able to assert my opinions much more freely during our evenings together. Even in the day-to-day running of the house, if I felt something could be managed better, I would suggest my idea to Edward, not fearing whether he would accept or reject it.

Edward noticed this change and teasingly said I must be the feistiest housekeeper in England. But beneath my brasher exterior, part of me still pined for Edward's affections and secretly hoped that Miss Sophia would be swept off her feet by a titled eldest son, and that in his subsequent heartbreak Edward would fall into my sympathetic arms—but all this seemed an unrealistic dream. If Edward had failed to find me attractive in the three years we had known each other, it was unlikely that anything would change his opinion now.

Indeed, enduring evening after evening on the theme of Miss Sophia, I began to question whether Edward and I had as much in common as I had previously supposed. I was surprised at his lack of concern for her liberal view on Sabbath observance, but when I tentatively raised the issue, he immediately accused me of being "too judgmental" and that "not everyone wears their Christianity on their sleeves," as if I was some sort of prudish Pharisee. This really hurt me, because it was not long ago, back in the library of Barton Manor, that we seemed wholly united in our spiritual thinking.

Within a fortnight of the Harringtons' departure, Edward received a letter from them inviting him, at his convenience, to be their guest and enjoy the shooting opportunities their estate afforded. Edward found it would be convenient for him to go almost immediately, so after a few brief deliberations with his farm manager and long deliberations over what to pack, he was off to Surrey, the hansom cab weighed down by a huge trunk and an assortment of guns.

The shooting must have been a success and the company congenial, as Edward stayed for ten days. Then, without giving us any

notice, he was back, but only to attend to some business affairs before he was off again to an estate of a Harrington third cousin twice
removed (or the like).

Thus the pattern for that winter was set: For the most part, we
servants were left to run the house. After a thorough clean-through,
I was at a loss to know how to keep the housemaids well occupied
and not allow ourselves to drift into slovenliness. By keeping fed,
clothed, tidy, and clean, we created a certain amount of work for ourselves, but when I began to contemplate darning old dishcloths as a
worthwhile occupation, I laughed at the ridiculousness of the situation. I did not want to lay off Clara or Molly because I was aware of
their families' dependence on their wages and besides, I would need
Edward's permission to do such a thing. Furthermore, at any time we
might be called upon to accommodate Edward's friends in return for
their hospitality. We were living the life of the servants in the parable,
knowing neither the day nor hour of their master's return.

## CHAPTER 20

THE WINTER SEEMED ENDLESS AND the days blurred into predictable monotony. My bedtime became earlier and earlier, as keeping my parlour stove burning just for myself seemed a waste of winter fuel. As soon as I was sure the Kemps were safely in bed, I took the oil lamp and checked around the house, stoked the kitchen range, locked the doors, and went to bed, often with a book. I should have enjoyed the enforced rest Edward's absence produced, but I was living with the daily suspense of wondering if his romantic hopes were being realised. I had laid the whole situation before the Lord many times and I should have left it there, but instead I kept mulling over the subject fretfully.

My daily highlight was taking Rex for an afternoon walk. Clad in warm clothes and stout boots and with an enthusiastic dog by my side, I could walk for miles over fields and through muddy woods, admiring the bare and bleak beauty of winter. In Rex I found a suitable companion; he shared my fondness for our master and seemed to miss him as much as I did.

Rex's energy and curiosity for the great outdoors, however inclement the weather, made every walk rewarding. His delightful habit of bounding ahead, then rushing back with a smiling face and wagging tail to check on me and receive a pat, never failed to lift my spirits and bring a smile to my face. On cold wet days I would try and delegate the walk to the garden boy, but the trusting, expectant look on Rex's face would melt my resolve and, somewhat unwillingly, I could not but oblige, warning Rex it would be only a short walk. But once we were out and had warmed up, any idea of cutting the walk short evaporated, so we often ended our walks drenched and covered in mud, but happy and refreshed.

From the waning light and gathering chill of the short winter afternoons, we would enter the somewhat stuffy warmth of the kitchen. For Mrs. Kemp, our entry signalled the approach of tea time, and she had the kettle steaming away on the range with a teapot at the ready. Mr. Kemp would rub Rex dry and say, "You look like you've 'ad a good time, me lad," as Rex's tail thumped happily against the kitchen floor. Then we would all sit down for a bit of bread and cheese, washed down with tea, before the housemaids left for home.

The Kemps seemed to relax and thrive during this quiet time at Biggenden. Mr. Kemp started whistling tunelessly again, and Mrs. Kemp was happy to do more cooking, "cos I know that you lot don't look down ya nose at me good, honest food." This made things slightly awkward for Agnes, who was keen to be the chief cook, but she had worked long enough with Mrs. Kemp to know how to handle her. Agnes cooked the food every other day, "just to keep me 'and in, in case we suddenly have some top brass as guests again."

Indeed, we had some top brass before the year was out. One Tuesday morning, a messenger boy cycled up the drive with a message for me from Edward. I was used to receiving such communications, usually only a line or two with instructions like "Please send my brown overcoat" or the likes, so I took the message and opened it without a second thought.

What I read was of far more consequence than brown overcoats. It said, *Be ready to welcome me home on Thursday, with my bride-to-be— the darling Miss Sophia!! P.S. Her parents are coming too.*

At my elbow Molly asked, "What does 'e need this time?"

I had to regain my composure, and with all the pretense of authority I could muster, I told her to ask all the staff to gather in the kitchen immediately. I must have looked shocked, because, when I entered the kitchen, I overheard Clara saying, "I 'ope 'e ain't gravely 'urt."

"No, Clara," I said almost imperiously, "Mr. Thorpe is not hurt. On the contrary, he has written to inform us of some happy news. He and Miss Sophia are engaged to be married."

At this the girls started clapping, but I raised my hand to hush them and went on. "Furthermore, he is bringing her here, along with her parents, on Thursday, and we have got to give them the very best of welcomes."

Then we settled down with excited chatter to decide on how we could impress our important guests, especially the lady who would soon be our new mistress. The news excited great interest in us all, and we seemed united and girlish in our curiosity to know the facts of the relationship, how he proposed, when they would marry, and most importantly to us—what sort of mistress she would be and if she would make many changes?

I suppose I should have curtailed this sort of gossipy talk, but the housemaids' questions were also mine. After Clara and Molly had gone home, Agnes and I went to the parlour to begin organising the menus and food orders for the next week. We had no idea how long our guests were staying or even what time on Thursday they would arrive so had to cover all eventualities. It was late into the night before we had settled on a satisfactory plan. This rush of activity was good for me, and I went to bed with my head full of thoughts of pounds of bacon and butter rather than that Edward was marrying and would never be mine. The Lord has many ways of being kind to us; some are strange, but all are effective.

The next day I awoke with a vague awareness that something was amiss. Then, all of the events of the previous day came flooding back. I lay in bed with a heavy heart and a sense of despondency, even my limbs feeling heavy and unwilling to move. I would have dearly loved to be a fine lady at that moment, able to give in to my feelings and lie morosely in bed all day, wallowing in my ill-fated love life, but I could not. I had work to do and staff to organise, so I heaved myself up to do my morning Bible reading and prayer. I prayed for strength and wisdom to get through the day, as usual, but also I prayed for special grace and submission in the unfolding events.

I wish I could report that I immediately felt special strength and help from above, but alas, this was not the case. Nevertheless, in a strange, unaccountable sort of way, the news of Edward's engagement was a relief after weeks of speculation. My loyalty to Edward had almost been a self-inflicted chain, binding me to Biggenden, putting him first in my every decision, but now I felt released, though somewhat afraid and daunted by my new freedom.

The whole house was spick and span, but the bedrooms needed airing and warming, so after letting in great gusts of cold November air, we shut the windows and lit the fires and then kept them roaring. The kitchen was a hive of activity as various delivery boys brought in their orders and Agnes set about making the ingredients into beautiful delicacies. Rightly or wrongly, we had gotten the impression from her last visit that Mrs. Harrington viewed us as inept country bump-kins. We were determined to prove her wrong and, to avoid any un-seemly disorganisation, we practised lining up outside the front door to welcome the guests. The gardeners acted, with great exaggeration, as dignified guests, and we curtsied to them and made appropriately welcoming noises before collapsing with laughter. Mrs. Kemp coerced the head gardener into giving Mr. Kemp a thorough wet shave, which made him at least look presentable, but we determined to keep his in-volvement with the visitors to the bare minimum. Rex came to see what was going on and looked at me beseechingly for a walk, but with great reluctance I had to delegate the task to the garden boy, wondering how long it would be before I would have the pleasure of a walk again.

Throughout Thursday we worked in a jittery, expectant way, ready at any time to throw off our aprons, smooth our extra crisp dresses, hide any loose ends of hair under our lace caps, and line up to greet our auspi-cious guests. Any movement on the gravel drive would send one of us scampering to a window, ready to sound the alarm. As the afternoon advanced, we took it in turns to stand guard near the hall window.

Just as we were sitting down to a cup of tea and Molly was drink-ing hers at the window, she cried, "Their coach is coming!" We rushed to take our well drilled places at the door. (I found Molly's cup of cold tea two days later behind the hall curtain.)

Mr. Thorpe (from now on I vowed to address him thus) sprang from the coach in his normal boyish manner, followed by a more cautious exit by Mr. Harrington, who went on to flex his back to re-lieve the aches from the country roads. Mr. Thorpe and the coachman together assisted Mrs. Harrington out of the coach; she looked exas-perated by their attendance but could not have descended without their help. Then Miss Sophia appeared, and with the lightest touch of Mr. Thorpe's hand, she elegantly stepped down and smoothed out her beautiful dress whilst saying something that made her fiancé laugh.

After barely a glance in our direction, the party swept into the house and we became busy attending to their wishes and needs. A second coach soon appeared with the luggage and, to our surprise, a lady's maid to attend the female guests. Whilst preparing afternoon tea, we had a quick discussion in the kitchen about where to accommodate the maid. Agnes volunteered to sleep at home, so her attic room was available, but it soon transpired that the maid intended to sleep in Miss Sophia's dressing room.

I hoped my face did not give away my blankness because, to my knowledge, none of the bedrooms could boast of a dressing room. Then, within seconds, I remembered that the room allocated to Miss Sophia did have a small room adjacent to it, which we called "the box room." After a bit of hasty furniture removing, we rearranged the room into an apology of a dressing room. We wanted to get a brass bed frame into the room, but the maid said it would be "out of keeping with the function of the room." Instead, she was willing to sleep on the bedroom's chaise longue, so we struggled and succeeded in getting it through the door way, all the while thinking that she was sacrificing comfort for elegance.

If we had ever entertained the idea that having a lady's maid to attend to the Harrington ladies would lessen our workload, we were quickly proved wrong. Bertha (for that was her name) made free use of the call bells with the excuse that she could not possibly leave her ladies to run and fetch what was deemed necessary. So poor Molly and Clara were forever running up and down the stairs to fetch (and

I give but a few examples) lavender water, raw egg for smoothing the hair, and someone to handle shoe cleaning. Bertha was deeply shocked when she found out there was no servants' hall and that we ate and sat in the kitchen of an evening. Such was her indignation that I thought it diplomatic to invite her into my parlour, and from then on she saw it as a kind of "pug's parlour" for the upper servants and used it regularly. My lack of privacy was irritating, but more so was the way she preferred to sit at dying embers in my grate rather than dirtying her pretty hand to throw on a log or pump the bellows.

At first I found Bertha's stories of working at the Harrington's interesting, but soon I began to suspect that most were stretching the truth considerably. She had never asked about my previous employment and did not know I had worked in a larger household before and could recognise a farfetched tale when I heard one! As she told her stories, Bertha was usually busy doing some fine work on one of her ladies' dresses or hats. She had been horrified to learn that we sent our laundry to several faithful village women to clean in their own cottages. I explained that their work was faultless, but she shuddered to think of *her* ladies' undergarments flapping around in a villager's garden for all and sundry to behold. This, of course, led to my parlour looking like a laundry room, with various items of clothing hanging to dry on a clothes-horse we had managed to find for the job. My desk was regularly covered with a blanket and used as an ironing board, despite the fact that I had more accounting to do and orders to write than usual. I was gradually learning that the wonderfully natural and spontaneous look that Miss Sophia prided herself in actually took hours of careful preparation and planning.

As Bertha was gradually taking over below stairs, the visitors were settling in above. During her previous stay, Mrs. Harrington had been a polite guest and expressed some wry amusement at the bachelor and provincial ways in which the house was run, but now she had a very different attitude. She was on a mission to sort the household out single-handedly before her poor daughter found herself the mistress of such an ill-run establishment. She seemed to think that Mr. Thorpe was a dear boy but slightly incompetent in knowing how to organise a house, and I soon got the impression she thought I was the main cause of the poor management.

Before she had been in the house forty-eight hours, I was summoned to Mr. Thorpe's study, where I was surprised to find a gathering of Mr. Thorpe (looking a trifle uncomfortable), Mrs. Harrington, and Miss Sophia. Mrs. Harrington was the self-appointed spokeswoman and instructed me to get my accounts book so it could be examined. Mr. Thorpe had never looked in the household accounts book, despite my asking. He always laughed off the matter, saying he trusted me entirely and, anyway, disliked wading through columns of figures. As I hastened to get the book, which I found under a pile of Bertha's ironing, I was thankful that I had kept up the accounts so meticulously. I also kept all receipts and invoices for two months, so I took those along too.

The ladies sat at the table, and Mr. Thorpe was pacing around behind them. If Mrs. Harrington had had her own way, I believe she would have made me stand throughout the interview, but thankfully Miss Sophia kindly invited me to sit down. Mrs. Harrington appeared to find my accounts disappointingly thorough, but she asked a few questions nevertheless, mainly to do with the amount of food required whilst Mr. Thorpe had been away. When I explained the number of staff we had, she immediately questioned as to who the Kemps were, and I explained their history.

"Oh really, Edward!" she exclaimed. "You are not running a charity. Surely it is time to move them on."

I looked at Edward, silently willing him to speak up on their behalf, but he merely smiled at his mother-in-law-to-be and said it was under consideration.

After making a few strong suggestions to Edward that the staff have less expensive cuts of meat and butter *or* jam but not both, Mrs. Harrington ploughed on in her investigations and began exploring our roles. She cross-questioned me about my daily tasks and all went well until she asked me what I normally did during the afternoons.

"I go for a walk with Rex, ma'am," I replied.

"Rex? Who is Rex? Is he a follower?" she asked, glaring at me suspiciously as if I had sinned.

"No, ma'am, in fact, I normally follow him. Rex is Mr. Thorpe's dog," I answered, noting a smile beginning to creep onto Mr. Thorpe's face, a smile that he hastily wiped away with his hand.

"What an unusual state of affairs—and do not be impertinent!" exclaimed Mrs. Harrington, leaning forward. "Why do you not delegate this task?"

"Why, ma'am, because I enjoy it, and the fresh air is beneficial."

"Enjoy?" she spluttered. "Enjoyment is hardly a reason. You should be guided by duty, not enjoyment. Do you think you are paid a wage to roam the countryside? Are you aware of these unorthodox arrangements, Mr. Thorpe?"

Mr. Thorpe shifted his weight from one leg to the other. "Yes, I am, and I am grateful for Reb— err—Miss Stubbs' care of Rex in my absence."

Miss Sophia intervened by saying, "Mother, is this intrusive investigation quite necessary?" only to be severely rounded on by her mother.

"My dear girl, one cannot be intrusive as far as servants are concerned. It is one's *right* to know their doings." Then, mixing her metaphors, "Details are the building blocks for the smooth running of any household." She fixed her steely gaze on me. "Stubbs, I hope you realise what a generous employer you are fortunate enough to have in Mr. Thorpe and that you do not presume upon his good nature."

I nodded demurely and said, "I am indeed grateful for his kindness, ma'am."

Mr. Thorpe, meanwhile, continued to pace to and fro behind the table, and somehow it was rather irritating. Miss Sophia must have felt the same, for she patted a seat next to her and said, "Darling Edward, please take a seat." When he did as he was bidden, she laid her hand on his knee and looked happier.

The interrogation then moved on to the roles of the other staff. Another snort of disgust came when I revealed that Molly and Clara had interchangeable roles.

"How utterly absurd!" Mrs. Harrington exclaimed. "How do they know their order of rank and where to sit at meal times?"

"Ma'am, we sit anywhere at meal times, and as for who does what, having both of them trained for all jobs gives us greater flexibility when we need it. For example, when entertaining guests, we can all clean, tend the fire, serve at the table, or wash up."

"My word, Stubbs, you are rather opinionated, are you not?" she answered scathingly.

I was pleased when Miss Sophia intervened.

"She has a good point, Mother."

Miss Sophia was quickly silenced by her mother's lengthy lecture on staff needing to know their place, watching their superiors, so working diligently to move up the ranks and be rewarded with more responsibility. "Rather than," she said, giving me a withering look, "being unguidedly given responsibility after very little experience and becoming conceited with their own perceived wisdom."

Then the Kemps and their role came up, and I knew we were skating on very thin ice. Mrs. Kemp's involvement by cooking for staff meals was satisfactory, but how could I explain that Mr. Kemp did little more than polish the silver, sharpen knives, and rub Rex dry? I stretched the truth as much as possible without lying, as I explained the Kemps' important contribution to the smooth running of the house, but the wool could not be pulled over the formidable matriarch's eyes, and once again she encouraged Mr. Thorpe to hasten their departure.

To conclude the interview, Mrs. Harrington reiterated to me the benevolence of Mr. Thorpe in being so understanding, if not *indulgent,* to his staff, and that this was not to be abused. She indicated that there would be changes in the future to increase the efficiency of workforce and to ensure no one "got above themselves." Then, with a dismissive wave of her hand, she said, "and that will do, Stubbs."

I removed myself rather shakily from the room. As I retreated to my parlour, I pondered over the event. Some things were now obvious. Mrs. Harrington did not like me, Mr. Thorpe would be of little use to help, and Miss Sophia might prove to be the best of them all.

But, I reflected, I could not count on this as her mother saw her as but a naive child and would not let her run her own household until she was sure it would be run in ruthless Harrington fashion.

The idea that maybe it was time to leave Biggenden began to grow in my mind, but what was I to do instead? And where would I go?

Of course, when I arrived at my parlour, I did not have the luxury of solitude; Bertha was there doing what I had rather grimly begun to think of as her never-ending fiddling about. For once, I had the courage to ask her to leave. I knew this would cause her a problem as she entered the kitchen only when absolutely necessary and then with an air of condescension. But right at that moment, I did not care for her petty sensibilities. She looked surprised, but after a big show of organising what she needed, she vacated the room. I slumped into my chair with my head in my hands, trying to take in how this new, heavy-handed management would affect the staff who, for all their minor failings, I considered my friends—something else Mrs. Harrington would not approve of.

At first, I felt slightly triumphant at managing to give coherent answers to the formidable lady, but then I happened to catch a glance of myself in the looking glass. There, on my left cheek, was a large streak of soot. I shuddered to think that I had been wearing this throughout the interview, and suddenly I saw how highlighted my servitude and lowly position. It reminded me that I could not dream of halting or even just slowing the fast flowing tide of change the Harringtons wanted to make, even though it would greatly affect the lives of all the staff and myself. Servants were two-a-penny and entirely dispensable: we either changed with the Harringtons or would be shown the door.

## CHAPTER 21

AFTER I HAD GATHERED MY thoughts, I asked Agnes if she could step inside my parlour. She was busy getting lunch ready and had only had a few minutes to spare, but it was long enough to give her a summary of Mrs. Harrington's thoughts. Agnes looked so downcast at the news that I felt sorry I had burdened her by confiding in her. She, like the other maids, had only ever been employed at Biggenden, and the thought of change scared her. Agnes' cooking skills had flourished over the last year: whereas I would be happy to call her an excellent cook, she felt uneasy even calling herself a cook, preferring to think of herself as a kitchen maid. The thought of her skills and produce being scrutinised by the fastidious and fashionable Harringtons made her feel so uneasy that she looked as if she would immediately "throw in the towel" and confine herself to her former duties. I fervently reassured her that not a word had been said against any meal by anyone in the room, but that did little to hearten her.

Agnes returned to the kitchen looking miserable. Oh, how I wished that I had not breathed a word to her! I needed to protect my staff, not lean on them for support. I briefly smiled to myself at the silly pun of not leaning on my staff, but then I tried to focus my mind on the business of the day.

The visit of the Harringtons continued as the party engaged themselves in indoor and outdoor pursuits, invited neighbours

178

around, and visited local notable families. We servants worked hard and long hours. We pieced together little tidbits of conversation we heard about the future of Biggenden. It was not ours to know the full plans and often probably got the wrong end of the stick, but as far as we could understand, the library was to become a billiard room, an extra wing might be added for a master bedchamber suite, and Miss Sophia was keen to have a conservatory. Rex was deemed unfit for indoor living and was banished to a kennel in the back yard. Men servants were to be employed as footmen because having maids answering the door and serving at the table was deemed too provincial. The attic above the new wing would house the men. I waited with bated breath for Mrs. Harrington to visit the kitchens and discover the Kemps' sleeping quarters, almost relishing her anticipated horror, but it seemed that she was not interested in our quarters as long as the food was up to standard. The only "below stairs" alteration she insisted on was the building of a laundry room so that washing would not have to be taken into the village.

I was curious to know Mr. Thorpe's opinion on the radical changes but was not to have the privilege of being privy to them. Once or twice he came to my parlour door with some request or other and looked as if he wanted to tarry and talk, but on finding Bertha there, he did not stay. His general demeanour was that of a man madly in love and willing to allow anything in order to get his prize. He was keen to get married as quickly as possible, but Sophia wanted a summer wedding, and her mother insisted that the building work should be completed first, believing that the dust and inconvenience of workmen was incompatible with an appropriate start to married life. Mr. Thorpe playfully chided his betrothed for making him suffer such a long wait; she relished hearing these loving arguments and answered sweetly but remained adamant.

What, you may ask, was Mr. Harrington doing while his wife was inflicting sweeping changes on the household? I had rather underestimated the man, thinking he was interested only in field sports and cigars, but soon my esteem for him rose. After a few days at Biggenden, he departed home, citing "other engagements." I later learned from Bertha that he was on a committee of benevolent gentlemen who had organised the building of a cottage hospital for the poor in their locality. Mr. Harrington had gone home in order to be present for the interviewing of candidates for a resident physician. I was glad to hear of his benevolence and hoped this trait would soon blossom in his daughter also.

Bertha's irritatingly frequent presence in my parlour and inability to work silently proved interesting at times. Once I had become used to her exaggerated devotion to the Harringtons, I learned to pick out relevant nuggets of truth. It transpired that the Harringtons' residence, Kenwood, was not as grand or large as I had visualised. Apparently, it was slightly smaller than Barton Manor and certainly had less acreage. They did not own a property in London, but rented the same house every year for the London season. I was slightly relieved to hear all this, as Mrs. Harrington gave the distinct impression that although Mr. Thorpe was a nice chap, he was slightly below their status and, although she was graciously overlooking the fact, she could never quite forget it and would be pleased if no one else did either.

The Harrington ladies stayed for ten long days, and then they departed to prepare Kenwood for the Christmas festivities. Mr. Thorpe tarried a few more days at Biggenden and caught up with estate management. He consulted his estate steward about the various proposed changes to the house, and between them they contracted planners who had links to reputable builders. Mr. Thorpe invited me to join him for evening drinks as in fore time, and I obliged, but without the romantic hope of gaining his interest, the evenings had lost their allure for me.

He was enthusiastic about the improvements that would be made to Biggenden and the prospect of settling down into contented married bliss. Previously he had in private been critical of and sarcastic about people similar to his future mother-in-law, but now he appeared to be much more accepting. Only once did he even hint at her over-dominating character by saying, "At least the forceful mother-in-law won't be living here." I replied, "How can you be so sure? Mothers often end up living with their youngest daughters," and watched with relish as he considered this awful possibility for the first time.

I had strictly instructed myself not to venture any opinion on the forthcoming changes or on the family he was to marry into during our evenings together. This resolution was hardly necessary, because, as usual (and now, with hindsight, it was so obvious), Mr. Thorpe did most of the talking and did not bother to ask about me, my welfare, or my personal opinions. His apparent presumption that I would be a permanent housekeeper at Biggenden irritated me. I could almost see with his mind's eye an image of a grey and wrinkly Mrs. Stubbs, the dear and faithful servant of the family, welcoming his grandchildren with freshly baked biscuits. All very comfortable and reassuring—for him. This assumption, more than anything else, galvanised my intentions to leave Biggenden, and to leave before Mrs. Thorpe and the inevitable Bertha arrived.

Yes, to leave was certainly my intention—but was it the right thing to do? I needed the Lord's guidance so much. It seemed as if He was slowly shutting the door for me at Biggenden. Or was the opposite true? Was I to stay there to help the staff through the changes ahead? Was I to sacrifice my own wants, swallow my pride, abandon any ambition, and just keep plodding on?

When I thought about our great Example, the Saviour and His self-denying life, any self-pity and self-will seemed wrong and unchristian. The Lord knew that all I hoped for in life was to have my own loving husband and family, but so far He had seen fit to deny me this blessing. Was He instructing me to wait, or was it a definite refusal? With an eternity of happiness ahead of me in the life to come, why was I so concerned about the few years or decades I had toiling here below? But heaven and eternity seemed so far away, so distant and intangible, while the cares and needs of daily life pressed with great reality.

Once again Satan used my spiritual struggles to suggest that God did not care. In my experience, whenever my faith lost its anchor hold on Christ, my soul was swept around like a little boat on a rough sea, battered from side to side and uncertain of the route or destination.

To make matters worse, Rev. Brinkhill seemed to think his congregation needed some spiritual sifting and preached sermon after sermon on false professors, presumption, and those "with head-knowledge" only. His texts were "Many are called but few are chosen," "Strait is the gate and narrow is the way," "I never knew you," and some of the verses in Jude about deceivers. These solemn and sobering verses pricked my wounded soul to the core, and I began to despair. I felt that my repentance had been too shallow, my understanding of sin too vague, my faith too weak, and my unbelief unpardonable. The vicar described a Christian conversion as such an emotional and dramatic change, a desperate sinner at his wits' end due to the burden of his sins, led to Christ and receiving forgiveness and immediate, immeasurable comfort, joy and peace—but I had not had such a deep experience and feared I had deceived myself.

Yet, in my dejection, I still clung to the Lord Jesus and like Peter said, "to whom else can we go?" I pleaded that, if I had never been right in my religious experience, I would be now. I started again coming to Christ with the huge burden of my doubts and fears and pleaded with Him to take me in as He promises to. I begged that He would remember His promise, "And He that cometh unto me, I will in no wise cast out." This was my prayer for a number of weeks, but it seemed as if heaven's door was shut against me, and my prayers returned unheard and un-regarded. All I could grasp onto for comfort was the fact that God never lies and that His promises are most sure. I remembered Pa's advice, "Trust our unchanging God, not your changeable feelings." I longed to have someone to talk to and remembered with sad longing the friendly conversations I had enjoyed with Mr. Thorpe at Barton Manor after evening services. How times had changed!

These spiritual agonizings did not fill my every waking hour; indeed, they only swept over me at bedtime or when I had more time to reflect, which would often be on Sunday. Even this caused me concern—surely a really convicted sinner would feel bad all the time! Yet most of the time I was busy with the mundane cares of running a household, and earthly care dominated my thoughts. I would determine within myself to wrestle with the Lord until He gave me relief, yet would fall asleep before I had hardly begun praying.

During this dark time, there was one source of relief the Lord kindly provided for me. I subscribed to the weekly sermons of Mr. Charles Haddon Spurgeon, a popular Baptist minister in London, whose presentation of the gospel was very similar to Rev. Ryle's, that is, warmly, urgently, and freely recommending Christ to all. He seemed to be able to stoop down to where I was and encourage me to see what a loving and willing Saviour Christ is. These sermons gave some peace and relief, but my general mood was that of despondency.

Indeed, on looking back on that winter, it was altogether fairly gloomy. The untimely death on 14th December of Prince Albert, our queen's beloved husband and consort, cast a mournful shadow over the whole nation. The weather was mild but rainy, so my walks with Rex were wet and muddy.

Mr. Thorpe was home for only a handful of nights to view the progress of the building work, preferring to spend his time at Kenwood or in the round of social engagements (he previously would have shunned) with the Harringtons. Making big structural changes to a property and even building extensions during the winter months is not advisable, but such was Mr. Thorpe's eagerness to get the work completed that he asked the workers to push ahead with the plans. Therefore, we were subjected to constant banging, crashing, raised voices, and in-trodden mud. We shut all windows, shutters, and curtains, but still the dust managed to permeate into the house.

The silver lining to this disruptive cloud was that the house was unfit for entertaining, so we had no guests to deal with. Molly and Clara found it no hardship to keep the workmen's tin mugs full of strong, sweet tea and would often tarry to banter far longer than necessary. Once again, I was finding it hard to keep them occupied because we could not do any thorough cleaning for as long as the disruption from the building work continued.

But then our workload increased in an unexpected way. The sister of Agnes's brother-in-law died tragically of a haemorrhage after a long and complicated delivery, leaving her husband with a new baby son and three other children under six years of age. Agnes's sister, Mary, lived close by, and although she had a large brood of her own, she helped the grieving widower as much as she could. This practical help even extended to giving suck to the young baby, as she had an un-weaned child of her own. George, the new widower, found it hard to accept his new son, who he couldn't help but see as the cause of his beloved wife's death, so Mary tactfully suggested she take the baby into her house to make it easier for everyone.

Agnes asked if she could work fewer hours in order to help Mary and the bereaved family. I readily agreed and, in a manner Mrs. Harrington would have heartily disapproved of, Mrs. Kemp, Molly, and I shared the cooking duties among ourselves. There was time enough for me to learn some elegant and elaborate dishes and to teach them to Molly.

Clara had been inspired by Bertha and was keen to gain the skills required to be a lady's maid, so I asked her to make new uniforms for Clara and herself. This task kept her occupied for many hours. Remembering happy evenings with Emma, I suggested Clara try styling our hair, and she had great pleasure in creating modern, gravity-defying styles. She had the enviable knack of seeing a certain hairstyle, remembering it, and being able to recreate it. Clara's hope was that Bertha would find Biggenden too rural for her liking and seek a more upmarket post, but I warned her that Bertha expressed deep devotion to the Harrington ladies.

"Deep devotion!" snorted Clara, hairpin in mouth. "She exaggerates everyfing, especially 'er *deep devotion*—only when it suits 'er."

Christmas loomed, and it quickly became obvious that Mr. Thorpe would not be celebrating it at Biggenden. Mr. and Mrs. Kemp were to go to their daughter's home for the day, and Molly and Clara would have the day off. Agnes would be with her family, so I braced myself for a Christmas alone. Maybe it would do me good to have a quiet day at home and to consider the real meaning of Christmas, I thought, but when Agnes realised I would be alone, she insisted that I join her family.

I put up a feeble protest about not wanting to intrude on a family occasion, but Agnes prevailed and I went—and what a lovely day it was! The cottage was packed full of children and grandchildren, all lively and enjoying each other's company. The women produced a lavish and delicious meal of roast goose, and after the washing up was finished, we all joined the children for games. We played blind man's bluff, hunt the thimble, pin the tail on the donkey, and endless rounds of charades. I had almost forgotten how delightful it all is: the loving and trusting attention of a toddling child, the uninhibited way of climbing up your leg, dribbling on you with a beautiful, dimpled grin, and an infectious laugh that encourages you to do silly things over and over again to an ever enthusiastic "'gen!"

At the end of the afternoon, I left the happy cottage, with baby sick on my shoulder, crumbs in my blouse folds, sticky marks on my skirt where a girl had wiped her candy-filled mouth, and the decision that I should mix with children more often as they enrich life so much—and washerwomen!

## CHAPTER 22

NEW YEAR BROUGHT A HANDFUL of letters from old friends. Emma was enjoying a life of travel with her lady. She was becoming well acquainted with many of the continental capital cities and rarely wintered in England. Miss Miller had accepted a new post as a school teacher in Broadstairs and hoped to begin in January. She sent the sad news that Mrs. Brown had passed away between Christmas and New Year. This was not a shock to me, but I wished I could have seen her one more time to express my gratitude again for her help in some of the darkest hours of my life. Mrs. Milton sent me a greeting card for the New Year, expressing the hope that I was maintaining a good standard of housekeeping and adding as a post script that she had just trained up all the housemaids to her satisfaction only to learn that one was moving on already!

The winter progressed as it had started—with long, wet, grey days. Mr. Thorpe came back to Biggenden for about four nights every three weeks to review the somewhat slow progress of the building work and to organise farm affairs.

On one occasion, I tentatively suggested we were rather over-staffed and that some of us might have some time off. I hoped Mr. Thorpe would suggest I take a visit to Pemfield. Instead, he advised me to give Molly and Clara a fortnight off on half-pay, but stipulated that I was needed to "be at the helm."

Molly and Clara viewed this enforced time off with mixed feelings. They were pleased to be free to do as they wished for a while, but they worried about the reduction in wages, which their families relied on heavily. I also felt for them, as a fortnight in February was not ideal for either relaxing or (more likely the case) helping their families with seasonal agricultural work out in the cold.

Unknown to Mr. Thorpe, I paid them their full rate out of my own pocket; they believed he had had a change of heart. I was annoyed that Mr. Thorpe had not seen fit to give me any leave at all since I had entered his employment, and I was annoyed with myself for not seeking it more vociferously.

So there we were, Mr. and Mrs. Kemp, Rex, and I in a mainly closed-up and dust-sheet-covered Biggenden. We all shared a common worry about the future—all, that is, except Rex, who was enjoying my less-divided attention. The Kemps sensed their presence was no longer valued but lacked neither will nor power to make any independent plans for their future.

I was pleased with their homely company in the otherwise empty house but wished they had more inclination to chat. Without the master at home, we did not receive a newspaper, and with so few mouths to feed, we had less frequent visits from delivery boys bringing us local news. There was very little to stimulate any conversation. I frequently told them of the people I met and chatted with whilst walking Rex, but whereas Agnes would in turn have supplied me with the family connections and background or an interesting anecdote of each person I met, the Kemps had no such knowledge, causing the conversation to stop there. The Kemps were not originally from the area but had moved to Biggenden with Sir Richard Tenson. Due to the long hours they had working for him, followed by their limiting infirmities, there were very few people around they could call friends.

In mid-March, just as it started to look as if the long winter would give way to a brighter and dryer spring, I went down with a heavy cold. Mrs. Kemp plied me with every tonic and healing concoction she could remember, but instead of getting better, I rather grew worse. I continued to be feverish, with a pounding head, blocked nose, aching limbs, and sore throat. I coughed, snorted, and tossed and turned my way through the nights, longing for the day; I would then drag myself around, croaking out instructions in the daytime, longing for the night. The maids urged me to take to my bed, and with too little energy to resist, I did just that.

Eventually, I started to recover, but was left feeling weak and tired. Had the household been busy or had there been a pressing need for action, I might have gained energy more quickly, but as it was, there seemed little need to push myself. I even absented myself from church, feeling disinclined to walk there, sit in the cold building, and listen to dreary sermons, when it was much easier to sit comfortably by a roaring fire, sipping tea and reading a lively and encouraging sermon by C.H. Spurgeon.

This slow and leisurely pace of life was rudely interrupted in early April by the master of Biggenden having the audacity to want to lodge in his own abode for a few nights. Unknown to me, when Clara greeted Mr. Thorpe, she said, "Mrs. Stubbs 'as been right poorly," and on meeting me, he found confirmation in my pale, lack-lustre face and seemed most concerned for my well-being. I was warmed by his anxiety on my behalf, until he said, "We do really need you to be well again for the wedding preparations." When he went on to ask what could be done to help, I had no qualms and did not hesitate to say, "I need a change of air."

It so happened that a few days earlier, I had received a letter from Miss Miller singing the praises of her new surroundings in Broadstairs, with its fresh sea air and beautiful coastal walks. No sooner had Mr. Thorpe agreed to my going ("Take three weeks, take a month, take as long as you require to get your strength back") than I sent a telegram to Miss Miller, asking if I could pay her a visit. A positive reply came remarkably quickly, and so I got packing, almost feeling my energy returning already.

The evening before I left, Agnes paid a call to Biggenden and came into my parlour for a cup of tea. She seemed uneasy and distracted, as if she had something she needed to share but did not know how to begin.

After she had drained her third cup of tea, she leant forward to place the saucer on the table and, studying the tablecloth, said, "I want to 'and in me notice today, Miss."

"Hand in your notice?" I repeated, trying to take it in. "Is it due to all the changes ahead of us?"

"No, Miss. It's because I am gonna marry George next munf."

"Marry George?" I stupidly repeated again. "Next month?"

"Yes, Miss. It's the right fing to do and will be good for the lit'le 'uns."

I felt truly shocked. Instead of doing the right thing and offering my congratulations, I just stared at her and asked, "Do you love George?"

Agnes took a long time to reply and finally answered, "George is a good man, and I 'ighly esteem 'im."

"But," I rudely pressed on, "do you want to marry him?"

"Why, of course, I does, Miss," she said. "I wonna be 'is children's new muvver, and it's an 'onour vat George asked me."

In my bewildered state I could have interrogated the poor woman longer, but thankfully common courtesy kicked in and I lamely said, "Well, Agnes, I will really miss you, but I wish you much happiness in your new job . . . sorry, I mean situation."

Agnes smiled warmly as she stood up. "An' I'll miss you too, Miss, but I am right glad to be ow' of 'ere before Miss Sophie and 'er muvver takes over." I smiled back knowingly as she continued. "George says we need to 'ave a right quiet wedding, ove'wise I would 'ave asked ya ta come along and see me wed."

"I would love to have seen you get married, but I understand George's wishes," I replied.

"And, Miss, I 'ope and pray ta see the day when you get wed yeself," said Agnes as she went to the door.

"Thanks, Agnes, we will hope and pray on," I said with a wry smile, suppressing a hollow laugh.

## CHAPTER 23

THE COLD, EARLY LIGHT OF the next morning saw me standing on the platform at the Tunbridge Railway Station, awaiting the service from London to the Kent coast with some apprehension. Never in my life had I travelled by a steam train before, and I began to regret choosing such a modern, dangerous mode of conveyance. I looked around at my fellow would-be travellers and was struck by their uniformly nonchalant air: here a man lit a cigar, there a man leant against a wall reading his newspaper, while others chatted calmly, hardly bothering to look at the giant, billowing engine as it came toward us and amazingly came to a halt right in front of us.

I followed my experienced companions into a carriage and a kind gentleman offered to lift my trunk onto a luggage rack overhead. I spotted a window seat and quickly sat down in the springy, cushioned seat and peered through the glass. With much whistling, great billows of steam, and a quick shudder, we were off.

Somehow I had expected the steam train to be like an unpredictably charging dragon, lurching around and difficult to be kept in control, but on the contrary, the train seemed dignified, steady, and controlled. The rhythmic clackety-clack of the wheels was relaxing and reassuring. I could not stop myself from smiling as I enjoyed the sensation of fast motion and watched the interesting scenery flit past the window. At every station the engine slowed down with a loud hiss to halt miraculously in a carefully calculated manner just where the platform was. People stood to greet passengers or to wave them off, porters hurried to unload crates and boxes, and young lads watched just for the fun of seeing the stoker and his fire.

As we rattled through the countryside, I once again looked at my fellow travellers. Many of them were reading, chatting, or sleeping, looking as relaxed and familiar with their surroundings as they might in their own drawing rooms. How amazingly sophisticated they all look, I thought, unlike me, who is scared she will get off at the wrong station, take too long and miss the stop, fall under the carriage, or fail to find a stage coach at the other end. Yet none of my worries came to pass, and by mid-afternoon I had alighted at Ramsgate Station and found a cab to Broadstairs.

As we approached the coaching inn at Broadstairs, I was pleased to see Miss Miller waving her handkerchief enthusiastically, and I felt most thankful that my travelling adventure was safely completed. As I clambered off the cab and received a rather stiff hug from Miss Miller, I was aware of the screeching of seagulls above us and a brisk breeze.

Miss Miller helped me to carry my trunk, and we set off down a cobbled street at a business-like pace. I wrapped my shawl around me and scampered after her. The wind freed some of my hair from its bun, and the loose strands whipped my face. As I licked my lips, finding they were salty, I felt very excited to be so near to the sea.

We turned a corner and there it was ahead of us: a vast expanse of choppy grey waves extending to the horizon, where it met an equally grey and threatening sky. Far out, it looked deceptively as if it was perfectly still and quiet, but at the shore the waves crashed against the rocks and sand, sending up a soaking spray and creating white foam. Each rolling row of waves seemed determined to beat the previous one in its vigorous advancement up the beach.

I stood stock-still, watching the amazing sight. Miss Miller smiled at my enchanted face and said, with the air of a seasoned seaside dweller, "Ah, the tide is coming in." We stood quietly side by side, admiring the power of the waves and their unstoppable progress.

I broke the silence by asking, "Do you remember teaching us about King Canute proving he could not stop the tide?"

Miss Miller laughed. "Yes, I do—a very difficult story to explain to children who have never seen the sea."

The coldness of the wind finally drove us away from the scene and into Miss Miller's small abode.

The little village school was a "Ragged School", run by the church and it was built behind the church and rectory. The little two-up-two-down schoolmaster's house was built alongside the school, but as no schoolmaster could be recruited for the small salary the church was offering, Miss Miller had been accepted. On entering the front door and turning right one stepped straight into the kitchen with a small range; turn left, and through a door one entered the best room, with a small hearth, two chairs, many books, and an old harmonium. This room was used only on Sundays. Just opposite the front door was a small flight of stairs leading to two bedrooms, one either side. The cottage had its own lavatory in the backyard but shared the school pump.

As we sat down to a warming bowl of broth, Miss Miller explained the reason for school's existence and the problems she faced. The school had been set up by the Ragged School Union, whose president was Lord Shaftsbury. The great novelist Charles Dickens was also an enthusiastic supporter of the Union, and as he had a house in

Broadstairs, it was fitting that a Ragged School should be established there. The schools were to provide free basic education, especially the four Rs (reading, writing, arithmetic, and religious education) to any children too poor and ill-clothed to attend any other school. The intended beneficiaries of this provision had mixed feelings about education; some families gratefully welcomed the opportunity, while others saw it as a complete waste of time. The latter argued that no one in their families had ever been to school, and they were no worse off for it; besides, they didn't want any "smart alec" in their family. There were plenty of useful jobs on fishing boats, at the beach, among the fishing nets, at the fishmonger's, or in the home for little hands to do rather than for them to waste their time "getting above themselves" with "book learning."

Not only did Miss Miller have to persuade her pupils that education was a good idea, but she also had to keep the generous benefactors happy. Some serious minds were convinced that only religious education, "education for eternity," was necessary, yet others wanted the lessons to be as practical as possible. Some even saw it as a training school from which they could imperially and conveniently pick suitable girls as servants. All had their own pet idea and wished to see it implemented. One kind lady wanted to ensure all the pupils had stout, warm boots for the winter, but unbeknown to her, many of these new, shiny boots were removed, sold, or pawned as soon as the children came home with them.

In spite of the conflicting demands placed upon her, Miss Miller appeared to be thoroughly enjoying the challenges of her new post. She had a group of older girls who were ambitious to join the ever-growing number of female shop workers. This was a new avenue of work opening up to women, and to many girls, it seemed very glamorous. The girls were determined to learn to read, write, and do calculations necessary for the job. Indeed, money calculations never seemed a problem for any of the children who, through working with their parents, had learned to be savvy and shrewd.

As we ate and chatted, I looked around the sparse room we were sitting in. Outside it was dark, the curtains were drawn, and the range was providing a good heat, making the room pleasant and warm, but yet there was no cosy feel to the house. This had nothing to do with the structure of the building; it was merely due to the fact that Miss Miller had no eye or maybe even desire for homeliness. I longed to make some cheap but colourful changes: the hessian curtains would be red and white gingham, the beige mat would be a multi-coloured rag rug, the wooden Windsor armchairs would have patchwork cushions, the walls would be adorned with cheap but colourful paintings, and on the windowsills would stand small plants. I viewed my imaginary changes with satisfaction, but that is where they were destined to remain, as I would never dare to suggest "unnecessary" change to my former schoolmistress.

I retired early to my chilly room (which could have been mistaken for a nun's cell, were it not for the lack of a crucifix) and unpacked my trunk. My belongings added colour to the whitewashed room and almost looked frivolous in such austere surroundings. I quickly changed into my night dress, threw my cloak on the bed for an extra layer and jumped into the bed, which was considerably more comfortable than it looked. After reading the travellers' Psalm and giving thanks for a safe journey, I soon fell into a deep sleep.

## CHAPTER 24

THE NEXT MORNING, THE UNFAMILIAR screech of the seagulls awoke me. I snuggled deeper beneath the blankets, waiting to hear signs of life downstairs. The light had hardly begun to steal through the thin curtains when the noise of Miss Miller stocking the range indicated that her day had begun. I reluctantly rose from the cosy bed, wrapped myself in my shawl, and headed down the stairs to get warm water for washing.

Miss Miller was already dressed, and I suddenly wondered if it was considered unseemly to appear in night clothes. As I later washed in wonderfully hot water, I decided it was worth breaking a few finer rules of etiquette to maintain such a luxury. Miss Miller, meanwhile, had made a pan of warm, milky porridge and, as the daylight strengthened and began entering in through the front windows, we ate breakfast together before her school day began. I was keen to help with the household chores, but Miss Miller would not hear of it. She employed a pupil's mother for a few hours every day to do her washing, cleaning, and some basic meal preparations. This was a mutually beneficial arrangement, as the woman's husband had a liking for strong liquor and the family rarely saw his wages. The money from Miss Miller went straight into the woman's pocket and almost immediately out again to keep the family fed.

With a whole day ahead of me and no commitments or duties, I felt my body and mind relaxing. I had a delightful hour to myself between Miss Miller leaving and her house-woman arriving, so I sorted out my luggage in a more orderly manner than the previous night and made a cup of tea that I enjoyed as I sat near the window with the now warm sunlight streaming on my face.

When I had drained my cup and tidied up, I wrapped up a roll of bread and chunk of cheese in a clean handkerchief, dressed in my warmest clothes, and left the cottage, determined to do a long coastal walk. The clouds and high winds had disappeared and the sky was blue. Instead of being grey and tempestuous, the sea was calm and sparkled merrily in the sunshine. Its blue mirrored the sky, and I was amazed at the difference in mood from last night. The pleasing sight and fresh atmosphere put a spring in my step, smile on my face, and energy into my limbs.

The little harbour was busy and noisy with fishing and bargaining activity, but the farther I walked, the quieter the shoreline became, until soon I was alone. I slowed my pace and walked to the newly emerging rock pools. It was interesting to lift up large stones and disturb the crabs, which scurried off sideways to hide themselves. My pockets soon became full and damp with interesting stones and shells. I was exploring the little pools for fun, but a small group of local women approached with wooden pails to pick mussels off the slippery, seaweed-clad rocks. Their reddened, swollen hands bore testimony to the harsh conditions they were used to battling against to earn a meagre living. Some women's swollen bellies indicated there would soon be another small mouth to feed and body to clothe.

I felt like an intruder, so I continued my walk along the shore line, watching the gentle waves retreating, revealing more golden sand, chalky rocks, and shallow pools. To my right, rising from the beach was the huge and impressive wall of white cliff that ran for miles, creating such a dramatic contrast between the sea and the dry land that I could easily imagine it emerging majestically from the waters on the third day of creation and wholeheartedly agreed with the Creator that "it was good."

The coastline was made up of a series of bays, some large and busy and some small and secluded. Each bay had a means for climbing the great cliffs; some had a properly cut out gulley and staircase, whilst others merely had a weather-beaten rope ladder dangling from the grassy top of the cliff. The ladders swung challengingly in the off-sea breeze—a challenge irresistible to school boys, of no consequence to hardy seafarers, but unthinkably dangerous to me. I imagined getting cut off in a small bay by a rapidly advancing tide and having to climb up a swinging, slippery ladder with water lapping menacingly at my feet, waiting for me to make a false move. With a shudder I (rather over-cautiously) promised myself never to walk along the water's edge when the tide was coming in.

Meanwhile, the sea was out almost as far as it would go, the sun was shining and the walk had given me an appetite, so I sat on a rock and ate my bread and cheese. As I sat munching, my mind wandered back to Agnes and her forthcoming marriage. She seemed so perfectly content with the arrangement, yet could not positively state that she loved the man. Was I expecting too much of life? Would I not be happier if I lowered my aspirations and learned to be content in every situation? Miss Miller seemed content in her little nunnery, and Agnes with her selfless, dutiful decision. How could she share her life, her house, her bed, even her body with a man she did not love? Again I shuddered, stood up and, shaking off the bread crumbs as if they were disagreeable thoughts themselves, continued my walk.

Rain clouds began to gather over the sea and the wind picked up, reminding me it was only April, so I changed direction and headed back to Broadstairs. The return journey seemed much quicker than the outgoing, and I was in the house before Miss Miller. I pulled my shell and stone collection out of my pockets and arranged them along the hitherto bare windowsill. I was pleased with the result and put the kettle on to boil. The tea had just brewed when Miss Miller entered, and she seemed pleased to sit down and relax. I was bursting to tell her of my walk, but she looked so exhausted from her day in the classroom that I kept quiet, and soon I was rescuing the half-full teacup from her lap as she nodded off.

The afternoon sun did not shine in the living room and the range had been burning low all afternoon, so the room was chilly. I found a blanket and carefully wrapped it around Miss Miller and then retired to my room and laid on the bed. Much to my surprise, I too quickly fell into a deep sleep. I awoke cold and hungry an hour later and was pleased to find Miss Miller had the range roaring to cook the meal and warm the house.

Much refreshed from our sleep and meal, we pulled our chairs by the range and sat down for an evening of handiwork and chatting. I was knitting squares for a blanket, and Miss Miller was embroidering a text. I burbled on about the delights of the sea, coastline, and the rock pools.

Miss Miller quietly put her needle down and said, "But there is a dark side to this seemingly happy community."

"Why, whatever do you mean?" I could not discern anything unseeming in this idyllic setting.

"Until 1840, local people lived in constant fear of smuggling gangs, but new laws slashing import duties to realistic levels put an end to all that—gradually. There was still a bit going on only ten years ago, but the memories and scars are still there, as are the family feuds."

Miss Miller explained the smuggling background. For generations, ruthless gangs of smugglers played cat and mouse with coastguards along the coves and bays. Innocent fishermen had been drawn into their grip by the promise of quick money or merely by being in the wrong place at the wrong time. Many a man disappeared for knowing too much and had either been forced to join the gang or ended up in a watery grave. Many a grieving woman had been relieved to hear that her husband's corpse had been found, washed up on the beach, rather than having to live in constant uncertainty of his fate.

The darkness gathered, and a gust of wind rattled the back door, causing me to almost jump out of my skin. We both laughed at my reaction, but it was clear that Miss Miller had a lot more to share.

"The gangs were so aggressive and ruthless that most men feared their treatment more than the hangman's noose, so they dabbled in criminality to stay on the right side of the smugglers. Everyone in the community knew something of what was going on, but no one knew how much everyone else knew, so no one fully trusted anyone. Coded messages were whispered in dark alleys. Half-truths and tall stories of captures, escapes, ghosts, and pirates were told at firesides until everyone was scared of his own shadow. This has left us with a community that dabbles in crime and trusts no one, Rebecca, especially not those in authority." Miss Miller shook her head with sadness. "Families hold ancient grudges against each other for crimes and violence committed by the previous generation, and this leads to frequent fights, even in the school playground. And children grow up knowing there is more money to be gained from criminal activities than from honest labour."

As I thought of the beautiful glistening sea, the stately cliffs, and God's amazing creation and then of the sad broken world we live in now, I realised again how awful sin is and how it has polluted God's wonderful earth.

## CHAPTER 25

LATER THAT EVENING AS I lay in bed, my overactive ears hearing every outside noise, I despaired of ever falling asleep, only realising I had done so when I woke up the next morning. Much to my disappointment, it was a wet day. Before she left for the school room, I asked Miss Miller if she would like me to do any baking. After some consideration, she replied that she rarely ate cake but that I could make some rock buns if I so wished.

Now some people enjoy rock buns, and it is nice that they do, but I find them crumbly, non-descript, dry, and hardly worth eating. They were the first thing my mother taught me to make, and having satisfied her that I had mastered the rubbing-in method, we never bothered with rock buns again. The only way to get an amount of pleasure from eating them is eating them when they are still warm from the oven, or failing that, dunking them in tea. To please Miss Miller I duly made a batch of rock buns and had them cooling on the table when she came in for lunch. I poured out a cup of tea to go with the fresh buns, but Miss Miller was busy finding a tin. She congratulated me on their appearance, but immediately stowed all the rock buns away into the tin, saying, "They will be a nice treat for Sunday."

Sunday! That was three days away. By then they would be most unpalatable and I sensed that dunking was strictly forbidden.

We ate bread and dripping with our cup of tea, and Miss Miller returned to her class. The rain had eased somewhat by the afternoon. I felt in need of escaping, so putting on my shawl, I left the house to explore the high street. Away from the noise and smells of the harbour and fish market was an altogether more upmarket row of shops boasting of a green grocer, an ironmonger, a dressmaker, and a bookseller. In the same street one could buy a bonnet, a basket, and a bread-tin.

I had not had the luxury of browsing such a comprehensive collection of shops since the day of our furniture auction. Now I had both the time and the means to wander around at my leisure, and I headed straight for the bookseller. A bell on the door jingled merrily as I entered, and an elderly, bearded man emerged from behind a pile of books and acknowledged my presence with a grunt. He then busied himself with sorting the tomes, humming and muttering to himself as he worked.

The ascetic atmosphere at Miss Miller's needed counterbalancing, so I headed for the Modern Novel section and was delighted to find *Shirley* by Charlotte Brontë. I had heard of Brontë and how she had surreptitiously succeeded in getting her novel published by using the male pseudonym Currer Bell, and I was curious to read one of her works. Rather guiltily—for my parents, like many evangelical Christians, did not like novels—I paid for the book and, hugging it close, left the shop.

A little tearoom just down the road looked invitingly warm and cosy as the wind and rain increased, so with all the courage of a fashionable town lady who buys books from the Modern Novel section, I entered and found a secluded corner. I was pleased to be served by a reassuringly homely waitress, and as I waited for tea and scones, eagerly unwrapped the book, keen to be entranced by the writings of a fellow vicar's daughter. Even as I read her warning, *Do you expect passion, and stimulus, and melodrama? Calm your expectations, reduce them to a lowly standard. Something real, cool and solid lies before you; something unromantic as a Monday morning,* my expectations rose, and I knew I was in for a satisfying read.

I did not do justice to the delicious tea and scones as I devoured page after page of the story, getting to know the inhabitants of the West Riding of Yorkshire. The gentle voice of the waitress, saying, "We are closing shortly, Miss," brought me back with a jolt to Broadstairs and the 1860s. I apologised, paid my bill and then, carefully secreting the book away in my shawl from the rain and from Miss Miller's observation, I set off for the schoolhouse.

Miss Miller was already at home when I arrived. She looked tired again but was more relaxed with the prospect of two days off ahead of her. I am ashamed to say that, at the realisation that she would be around for the next two days, rather than feeling glad of her companionship, my first thought was "I will have fewer opportunities to read." I chided myself for this selfish thought as I hid *Shirley* under my pillow and went down to help with the preparation of the evening meal. Later that evening I sat with my inevitable hand-work, inwardly rebelling against the plight of women. How was it that men could sit idly in front of a fire in the evenings, doing exactly as they wished, while women had to keep their hands occupied with some useful needlework?

I thought the evening would drag, but Miss Miller began reminiscing about Pemfield, and we ended up having a delightful evening as we chatted about old times and dear friends. I especially appreciated being able to talk about my parents with someone who actually knew them. As we recalled various events, the Sunday evening hymn singing and the winter evenings at the vicarage, my heart ached for my dear pa and ma. But the pain was not as intense, tearing my heart as it used to. Rather, it was a warm ache that one would not really be without, as it was the price one pays for loving and being loved unconditionally.

Saturday dawned bright and sunny, so we set off to explore the shoreline toward Margate. I had only walked the opposite way, so this was all new to me, but it was one of Miss Miller's favourite walks. We passed three beautiful bays before arriving at Botany Bay, where we sat on the cliff top and ate our lunch before returning to Broadstairs, tired but satisfied.

On Sunday I was curious to attend Miss Miller's church. She had warned me that, although the vicar was good man, he had a curate whose preaching left a lot to be desired. As a robed man entered the pulpit, the expression on Miss Miller's face told me that this was the curate. He was young, handsome, and flamboyant with a great gift of oratory.

At first I thought Miss Miller was being rather prejudiced against him, but as the sermon progressed, I began to realise that although he used impressive words and flowery language, his message had very little substance. If salvation were to be obtained by good works, his preaching would have been faultless. With warm words and glowing compliments, he congratulated the attentive congregation for their generosity and the good works done for the poor in the community, giving them all a verbal pat on the back. He could have charmed the birds from the trees as he expressed his gratitude for being assigned to such a noble—or in my opinion, condescending—congregation. His buttery words were effective in making the hearers dig deeper into their pockets for the collection, allowing them to go home with a warm, smug feeling of charity bestowed.

Over the midday meal, I expressed my surprise at the class of the congregation. I had expected the local fishing community to be there, but instead it was the upper class. Miss Miller had also been disappointed when she first realised that although the church was busy supporting the Ragged School and other worthwhile endeavours for the disadvantaged, if one of these beneficiaries did want to come and worship with them, they would receive a less than warm reception and be considered not to know their place.

The Lord's Day seemed long and quiet as we sat in the cold best room, reading the somewhat wordy works of Puritan preachers. As I sat, book in hand, daydreaming, it struck me how distant Biggenden and Mr. Thorpe now seemed. I was learning that I could easily enjoy myself away from his presence and influence, and I could think about his impending marriage with the emotional indifference of an ordinary housekeeper.

I was still only twenty years of age, old enough to make more informed decisions than when I was an inexperienced lass at Pemfield, but young enough to have many opportunities ahead. Opening a small tearoom seemed a nice idea, and I toyed with the idea of selling delicious cakes and pastries from a sweet little kitchen to a loyal and admiring clientele—until Miss Miller's snoring brought me abruptly back to reality.

# CHAPTER 26

AS MISS MILLER SNOOZED, I pondered again the confusing subject of unanswered prayer. For many years, my daily—maybe at times hourly—prayer was that God would grant me a godly and suitable husband. It was my heartfelt desire that I could be a helpmeet to a man as we served the Lord together. This prayer was so far unanswered. Was I wrong to keep on praying? Was it arrogance to think that I could be useful, spiritually, to a God-fearing man? I had seen a lovely example of this in my own parents and knew what a strong team they had been for the Lord. Was I just saying I wanted to be a spiritual and practical help to a husband as a bargaining tool to have my own way? Deep in my heart I knew this was not the case. I genuinely wanted to work for the Lord—but was I dictating *how* by more or less saying "I want to work for God's glory, but only in a marriage relationship"?

My thoughts spiralled around in my head until Miss Miller stirred. Upon her waking, I went to get her a cup of tea and an (in my opinion) by now stale rock bun.

We attended the second service, not out of any great desire to be there but because it was expected of someone in Miss Miller's position. I sat bolt upright on the wooden pew, looking at the preacher, but my mind was far away in Yorkshire with Brontë's Shirley and Caroline. Afterwards, we returned to the appointed place to sit on a

Sunday—the best room. Miss Miller finally lit the little open fire, and we sat around it, toasting crumpets.

As usual, the eventide made Miss Miller chattier, and we were soon discussing the benefits of public ministry on one's own spiritual health. Without much thought I asked the question that had been vexing me for a long time: "What do you think of the question of unanswered prayer?"

As soon as I blurted it out, I regretted bringing up the subject and determined to keep the conversation general. The last thing I wished to do was introduce Edward into the discussion. The question hung in the air as Miss Miller gave the subject her full attention and eventually provided a clear and helpful answer.

"The first thing to consider is God's revealed and secret will. If the thing you ask for is against His revealed will—that is, if it is condemned in Scripture—then it is clearly wrong to ask for it, and you can take the answer as a straightforward no. Yet if it is something recommended or encouraged in the Bible and you really desire it and desire it with a genuine, godly motive, then so-called unanswered prayer may be a delayed yes.

"We are not to try and second-guess the Lord's secret will for our lives. The thing we can be most sure of is that, if anyone seeks salvation in Christ, he will receive it: this is very clearly promised, also that for believers all things will work together for good, because that is promised as well."

"But how do you know that your intentions and motives are right?" I asked.

Miss Miller looked into the fire, thought for a while and then said, "I do not know. Christians remain such a mixture of good and bad that we never do anything with a motive that is one hundred percent pure, do we?"

As I silently nodded in agreement, she continued, "And that is why we need such a compassionate and forgiving Saviour."

"But I wish I was more like you," I moaned. "You seem content with your life here and with the work God has given you, doing it with such diligence and self-sacrifice." And before I could stop myself, the whole story of Edward—my love for him and his forthcoming marriage—came tumbling out. "How can you be so happy, being single?" I asked in tears.

Miss Miller turned her eyes from the fire, leant forward, and looked at me intently. "Oh, my dear Rebecca," she said, "You misjudge my character in a far too favourable manner. I have never had any desire to marry. I have no brothers, and my father squandered our money in gambling. Since my childhood I have almost despised men. In fact, I find it hard to trust anyone and prefer solitude to society. I am happy alone."

"But . . . teaching is sociable," I uttered in surprise.

"Not really, it is not the meeting of two minds on an equal level, but the imparting of knowledge. The relationship between a teacher and a pupil has clear boundaries and objectives, and that is how I prefer to operate. I often wish I had a sociable nature like yours, which seeks out friendship, but I do not."

"Do you want more friends?" I asked, frantically trying to understand her.

"No, to be honest, I do not. I sometimes think I *should* want more friends and that it is wrong of me to be so self-sufficient, but it is not in my nature to want companionship. I hate small talk and mind-numbing social gatherings. I do not feel a need to have a 'soulmate' to whom I am duty-bound to open up my heart and bare my soul."

"So are you happy as you are?"

"Happy is a strong word. I would prefer to say I was content. Yes, I am content." Then Miss Miller put on her teacherish look. "But, Rebecca, you must remember the chief end of man is not to be happy in this life, but to 'glorify God and enjoy Him for ever.'"

At that moment, I had no intention of being drawn into a discussion of the Shorter Catechism. I had more delving to do. "Do you feel fulfilled, though?"

Miss Miller paused and needlessly stoked the fire. After some time she looked at me with a wry smile. "As you know, I am no expert in the etiquette of friendship, but since you have entrusted me with your secret about Mr. Thorpe, I am obliged to reveal my own struggle to you."

I smiled encouragingly and said, "Not 'obliged,' but I am all ears."

"I have never told a soul about this before, but I have a burning desire to go to Africa. To teach African children in a mission school."

I stared at her, stunned by such an adventurous idea.

"Yet," she continued, "it seems so unlikely that a Missionary Society would take on a single lady. I pray daily about this desire, maybe with the fervency you pray for a husband, but so far the Lord has seen fit not to open up a door for me to go. My youthful vigour is behind me, and I have far less now to offer than when I first started praying about it, but I am still in England. I sometimes question my motives: do I really want to go for the good of the African children and for God's glory, or is it just the adventure it would bring, the thrill of escaping from our over-structured society?"

Miss Miller's face lit up, and she had an unusual animation about her as she described the books she had read on Africa, its people, climate, landscape, and wildlife. She wanted to learn an African language, but as the continent is so vast, she didn't know which would be the most useful. She had started learning some basic Swahili. Through reading the "Missionary Record," Miss Miller had learnt of Mary Ann Aldersey, the first single woman to go to China as a missionary and who had succeeded in founding a girls' school in Ningbo. She had found the story very inspiring, but she was so unsure of her motives that she wanted clear guidance before she took a step forward.

"Maybe the Lord wants someone with a larger heart than mine for the work," she said with a sigh. And there we sat, two women in a little cottage in Broadstairs, both dreaming of our hopes for the future. Our dreams were poles apart from each other, but the intensity of longing united us.

## CHAPTER 27

THE DAWN OF A NEW day and working week saw Miss Miller snap back into her "business as usual" mode. As I appeared in the kitchen, she presented me with a paper bag full of my shells and stones.

"I think they are thoroughly dry now," she informed me.

I should have known better than try to decorate her house, and I meekly took them to my room. The day was fine and bright, and I planned another walk toward Ramsgate, but first I had business to attend to. I headed for the dressmakers to get measured for a new summer frock.

The shopgirls were so friendly and full of advice and ideas of matching fabrics, contrasting lace, and ribbons that my original idea of a plain frock soon went out of the window—along with my original budget!

By the time I had finished at the dressmakers and had brought a hot pasty for lunch, it was eleven o'clock. I was unsure of the tides so decided to take the cliff path to Ramsgate rather than walk along the shore.

It was easier walking along the path, and before long I reached the outskirts of Ramsgate and headed for the harbour to eat the pasty. On the way, I noticed a road sign, "Regency Road." That vaguely rang a bell in my memory, and as I sat eating I suddenly remembered why.

Of course! Uncle Hector regularly sent us postcards from 42 Regency Road while taking the seaside air for his chest complaint. He normally went in early spring—about now.

I briefly thought that he might be there now and that I should look him up. Then I decided not to. After all, he had never been nice to Pa. I had lived in fear that Uncle Hector would track me down, claim to be my legal guardian, and force me to live with him until I was twenty-one, but now I had only a month before I would come of age. I no longer had to fear a sort of legal kidnap.

As I passed the road sign again, my conscience smote me: "Rebecca Stubbs, here you are within what may be a stone's throw of your only known blood relative, and you are too selfish to pay him a visit. What would your parents think? Your mother would say you had become self-indulgent, with your fine frocks, seaside vacations, and novel reading."

At that, I turned around and tracked down number 42. The guest house had a very pleasing appearance and was one in a row of large, well-maintained, bay windowed, whitewashed houses with red roof tiles.

A young housemaid answered the door, but she did not know if Mr. Hector Stubbs was in residence and hurried off to get the landlady. A buxom, middle-aged matron came to the door and knew immediately who I was talking about, and furthermore said that he was reading in the drawing room. She invited me in, and I followed her along a wide hall to the elegant drawing room.

I barely had time to think before I stood face to face with Uncle Hector himself. With tears in his eyes, Uncle Hector hugged me long and hard, as if I were the long lost prodigal son. Such close proximity revealed that Uncle Hector, despite his chest condition, was looking hale and hearty and exactly as he always did—double chin, ruddy cheeks, waxed moustache, and all.

He drew a chair for me, close to his, and holding my reluctant hand in his two soft, plump hands, he exclaimed, "My, how my little Becca has grown into a fine, young lady! How much like my dear brother you look."

He did not call for the fatted calf to be killed, but he rang the bell and ordered afternoon tea for two. The buxom landlady sensed the significance of the occasion and brought in the platter of sandwiches and tea-bread herself.

"Mrs. Wickens," said Uncle, "I have the great pleasure of introducing you to my dear niece Rebecca."

Mrs. Wickens warmly shook my hand and said, "I've heard all about you and your dear departed parents from Mr. Stubbs. He was so terribly fond of them and can't praise them highly enough."

I tried not to show my astonishment or slight amusement.

As we settled down to our lavish tea, Uncle Hector bombarded me with questions about the last four years. He was shocked to hear I had become a domestic servant. On one occasion he had written to Mrs. Brown, asking her of my whereabouts, and she had replied that I was staying with good friends.

"Obviously a blatant lie!" sputtered my uncle. I tried to justify her reply by saying I did have many friends at my work, but he just shook his head, making his chins wobble, and muttered to himself, "A Stubbs in domestic service. Unthinkable."

I tried to be vague about my present position and emphasised that I had a lot of freedom and influence, but this did not satisfy the

Stubbs pride. He was slightly mollified when I explained that I was about to give notice to end the employment. As soon as possible, I turned the conversation to him, and once on his favourite subject, he soon brightened up and talked energetically about his London life, his many vacations, and his doctor's orders, whilst consuming vast amounts of cake in large mouthfuls.

Once the platter was emptied and the teapot drained, Uncle Hector sat back and lit a cigar (as recommended by his chest physician). I chuckled as I asked him if he remembered how much Ma had hated the smell. He remembered and also revealed that when Ma had retired for bed, Pa would secretly join him for a puff.

I smiled as I thought of the naughty-boy expression and mischievous twinkle in his eye Pa may have had. At least Pa had enjoyed some parts of his brother's visits. One thought of my parents led to another, and before I knew it, we had spent the afternoon recalling memories of them.

Instead of constant criticism of Pa, Uncle Hector had nothing but praise. Ah, he remembered their warm hospitality, their unflagging diligence, and Christian love. His dear brother had been such a faithful preacher, so well read, so wise, and his sister-in-law a rare gem, such a good little housewife, such an admirable cook.

Sometimes I looked at him, trying to detect some insincerity in his face or speech, but no, these gushing praises flowed from a genuine heart. Every now and again I looked through the window at the falling sun and made an attempt to go, but every time Uncle Hector launched into some hitherto-unknown-to-me story of my father and I sat back, intrigued to hear it.

At dusk, I could leave it no longer, and with fearful thoughts of highwaymen and pirates, I asked for my shawl to be fetched. Uncle Hector would not hear of me walking back to Broadstairs (he made it sound like a huge journey) and organised a private carriage to convey me door to door. But before I departed, he entreated me to come again as soon and as often as I could.

"I am not having you just disappearing out of my life again!" he warned.

I dutifully kissed him good-bye and assured him I would not disappear but would be back in a few days for more stories. I was rewarded by a flush on his fleshy cheeks and a stroke of my arm.

## CHAPTER 28

MISS MILLER WAS SURPRISED TO see me arrive back in style, carriages being rarely seen in her narrow back street. She was a very satisfactory and attentive listener as I recounted the afternoon's events. My final week in Broadstairs flew by at an alarming speed. I finished reading *Shirley*, and now that my appetite was thoroughly whetted for Charlotte Brontë's writing, I returned to the book seller and bought Brontë's first and more controversial novel, *Jane Eyre*.

Day by day my new summer dress took shape and the final result was delightful. I felt almost like Miss Sophia herself! I smiled as I imagined Mrs. Harrington declaring it entirely unsuitable for a woman in my lowly position. Soon I would be forever away from her criticism and censorship. Alas, my frugal budget was thoroughly trampled underfoot when the dressmaker recommended a contrasting bonnet and gloves that perfectly complemented the frock. It seemed utter folly to buy the dress without them.

Three more afternoons saw me in the plush, smoky drawing room of 42 Regency Road. When Uncle Hector was not in the mood to talk about himself or his brother, we played board games. He tried to teach me bridge, but I could not grasp the complicated rules and thought that the best role for me was the dummy.

I suggested we stroll together along the promenade, but it seemed that Uncle Hector lived a fairly sedentary lifestyle and preferred not to over-exert himself. I could not help wondering how the Ramsgate sea air could benefit his lungs whilst he was cooped up inside, but politeness prevailed and I kept these thoughts to myself.

On our final afternoon together (I was leaving for Biggenden the following day), Uncle Hector begged me to come and live with him in London.

"My dear Becca, I would treat you like my own daughter. You would lack for nothing. You would never have to work again. Your parents would have whole-heartedly approved of the arrangement—which is more than can be said for your current situation." His pudgy white hands grasped mine, trapping them as he continued. "You could accompany me on my visits to Bath and Tunbridge Wells to drink from their healthy water springs and mingle with high society. I could arrange tuition for you to be instructed in painting, history of art, musicology, or whatever your heart desires."

As I looked out of the window, trying to formulate a diplomatic reply, I knew that I would feel like my hands right now: trapped. In my mind's eye I saw the London house with thick, squishy carpets, sturdy wooden furniture, and heavy velvet curtains preventing the sun's rays from warming the rooms. A stale smell from lack of air, the aroma of cigar smoke, old men and port filled every room. I imagined being a dutiful hostess to all his aged (maybe groping) friends as they came to play bridge or discuss politics. What a gilded cage it would be!

I was beginning to taste freedom, and what an enjoyable taste it was! I was not prepared to give it up yet, especially not for a verbose uncle and London. I was utterly determined to say no there and then, but as I turned my gaze from the window to his beseeching eyes, my resolve floundered. I did the cowardly thing and told him I was not free, as yet, to do as I pleased but that I would consider his proposal carefully and write to him with my response.

Uncle Hector took this answer rather more positively than the spirit in which it was given and seemed satisfied. With mixed feelings I extracted myself from his embrace and whiskery kiss and climbed into the carriage. A feeling of sadness at saying farewell to a loving relative was almost outweighed by a feeling of relief that no one could force me to live with him.

That last evening at Broadstairs was mild, still, and dry. A full moon shone in the cloudless sky. After some persuasion, Miss Miller wrapped herself up and came with me to sit near the cliff edge. The moon was so bright that we felt safe to venture outside. We sat in companionable silence, absorbing the peaceful scene around us. The darkness had silenced the seagulls, the calm sea lapped at the shore, and the beach was deserted. The shining moon was reflected in the still sea, creating a shimmering track that seemed to come directly to where we sat.

A multitude of stars twinkled at us. The tranquillity of the sight and the sense of the universe's magnitude impressed me with awe for our great Creator. The benevolent and powerful God who counts the stars and knows their names in His great goodness sent His Son to save us. He is worthy of my wholehearted trust and confidence to save body and soul, both for time and eternity. A deep sense of peace and happiness filled my heart as I committed myself once again to my God and to His wise and loving plan for my life, whatever it might be.

As I gazed at the stars, which had shone for thousands of years, my little life and its concerns seemed very insignificant. In another hundred years (unless the Lord returned), the same stars would still be shining and the tides still ebbing and flowing, great constants un-affected whatsoever whether I married or remained single. The only thing that really mattered was my relationship with Jesus Christ, to be loved and forgiven by Him, and I rejoiced to feel a glow of that everlasting love already.

The slight sea breeze eventually penetrated through our thick cloaks, and Miss Miller and I were obliged to head indoors. An awk-wardness fell over us; we both knew this was our last evening to-gether, but instead of producing an easy flow of conversation, our communication seemed stilted and forced. I really wanted to show my appreciation for her kindness and friendship, but one look at her business-like face as she checked her weekly timetable made it clear such sentiments would be dismissed, but these things need to be said anyway so, taking a deep breath, I expressed by gratitude for her hos-pitality and company.

As predicted, she brushed it aside with a "don't mention it" but went on to say she would miss me. Putting down her work, she urged me to come back once I had finished working at Biggenden and whilst I was seeking other employment. I was delighted with the idea and readily agreed to it.

"Unless you are in Africa," I laughed.

"Unless you are married," she replied.

## CHAPTER 29

THE SADNESS OF LEAVING BROADSTAIRS and Miss Miller (and even my nun's cell bedroom) was tempered by the hope of seeing them all again in the near future. Miss Miller watched my carriage disappear up the cobbled high street before wandering back to the school room to commence the working day.

As the steam train chuffed its way through Kent toward Tunbridge, the cares and concerns of daily life at Biggenden Manor came to the fore of my thinking. I shrank from the thought of handing in my notice, but somehow the very presence of my new books and dress in my trunk—symbols of new independence—gave me courage and determination.

As planned, I got a ride back to Biggenden with a farmhand who had been selling milk, butter, and eggs at Tunbridge market. My trunk and bags were thrown on the wagon, along with the empty churns and baskets, before we trotted off.

I tried to shake off the feelings of servile dutifulness and loyalty that engulfed me as we progressed up the drive, but when the Kemps and Rex gave me a hearty (and tail thumping from the latter) welcome, my plans of independence and freedom suddenly seemed selfish. After a much needed cup of tea, Mrs. Kemp eased herself out of her chair and limped through the house to show me what the builders had done.

The outside work was now complete, leaving only the inside painting and decorating. It seemed highly likely now that everything would be shipshape for the grand arrival of Mrs. Thorpe. Mrs. Kemp's attitude toward the "so-called improvements" was an amusing mixture of disapproval and grudging admiration. I was impressed with the extension but wished it blended in better with the more austere character of the original rooms.

As we paused to admire the view from the conservatory, Mrs. Kemp broke into my thoughts.

"We're moving owt."

I turned to look at her. "You're moving?"

"Yep, it is decided," she said, her face resolute as if I was about to remonstrate. "Me an' Arfer are moving in with our Sally." (Sally was their daughter.)

"But I thought her cottage was full," I replied.

"It were full, but me oldest two granddaw'ers 'ave gone inta service, so naw there's room fer us. We ain't got much stuff ta take wiv us, and we wanna be gone before yer wedding."

"Was this your decision, or did Mr. Thorpe ask you to go?" I queried, my eyes narrowing at the thought of him, under the direction of his mother-in-law-to-be, unceremoniously asking them to pack their bags.

"Well, 'e said we woz free to go if we wonted, an' so we fort abowt it and decided we wanna move before fings 'ere change too much."

I nodded. "And I think you are very wise."

"An' you, young gal, must look arfter yeself too," she said, looking at me with motherly eyes.

I nearly told her of my plan to leave, but then I imagined her shouting this communication into Mr. Kemp's deaf ears, along with the instructions "but keep it ta yeself," letting anyone around into the secret too. So I just said I had a few ideas and thanked her for her concern.

When the Kemps had retired to bed, I sat in my parlour and went through a pile of paperwork. I was pleased to see that Clara had kept a list of ingredients she had used, along with the relevant bills and receipts. My heart sank when I read an invitation (or rather, summons) from the church warden's wife, asking me to help at the annual Sunday school outing.

My lack of success at the Ladies' Mission evenings ruled me out from being invited to help with the many jobs that the good ladies of the church did, but, the reputation of the Sunday school outing being as it was, they had to scrape the barrel when looking for volunteers and approached me. I had gladly accepted the year before, imagining it to be a civilised and enjoyable little picnic with well-behaved children in their Sunday best—and that is how the day started.

We had gathered in the church yard, the girls in newly washed spring dresses and the boys wearing their best suits and shining boots. Then the vicar, Mr. Brinkhill, in full clerical garb and holding aloft the Sunday school banner, ceremoniously led the way as we marched through the village toward the designated meadow. Villagers waved at us from their garden gates and more children ran to join the parade. Rousing Christian hymns were sung, like "Onward Christian Soldiers," but before we had left the village the singing degenerated into shouting and the hymns turned into a bloodcurdling war-cry against all Baptists, Methodists, or Papists. The vicar, absorbed in keeping the heavy banner erect and occupied with his own marching, was oblivious to the riotous behaviour. Heavy laden with baskets of food, three ladies and I trailed apologetically behind.

The appointed meadow seemed to be the one farthest from the village, and we lost sight of the children as we struggled with the provisions. At last we arrived. Once the vicar had ponderously decided where we would "set up camp," we spread our blankets and prepared the food. The children fought their way to a place on the blankets, stomping on each other as they went, and once we all sat down, the vicar said the longest grace for the food that I had ever heard. The bread, cheese, pastries, and biscuits soon disappeared into over-stuffed mouths and pockets, and gallons of milk were drunk.

Agnes informed me that the traditional beverage for the occasion had always been the vicar's wife's homemade elderflower cordial, but one year the bottles had fermented, causing the children to go home half drunk. The vicar's wife vehemently denied any connection and suggested that the children had a touch of sunstroke, but as it had been a cloudy day, no one swallowed that story. The tale of the tipsy children spread around the village like wild fire, becoming more and more exaggerated with the telling. From then on, only milk was provided.

After the picnic, I expected some structured entertainment to take place, but on seeing the vicar settling down under a tree with a book and the ladies busying themselves with the leftovers, I realised the children were just left to their own devices.

The meadow was on an undulating slope, so that the lower half could not be seen from the picnic area. The boys headed straight for this spot, out of sight but not hearing, and soon raucous shouts indicated that something lively was going on. None of the other grown-ups seemed to notice the noise, but I went to investigate. The boys were playing British Bulldog. Not the relatively gentle variety we used to play in the school yard, but a full blown "shoulders on the ground" version. A big burly lad stood in the middle, calling the name of a small, puny boy who had to run past him to the other side of the field. The big lad would have to catch the runner and bring him down to the ground. If the runner happened to get to the other side, everyone would run across. Anyone caught would join the catcher in the middle, making the game harder and harder. As I watched, a huge muscular boy tripped up a small lad, flinging him to the ground. The little lad arose with a bloody nose and a face covered with fresh cow pat. I was about to rescue the victim, but then I saw his eyes flashing through the cow pat, and with the brutality of an ancient war-painted Briton, he hurled himself at the legs of a youth twice his size, bringing him crashing to the floor. At that point, I remembered that discretion is the better part of valour and retreated up the hill to sit with the other women.

The girls entertained themselves in a slightly more civilised manner and foraged the hedgerows for flowers and created small posies for the ladies and each other. Once they had exhausted this activity, they made up various skipping games and clapping hand rhymes. Near the end of the afternoon, they were clearly bored, challenging each other to pick as many stinging nettles as possible without getting stung.

I was relieved when the vicar finally closed his book, heaved and stretched himself into a standing position, and ordered everyone to march back to the village. The troop that arrived back at the church yard was hardly recognisable as the smart one that had left a few hours earlier. The girls' neat plaits were dishevelled, their dresses creased and stained, some even ripped, while the boys looked like the victims of a natural disaster. The waiting mothers seemed unperturbed by the appearance of their offspring, and each reminded their charges to say "thank you to the kind vicar" before they headed for home, every child clutching a small bag of sweets.

So it was with reluctance that I put pen to paper and wrote back to the church warden's wife, agreeing to help. To make matters worse, the event would take place on my twenty-first birthday. What an awful way to spend the day! Then I reminded myself that I no longer celebrated birthdays anyway so should not to fuss about it.

First thing the next day, I received a telegram from Mr. Thorpe informing me he would be returning that evening. I hastily ordered a better cut of meat and made certain his room was heated. By the time he arrived home, tired and hungry, Molly and Clara had already gone home and his meal was spoiling. He declared himself too exhausted to eat a large meal and asked for bread, cheese, and pickles to be sent along to his study. Mr. Kemp eagerly cleared up the somewhat dried out supper.

I served the food and, just like old times, Edward invited me to sit down and chat. The study was (as yet) untouched by Harrington hands, and as we caught up with each other's news, the cosy atmosphere of bygone evenings pervaded, making me feel even more traitor-like to contemplate leaving. I did not want to spoil the congenial nature of the evening and said nothing about my plans, but listened attentively to his.

## CHAPTER 30

THE NEXT MORNING, I BRACED myself for action with the notion that the sooner he knew, the sooner he could plan a replacement, and once again headed for Mr. Thorpe's study. With great sense of purpose, I knocked on his door only to find him in deep discussion with his land steward. The next time I tried, it was the builder, and so it went on throughout the frustrating day. I had almost given up for the day when, at tea time, Mr. Thorpe caught up with me in the hallway and asked if I wanted to see him.

My well-rehearsed speech had vanished from my mind and my mouth went dry, but as soon as we were safely within the privacy of his study, I said, "I would like to give notice of leaving your employment, please."

Flabbergasted, Mr. Thorpe looked at me. "You, give notice?" he sputtered. "But why?"

My mind was far from clear, but while rubbing my sweaty palms on my dress, I said, "I have enjoyed working for you, sir—and am grateful for your kindly friendship toward me—but with all the changes afoot for you and Biggenden, I feel that it would be for the best for all if I left."

Mr. Thorpe slumped in his chair with his chin on his chest. Then, looking both despondent and accusing, he asked, "How could you do this to me?"

"I think it will be best for you all," I repeated.

"And who, pray tell, is *you all?*"

"You, sir, your bride, the new staff, and the Harrington family."

Mr. Thorpe sat up straight. "Has Mrs. Harrington suggested this move to you?"

"Not at all, sir, though I imagine she will approve of it."

"Be that as it may, Rebecca, but the point is that I need you and your sensible guidance."

"But, sir, you will have your wife to offer you sensible guidance."

Mr. Thorpe studied his finger nails a while before replying. "My darling Sophia is an accomplished young lady, but I could not rely on her for sound advice or well-considered reasoning."

My astonishment made me say too much. "But, sir, surely to have confidence in your spouse's opinion is of utmost importance in a marriage?"

This statement clearly annoyed Mr. Thorpe, and he rather savagely retorted, "This just shows how little you know of love. You always have been surprisingly dim on the subject."

I was both hurt and perplexed. I needed to get out the room, so I edged toward the door.

"So is that your final decision, Rebecca?"

"Yes, sir, it is. I really should be seeing to the staff," I replied, disappearing out the door before he could reply.

During the next few days, Mr. Thorpe tried every possible tactic to make me change my mind. One hour he would declared me selfish; the next, unchristian; then thoughtless; then too ambitious. He sometimes begged with boyish playfulness, sometimes scolded me with severity and sometimes whined pathetically. I could easily withstand the scolding and whining, but his boyish playfulness was so like the light-hearted banter we used to enjoy in pre-Harrington days that my heart softened and my determination weakened. I so distrusted my ability to stand firm that I decided that the only way to force myself to stick to my resolution was to tell the staff of my intentions.

The Kemps digested the news as they did their dinners—with silent approval. Clara and Molly were both shocked—probably imagining, like Mr. Thorpe, that Spinster Stubbs would be at Biggenden for aye. They were also apprehensive about who might replace me, fearing some sweeping regime changes.

Our immediate priority was the rehousing of Mr. and Mrs. Kemp. We all worked hard to pack up their belongings, marvelling at how many possessions they had managed to fit into their strange pantry bedroom. I had never actually been inside the room before and was horrified to see the conditions they had endured. The outside wall was damp, and mildew covered the plasterwork. Their earthly goods looked sadly dishevelled and pathetic loaded onto a donkey cart, and their owners looked equally uprooted. The housemaids and I tried to make the occasion as cheery as possible, but we all knew life at Biggenden would never be the same again.

The Kemps were more than happy to live with their daughter, but this did little to make the move, which also marked the end of their working life, any easier. Despite Mr. Kemp's very minimal involvement in the running of Biggenden, he still saw himself as the man of the house. As he left the house and was helped up onto the wagon bench, he seemed to diminish and looked like a frail old man who no longer knew his role in life. Mrs. Kemp bustled about, ensuring all her breakable possessions were adequately wrapped up—including her husband. She tried to look calm, but an uncharacteristic clumsiness and talkativeness gave her away. She kissed us all and then was heaved up to sit next to the driver. Her voice cracked and her bottom lip trembled as she called out her final instructions. We waved them out of sight, vowing to visit them often before we returned to the empty kitchen with damp eyes.

Our next job was to thoroughly clean and whitewash the pantry, but for just a while, all we could do was put the kettle on and flop into chairs. All that could be heard was the kettle as we sat in silence, each pondering our loss. The kettle's whistle jolted us back to life, and as we drank our tea, we reassured ourselves and each other with "It will be nice for them to be with their grandchildren" and similar platitudes. I inadvertently lightened the mood by knocking on the pantry door before I entered—old habits certainly die hard.

## CHAPTER 31

THE HOUSEMAIDS SEEMED RELUCTANT TO leave me alone in the house that evening. The house felt large and gloomy, despite the fact that Mr. Thorpe was in residence somewhere. So absorbed was their employer with other matters that he was not aware of the Kemps' departure, and somehow I felt loath to inform him.

It seemed strangely awkward to acknowledge we were alone in the house, so I continued as if all was normal. The next day was worse as, being a Saturday, the maids had a half day. I cooked a small meal and served half in a silent dining room and half in a silent kitchen.

By now Mr. Thorpe had realised the Kemps had been rehoused and even visited the newly reclaimed and whitewashed pantry. As we stood in the unnaturally quiet kitchen, I ventured to ask if anything should be done to recruit more staff before the wedding, imagining some of the responsibility would fall to me, but he assured me all was in hand; Mrs. Harrington was overseeing the promotion and transfer of some of her loyal and trusted staff. The new housekeeper would arrive in June, followed by the kitchen staff and male servants in July, around the time of the marriage, ready to be fully operational when the happy couple returned from their bridal tour of the continent.

I digested this information with interest, marvelling again at the domineering efficiency of Mr. Thorpe's future mother-in-law. I could almost see the glint of satisfaction in her eyes as she learned I was leaving Biggenden and then plotted how she could use this void to ensure Biggenden was run more along Harrington lines. Biggenden would be a small colony of the Harrington empire, and to ensure its loyalty, she needed trusted and obedient generals on the ground to keep the natives in check.

Mr. Thorpe's only request was that I stay on until September, when he returned from his trip. He was anxious not to leave Biggenden and Rex alone with the new crew. With a wry smile, he also said he hoped I could educate the housekeeper in "Biggenden ways." I happily agreed with these terms, as my future plans were by no means decided, and I was anxious that our parting be amiable. Now that he had come to terms with my imminent departure, Mr. Thorpe was touchingly interested in my future and what I hoped to do. I did not want to worry him with my uncertainties so, without lying, I led him to believe that Uncle Hector's offer was rather more appealing to me than it was. My pride forbade me from explaining how I would be earnestly searching for a way of making an independent living.

As we chatted about our futures, Mr. Thorpe sat down at the long kitchen table and suggested that we have a cup of tea "for old times' sake." Over tea he described his planned route around the continent and all the sites and cities he hoped they could visit. I looked at his boyishly animated face and felt a surge of love for him again, but this time it was not the exciting "in love" feeling but rather the friendly warmth and concern one may feel toward a close but sometimes irritating brother. The life he was dreaming of with his glamorous bride sounded nice, but it was not what I would enjoy. I could have imagined myself as the wife of a rural landowner who enthusiastically followed the farming almanac, but not as one who enthusiastically followed the social calendar of the upper class. I felt content that we had shared some good times together, but it was clear that now our lives were naturally drifting apart. I did not know my path ahead, but I knew who was making the path and had full confidence in His wisdom.

That afternoon, Edward left for Surrey to see his beloved Sophia again, and I was left alone in the house for the first time. As the daylight dwindled, I locked all the doors, then checked and rechecked them. I tried to rationalise my unease away by telling myself that Mr. and Mrs. Kemp had hardly been the most able security guards, but such logic did little to help.

I normally enjoyed the solitude of my parlour, but with the awareness of an empty kitchen next door, my enjoyment evaporated. Instead of settling down in front of the stove, I paced around restlessly. The silence had the opposite effect on the noticeably noisy clock, and its hands crept around the face at an unusually sluggish pace. The evening dragged on, and when I could bear it no more, I made a bed of old blankets by the kitchen range for Rex (an arrangement he thoroughly approved of) and went to bed. My normal prayer request for protection during the night hours was pleaded with great earnestness that evening, and thankfully the Lord not only protected me and the house but gave restful sleep as well.

## CHAPTER 32

IT WAS WITH AN AIR of reluctance that I prepared for church the next morning. A mere tickle in the throat or suggestion of a headache would have been an excuse sufficient to skip the morning service, but as I was in good health, I fastened my bonnet, donned my cloak, and left the house. The morning sun shone brightly upon the lush foliage and bluebells. In the orchards the fruit trees were covered in blossom. The beautiful spring sights drove away some of my negativity; if I could not enjoy the preaching, at least I could enjoy creation's message. By and by I caught up with Mrs. Brookes and fell in step with her. She updated me with the family news, especially of Agnes' recent wedding.

"And that were the last sermon the Rev'rent gave," she said.

"Oh," I said, surprised. "What has happened to Reverend Brinkhill?"

"'Aven't you 'eard? Why, 'e's fallen over en broke 'is leg—right bad."

"Poor man!" I gasped. "So what about preaching?"

"Impossible. 'E can't preach for munfs. The bishop 'as sent in a curate to take 'is place."

Now, I would not wish a broken leg upon anyone, but I had an unholy wave of joy at the thought of the vicar being unable to preach. I tried to check this feeling and sound sincere as I answered that I hoped his leg soon mended.

"Naah," came the pessimistic reply. "'E's the wrong side a sixty ta make a quick recovery."

By now we were at the church porch, so we separated to our normal pews. I prayed that the bishop had sent a good man to the parish. Instead of a feeling of having to endure the service, I felt anticipation. My hopes were not dashed when an energetic man opened the vestry door, walked determinedly up the pulpit step, and opened the service with prayer. His prayer was warm and reverent and bore the marks of a man who knew that he had the ear of Almighty God. He read the Bible with expression and reverence, raising my hopes further that we were in for a good sermon. He preached from the well-known parable of the prodigal son and held our attention well with relevant illustrations, interesting observations, and good eye contact. His description of God as the loving father was heart-warming as he drew parallels between the ways in which they welcome wayward sinners.

He hit the message home by warning us that we need not be "in a far country" to be far from our heavenly Father, but sitting piously in a pew with our hearts somewhere else. "We don't need to be living riotously, but if we are not in fellowship with the Father, then we are far away."

From Isaiah and the New Testament, he pointed out some lovely passages that showed the heavenly Father's loving heart and willingness to welcome sinners. He urged us to come home to the Father and experience His forgiving love.

He was not the most polished or eloquent preacher I had heard, but his earnestness and warmth shone through, making him a compelling speaker. My soul sang for joy as he quoted, "In thy presence is fullness of joy; at thy right hand there are pleasures for evermore."

Then we were suddenly brought back to earth by practical arrangements. Much to my surprise, the curate said, "Now we will take a few moments to privately think on these things while our band members tunes their instruments in preparation for the final hymn." Looking up, he smiled at the musicians and sat down. I did continue thinking about the sermon, but I also wondered how the curate had reacted to the band's interruption the first time he preached and was impressed by how he had decided to handle the situation. After a few minutes of screeches and scratches from the balcony, the noise died down, and the band leader called out "Thanks, parson," at which the curate stood up and said, "Thank you, gentlemen," before continuing his sermon for another five minutes, pressing home the urgency of being reconciled to God.

I walked home alone with a thankful heart for the invigorating sermon and a welcoming God. I also thought about the curate. I gathered his name was Rev. Hayworth. He was neither young nor old, and the best way I could describe him was as a "family man." His brown hair had tints of grey around the ears, and his kind brown eyes and friendly face showed evidence of life experience and maybe hardship. I imagined he was a capable father of a young family and was the husband of an able, godly woman.

When I got back to Biggenden, it was strange unlocking and entering a deserted house. After a meal of cold meat and vegetables, I was pleased to get out into the spring sunshine and walk Rex. The day of rest passed slowly, and I leisurely walked, read, and then dozed until the evening service.

The evening service was as good as the morning, and once again our new curate preached an instructive and heart-warming sermon.

As I listened to his fervent praying, I felt rebuked for my sluggish and distracted bedtime prayers and resolved to do better. At the end of the service, before the benediction, Rev. Hayworth gave out a notice: "I have been asked to remind you of the Sunday school outing due to take place next Saturday. All Sunday school scholars are warmly invited, and I look forward to joining you on this happy occasion."

My reaction to this announcement was mixed. I felt glad he was coming, but I also felt sorry for his misguided enthusiasm, stemming from his ignorance of the true nature of the event. With curiosity and some amusement, I wondered how he would handle the situation and began to almost look forward to the trip.

But that week I was not given much time for conjecture. Monday afternoon brought an urgent message from Mr. Thorpe, announcing that he would be arriving on Tuesday afternoon with Mr., Mrs., and Sophia Harrington so they could view the building work and plan the décor. They would be staying until Friday, along with three servants.

Clara, Molly, and I flew into a flurry of domestic activity. The garden boy was roped in to be a messenger as I sent orders and then amendments of orders to all our normal suppliers. Molly's younger brother was bribed with promises of regular cake to keep all the bedroom and reception room fires burning. He did such a sterling job that we became more concerned about chimney fires than damp, cold rooms. My insistence in keeping the house clean despite its being empty paid off, and Clara had only to do some cursory cleaning and straightening up, while Molly and I set to in the kitchen.

How we missed Agnes's expertise as we thumbed through the flour-covered recipe books, trying to construct a suitable menu! Then Mrs. Brookes' youngest daughter, Violet, was offered by her mother as a temporary scullery maid, so we fitted her up in an over-large uniform and got her busy at the sink. Beds were made up in the attic rooms for the Kenwood housemaids and Clara, Molly, and Violet, who had to live-in for the duration of the visitors' stay.

As instructed by Mr. Thorpe, a carriage was sent to meet the visitors from Tunbridge Railway Station, and the farm wagon was also sent for the staff and all the luggage. We were taken by surprise when one of the servants turned out to be a footman. Clara and Molly giggled when he took his overcoat off and revealed a ridiculously showy uniform. He showed his superiority by studiously ignoring their stares and chuckles. Like an exotic bird among sparrows, he looked completely out of place among the likes of us. But we did not have time to stop and stare but had to scurry around making our guests comfortable and provide them with refreshment. The groom and gardener quickly helped me get a bedroom ready for the footman in the new men's quarters.

When I met Mrs. Harrington in the hallway, she acknowledged my presence with a triumphant air of one who has got her own way, saying, "Ah, Stubbs, I understand you are leaving."

"Yes, ma'am, I am."

"Well, I am pleased you knew the limits of your capability," she purred.

I snorted but quickly turned it into a cough as she swept into the sitting room, smiling to herself.

Of course, Bertha was back. This time I had prepared my parlour for her intrusion, clearing the desk, ready for her ladies' delicates. The other maid was Hilda, an under-cook at Kenwood who was considered worthy of a promotion to head-cook at Biggenden. Hilda marched into our kitchen ready to take command of dinner preparations, but halted when she saw that the task was almost completed already. If she was impressed, she hid it well by criticising the combination of dishes. She wanted to throw out our meal plans for the next three days and order food for her own menus.

Molly looked as if she was about to use her wooden spoon on haughty Hilda, so I intervened by explaining how wasteful a change of menu would be because we had already procured most of the ingredients. Finally, common sense won, and after making a few unnecessary changes, Hilda reluctantly gave in. But she still thought she was queen of the kitchen and insisted on moving the kitchen utensils "to their right place," making it impossible to find anything.

Upstairs, there was also friction about the right place for things. The Harringtons possessed various items of furniture that had been in the family for generations, and they wished Mr. Thorpe and Sophia to have some of these at Biggenden. Her doting parents agreed to let Sophia have whatever heirlooms she wished, and as they walked around the empty space, discussion took place as to what would look nice where.

They were unitedly impressed and delighted by the new rooms, but they were un-united in how to fill them. Any suggestion from anyone else was immediately squashed by Mrs. Harrington. It soon became clear that Sophia was welcome to any family heirloom—as long as it was not one of her mother's favourites. It became yet clearer that most of them were her favourites and "would not stand the journey." Mr. Harrington huffed and puffed about his wife's unreasonableness and then disappeared outside to inspect the workmanship of the brickwork.

Mr. Thorpe later told me that he feared that the rooms would be filled with ugly rejects from Kenwood, so he had quickly suggested that locally made, bespoke furniture would suit the extension very well, and Sophia, always the peace-lover, readily agreed.

During their three-day visit, I had very little time or opportunity to study Mr. Thorpe and his fiancée, but the few brief times I saw them together, I was reassured of their utter devotion to each other. Miss Sophia looked childishly enchanted by the improvements to the house, and according to Bertha, she was counting off the days until she would become Mrs. Thorpe. She told Bertha it would be "such fun" to be mistress of a household and "so grown up" to be a wife.

Bertha was not so smitten with the idea, as she would also have to move to Biggenden and live among rustics. The only consolation was that now a sizeable team of staff was also coming with her, so she would at least have some "decent company." I expressed my hope that they would be nice to Molly and Clara, but she just shrugged and said, "If they don't like us, they can leave."

In the kitchen, things were gradually improving. On Wednesday evening while preparing the lavish meal, Hilda got flustered over lumpy sauce and ended up in tears. Molly came to the rescue by sieving it all and adding more cream, thus gaining Hilda's gratitude and respect. Through her sobs, Hilda explained she had only been keen to keep her own meal plans as they were dishes she was confident in preparing, and Molly cheered her up by saying that was exactly why she had fought hard for her own too! From that moment onward, they worked well together, exchanging tips and ideas.

Poor young Violet worked harder than ever before in her life, washing everything from delicate glasses to fatty pans in the old stone sink. Her hands became red and raw from the hot water, carbolic soap, and baking soda. Every night I plastered her hands with lotion, but it gave only temporary relief. By Friday, she was tearfully grateful to receive her wages and run home.

Meanwhile, Clara was working closely with Lawson the footman and continued to be fascinated with the amount of work he got through in such a gliding, unhurried manner. He had no doubt about his own importance, performing every task with the air of one doing the world in general and us in particular a great favour. By the end of his stay with us, we had no more idea of his personal character, his likes or dislikes, than when we first met him.

It was with happiness and relief that we waved the Kenwood staff off on Friday morning and retreated to the kitchen for a good "chew over." Molly and Clara had a commendably stubborn streak, making them ready for the challenge of working with the "toffs," as they called them. They laughed at their superior attitude, saying, "They fink, cos they work for 'em, that they're the upper clarss too."

They were soon comparing the peacock-like Lawson with their male friends and neighbours. His thin, white-gloved hands and their muscular, mud-engrained fingers. His smooth delicate steps and their lumbering strides. The lively conversation ended with them both declaring they preferred "real men, like our village lads," and silently I had to agree.

I let them linger at the table for longer, but I had to get busy making biscuits, as promised, for the Sunday school outing the next day.

## CHAPTER 33

THE MORNING OF THE SUNDAY school outing dawned bright and dry. I bade my reflection in the looking glass happy birthday and then resolved to forget the fact. After organising the diminished household (Clara and Molly stayed on to continue tidying up, and Mr. Thorpe was still in residence), I prepared myself for the picnic. I deliberated as I took off my uniform. I knew I really should wear an old frock, but the new blue one looked so tempting and so suitable for the beautiful weather. But it seemed foolish to wear a new dress; it could get grass stained or even pulled on brambles. Then I thought of the new curate. Maybe, just maybe, he was single. Maybe, just maybe, he was looking for a wife.

As I brushed my hair, I tried to dismiss such ridiculous thoughts and remind myself that some preachers follow Paul's example and stay single for the good of their calling. Anyway, who would want old Spinster Stubbs, even if she was in her best dress? With these admonishing and sensible thoughts, I reached into my wardrobe and put on my dress—the blue one. "To celebrate my birthday," I lied to myself.

The church yard was heaving with excited children when I arrived. I edged my way through them to the capable, basket-laden matrons, and we exchanged pleasantries. Through the side gate entered Rev. Hayworth, not in clerical garb, like Rev. Brinkhill thought seemly to wear for the occasion, but instead wearing a normal jacket and trousers. But the boys were not looking at his outfit, for all their eyes lit up as they saw what he carried under his arm: a new, leather football. This ball created more compliance than any stern outfit could have done, and he soon had them all assembled for the procession. When announcing that he was looking for some strong boys as volunteers, the normal ringleaders in trouble-making quickly came forward. The biggest boy had the honour of walking ahead with the banner, and the others, the "privilege" of carrying our food baskets.

Unburdened of our baskets, even the stoutest woman could keep up with the procession, if not sing along with the children. Our voices from the back and Rev. Hayworth's from the front, along with the desire not to fall out with the owner of the football, ensured that only the correct version of each hymn was sung.

At the appointed meadow, Rev. Hayworth halted the procession under a large old oak tree, and we prepared the blankets and food. After a short but thankful prayer, he (rather unnecessarily) urged the children to eat their fill. As usual, the baskets were emptied at an alarming rate, and the children gobbled up the food as if it was a race. Before the curate had hardly started his meal, the older boys were pestering him for the football, but instead of handing over the ball, he got up and went to organise the match himself. The lads were quickly divided into teams, and discarded jackets were used for goal posts.

The boys were happily entertained, but after watching for a bit, the girls grew bored. They half-heartedly made wildflower posies for us and each other and put bluebells in their hair, then mine, but before long they had reverted to their old game of picking stinging nettles. I felt sorry that nothing was organised for them and was just wondering what I could do about it, when a couple of girls asked me if I knew any country dancing.

"I know only a few that I learned at the harvest supper," I told them apologetically.

"Oh, please, miss, won't you teach them to us?" the tallest girl urged, with additional pleading coming from her friends.

I wavered and looked across the field; surely this fatherly curate, now only in his shirt sleeves for his energetic involvement in football, would not condemn me for a few innocent dances with the girls? As I was watching, he stopped running, swept his hair back from his warm face, and laughed heartily at the antics of one of the players. I wavered no longer but got up enthusiastically and organised the girls into couples and sets to learn some sequences. The older girls knew more than I, and soon we were singing, clapping, and dancing, in and out, up and down, just like at harvest.

The younger and shyer girls watched us eagerly and then were persuaded to join in. In the distance, I could see the disapproving looks on the older women's faces. This was not 'normal' for a Sunday school outing and therefore hardly proper, but one look at Rev. Hayworth made me insensible to their censorship and determined to give the girls an enjoyable time.

The outing could have run overtime if it were not for the church-warden's wife marching to the football pitch and indicating it was time for a cup of milk and walk home.

As we drank our milk, Rev. Hayworth approached me with a warm smile. "Thank you Miss . . . er . . . er—"

"Stubbs," I provided quickly.

"Miss Stubbs, for entertaining the girls so well. I am sure they much appreciated it, and I—"

He was called off by Mrs. Brinkhill to organise the march back. By now I was sure I liked our new curate very much indeed, and that feeling put a spring in my step . . . until I overheard the churchwarden's wife say to Mrs. Brinkhill, "Yes, and poor Mrs. Hayworth, in her situation . . ."

I did not hear what this situation was, but I had heard enough to crush my new hope. There was a Mrs. Hayworth already.

At bedtime I removed the forgotten bluebells from my hair. They were now wilted and crushed, just like my newly born but now withered hope. I was annoyed with myself that I could feel so deflated after a hope only a few hours old had been dashed. But the combination of disappointment and tiredness from the busy week ensured that I shed a few tears into my pillow before falling asleep.

The next day was again bright and warm, bringing a new optimism. I was slightly disappointed when Rev. Hayworth announced his text to be in Proverbs, making me believe that we would probably have a moralizing sermon, but then he preached from the eighth chapter about wisdom. He proved clearly that the wisdom spoken of was Christ and went through the verses explaining to us Christ's invitations, His truth, His immense value, and His power. He went on to show His eternal Sonship and how Christ was present at the creation of the world. He rounded off his uplifting sermon by speaking of Christ's willingness to dwell with sinners from the phrase "and my delights are with the sons of men." His argumentation was such that by the end of the sermon, it seemed utter foolishness not to put one's whole confidence in such a great Saviour.

That evening as I sat listening to another excellent sermon from Rev. Hayworth, I was resolved to visit the "poor Mrs. Hayworth." I looked around the congregation to see if there was anyone new who would fit that description, but seeing none, I decided her "situation" was pregnancy (an unsaid word among refined older ladies) and that she was probably feeling too nauseous to attend church.

The wife of such a decent man had to be a nice person. Once I had forgiven her for marrying him, I would probably enjoy her company and maybe even find the kindred spirit I longed for in this community. So as soon as I was free from duties, which was not until Wednesday afternoon (Mr. Thorpe being invited out to dinner), I baked a batch of ginger biscuits, as they are good for nausea, smartened myself up and, having asked Agnes' mother for directions, set off for the cottage.

It was quite a long walk, as the only suitable house the church had been able to provide was in a small hamlet the other side of the village, but the colourful hedgerow and the melodies of the songbirds made it very pleasant. The last of the bluebells were joined by buttercups, yellow rattle, and cow-parsley. It was tempting to make a posy, but I knew they would lose their beauty as soon as they were picked.

When I arrived, it seemed that I had come to the wrong house. It was a tiny cottage, hardly big enough for a young family. I knocked at the door and had a long wait before it was eventually answered by an old lady. Now I knew I had been mistaken.

"Sorry, but I was looking for a Mrs. Hayworth," I said apologetically.

"Then come in, my dear; that is me," she sweetly replied.

"But . . . I . . . the minister's wife . . . " I stupidly blurted.

"No, I am not the wife. I am the mother," my hostess explained and laughed.

Before I knew it, she had me seated and was putting the kettle on. I tried to gather up my whirling thoughts as she did so. When she turned around to speak to me, Mrs. Hayworth was still smiling. She had a beautiful face, full of laughter lines and expression. Her eyes were brown and friendly, just like her son's. But they were also bloodshot.

"You must excuse the drawn curtains and dimness," she said. "Only a month ago I had cataract operations, and I must avoid bright sunlight."

So that was the "condition" that kept her from attending the church picnic!

I asked her how she was recovering, and she enthused about how she could now see better than she had for years but said she still had to avoid strenuous exercise and exertion, which was awkward when one has just moved house.

"But tell me about yourself," she said. "I am intrigued to know who you expected to find here."

My mind had been working fast. Unless I told the full story, I could easily appear to be one of those man-grabbing women who sometimes plague single men of the cloth. Somehow I knew that this happy, sparrow-like lady would find the situation amusing, so I told her how much I liked her son's preaching, how I had wrongly concluded that he had a wife who was ill, and how I decided to pay a visit.

Dear Mrs. Hayworth laughed heartily, and on seeing the ginger biscuits and putting two and two together, she laughed even longer until I feared for her eyes.

"But your mistake was my gain, my dear," she said. "I like meeting people, but what with my eye condition and being so far from the village, we are living a rather secluded life. Jack keeps busy in his study or visiting the sick, but we have no visitors."

Mrs. Hayworth was not nosey or gossipy, but it was clear she loved finding out about people and soon had heard all about me, my work, and my parents. But the conversation was not just one way. She explained about her family too. She had been a widow for seven years. Her husband was a vicar, and she had a son, a daughter, and Jack, her youngest. Her two other children were married with six offspring between them.

She relayed all this information in a chirpy and optimistic style. She was clearly full of energy and enthusiasm. We could have sat chatting all afternoon, but I felt I was holding her back from scurrying on with some task and made a comment to that intent.

"Oh no, my dear," she assured me. "I am having a lovely time." Then as she thought a bit, she said, "But I could make use of you, if you don't mind. Look around and see how bare this room is. Jack has started unpacking, but he has done only the essentials. And his 'essentials' only include the pots and pans and all his books. Somewhere deep in a crate are my knick-knacks, which are clearly not essential to him but make a house look like a home. Would you do me the kindness of digging around for them? Jack and the physician completely forbid me to do such things."

I readily agreed and was soon pulling out all kinds of plates, ornaments, and pictures from crates, listening to the interesting stories behind each one. We were so engrossed in our task that I did not hear the door open and Rev. Hayworth enter. On seeing him, I felt foolish again and wished I had not come, but this feeling soon disappeared as I witnessed the teasing banter between mother and son.

"I have conscripted Miss Stubbs into getting out my so-called clutter," said Mrs. Hayworth.

"Yes, I see you have a new partner in crime," answered her son. Then turning to me, he laughed and said, "You could have at least started by putting my books in order."

"In order? Have they ever been in order?" teased the mother, putting on the kettle for the second time.

As we sat down to more tea, Mrs. Hayworth looked around contentedly at her afternoon's work. "Now this place is beginning to look more like home," she said with satisfaction.

Rev. Hayworth looked at me. "Thank you, Miss Stubbs, for your help. These things mean a lot to my mother, and sometimes I fail to appreciate that."

"Oh, don't you start berating yourself, my dear," Mrs. Hayworth said, stroking her son's knee. "You can't help being a man."

We all enjoyed a laugh at that. The laughter continued as Mrs. Hayworth explained how I had come looking for the curate's wife and not his mother. I blushed as she told the story but was pleased my reason for being there was explained. Once we had finished tea, I made a move to go.

"Now you have found your way here, you must come again soon, my dear," urged Mrs. Hayworth.

"Indeed, you must," echoed her son.

I put on my shawl, and Rev. Hayworth fetched his coat. "I'll walk you home," he said.

"But, sir, you have only just come in, and it is the other side of the village," I protested, but my heart skipped a beat.

"I am not averse to walking." He smiled, donning his coat and opening the door for me.

I feared that, without his mother, conversation would be rather awkward, but I was relieved to find this was not the case. Rev. Hayworth was as interesting and interested as Mrs. Hayworth, and our conversation flowed as we walked along the now darkening lanes.

He had done a few years as an apprentice at a joinery firm, having always had a love for carpentry. But after the death of his father, he had become more and more convinced that he should train as a vicar. He resisted this thought for a long time due to his enjoyment of his apprenticeship, but at last he gave in to the Lord's promptings and applied to do his ministerial training. He studied at Cambridge and had been a curate for a couple of years.

Having been under the authority of various vicars, some good and some awful, he now longed to have his own parish. "Preferably one without a dominating landlord or church warden to obstruct my every plan."

He found my story from vicarage to servants' hall astonishing and asked me what my parents would have thought. I had often asked myself that question, but no one had ever asked me. I was slow to reply but answered, "They both had a stubborn, independent streak about them, so after being shocked at how hard my life was as a housemaid, I think they would have approved."

"But why did you stick at being a housemaid for so long?" he asked.

Again, this was difficult to answer. "I suppose it was to prove to myself I could, and also due to the friendliness of the staff. But most of all, I think that sheer hard work was good for me when I was in such a raw state of bereavement."

After a long pause, my companion replied, "I think I understand. When my father died, I flung myself into carpentry during the day and studying New Testament Greek in the evenings as an escape."

"Oh, I am pleased I am not the only one," I confessed. "I thought that as a Christian and with the firm belief my parents are now in glory, maybe my escapism was somehow wrong and inconsistent."

I expected some preacherly lecture on not mourning as those without hope, or something equally as relevant and true, but instead Jack (what a lovely, homely name!) just said, "Then I am wrong and inconsistent too, but I don't think that is how the Lord sees it."

All too soon we were at Biggenden Manor, and I was unlocking the kitchen door. "Sorry you have to walk all the way back through the village again," I said.

"It is a price worth paying," he replied. "I hope you will visit us again soon."

"Maybe I can come next week," I suggested.

"Why not later this week? Mother did so enjoy your company." With a laugh he added, "There are plenty more boxes to unpack!"

Pleased that he wanted me to return sooner rather than later, I asked, "Would Saturday suit?"

"Yes, we would be delighted," he said, and with that we said good night, and I closed the door.

I had so much to think about. What a lovely family they were! Rev. Hayworth's questions on our walk showed interest and insight. But what did he mean by "It is a price worth paying"? Was it for his own pleasure, or for his mother's? However much I liked his mother, I fervently hoped it was for his own!

I did not have the luxury of a private mull-over for long, for Mr. Thorpe bounced into the kitchen.

"I beat you back!"

"Indeed you did, sir," I said as I removed my shawl.

"And discovered your little secret," he said slyly.

I blinked in surprise. "I have no 'little secret.'"

"Then who walked you home tonight?" he asked, following me across the kitchen to the table.

"Someone."

"Someone, who?"

"My friend's son."

"And does the 'friend's son' have a name?"

A small smile escaped. "I believe he does."

"And may I know his name?"

"I would prefer not, sir."

"Aha, then you *do* have a little secret!"

I shrugged my shoulders. "But there is nothing interesting to tell."

"But will it get interesting?"

"How should I know?"

"Do you want it to get interesting?"

"Oh, sir, don't tease me."

"I'll take that as a yes."

I kept silent.

"And I will watch with interest."

"Do not get your hopes up."

"Are you speaking to yourself or me?" he said with a small chuckle.

And with that, much to my relief, he left the room, laughing at his wit and my discomfort, leaving me feeling I had said little but still too much.

## CHAPTER 34

I COULD HARDLY WAIT TO return to the little cottage. Not for a long time had I been made to feel so welcome and accepted. I was surprised how freely and deeply Rev. Hayworth and I had talked, even though we were only newly acquainted. Yet as I walked to their house the following Saturday afternoon, I was full of misgivings. Saturday was a busy day for ministers as they prepared their sermons. My visit might be a rude disruption he would be too polite to object to.

I tentatively knocked on the door and was soon wrapped in Mrs. Hayworth's warm embrace and ushered in. Her genuine delight at seeing me was reassuring, but I was right about the studying.

"Now we must keep quiet, for Jack is busy in the study," she warned.

We started once more to empty boxes and fill the cupboards, all the while chatting about the contents and their histories. Mrs. Hayworth was such a busy, lively little lady that the enforced rest was a great trial to her. She would have lifted the heavy packing boxes or balanced on chairs to arrange things, had I not objected and insisted on doing it myself. Before long, the study door opened and out came Rev. Hayworth.

"I hope we didn't disturb you, dear," fretted his mother.

"Not at all. I've finished," he replied and then turned to greet me.

As we sat down for a drink, Rev. Hayworth took a journal from the table. "I have got something you may be interested in," he said, smiling at me, "but let me first explain. When I heard your surname, it seemed to ring a bell, and as you spoke of your father, I remembered reading his obituary, so I had a look for it."

"Hayworths never throw anything away," chipped in his mother.

I gasped. "I never knew anyone had written an obituary!"

"And here it is," he said, handing over the Diocesan Gazette of summer 1858.

I took it eagerly and, with a lump in my throat, began to read the story of my dear father's life. Some of the facts were new to me, but much was well known. The writer seemed to have known my father well, but the exaggerated praise of his virtues, transforming him from mere man to some angelic figure, rather jarred. By the time I got to the rather misinformed sentence that read, "his only daughter is being cared for by friends," I was almost certain I knew the writer. Sure enough, it was none other than Uncle Hector.

It is rather unusual to chuckle at one's father's obituary, so I had to explain the cause of my mirth to the Hayworths and relayed a few stories of Uncle Hector's unwanted visits, and soon they were laughing with me. Despite its sugary style, I gratefully pocketed the obituary when it was offered and kept it as a treasured possession.

As previously, the conversation flowed naturally and freely. My new friends seemed to share my ideas of what in life should be taken seriously and what is best laughed at. This, in my reckoning, made them "sensible people." Too many people in my opinion fail to get the balance right, rendering them either sanctimonious or foolish, but with the Hayworths, I feared neither extreme. Mrs. Hayworth was lively, interested, and wise. As for her son, to my taste he was all a good man should be: God-fearing, intelligent, kind, humorous, and, to crown it all, also very handsome. I was also pleased to notice that, rather than the slender, effeminate hands otherwise good-looking men often have, Rev. Hayworth had muscular ones with broad, blunt fingers. They were the hands of a carpenter rather than a preacher, more suited to a plane than to a pen. Instead of feeling shy and inferior in their sparkling company, the Hayworths made me feel free and vividly energized.

I secretly hoped that Rev. Hayworth would offer to escort me home again and was delighted when he did. As we walked companionably down the lanes, I was acutely aware of his masculinity, and that awareness made me feel wonderfully feminine. It was a delight just to look down and see his broad leather boots in step with my daintier ones.

*You are as romantically silly as Molly and Clara put together,* I told myself, whilst trying to formulate a reply to a question he asked about my work. We both slackened our pace as we neared Biggenden, so the last quarter of a mile took twice as long as it should have done. When we did arrive at the kitchen door, we both seemed awkward and untaught in the normal social interaction of saying good-bye.

"I hope you get on well tomorrow," I said.

"Yes, thank you," he replied. "I would value your prayers." Then he hesitated. "Miss Stubbs, do you have a ... err ... a follower?"

"No, I don't," I answered, feeling suddenly shy.

"That's good," he said with a hint of relief in his voice.

"Yes, it is," I replied with what I hoped was an encouraging smile.

"Good night to you, then."

"Yes, good night to you, sir."

I shut the kitchen door and leant against it with my hands pressed to my heart. His last question gave me so much hope. But what a silly reply I made. "Yes, it is." Could he have concluded from it that I was not interested in men and marriage, preferring a nun-like existence? I spent the evening either smiling or fretting, wholly relieved that I had the house to myself and no one to witness my strange behaviour.

When I went to bed, I prayed long and earnestly, thanking the Lord for the friendship I had with the Hayworths and pleading that I could become Jack's wife. "Please do not try me with this relationship," I prayed.

Listening to Rev. Hayworth's sermon the next morning was a rather strange experience. Most of the time I could concentrate on his excellent preaching, but every now and again, my mind drifted. Last week I had imagined the man in the pulpit to be happily married, but this week I saw him as highly marriage-able, which made it slightly harder to maintain eye contact when he looked in my direction. But then he seemed to avoid looking at my pew this week, giving more attention to the people on the right. I chided myself for lack of spirituality in admiring the minister and tried to focus on the message. A woman who cannot concentrate on a thirty-minute sermon is hardly suitable for a man who has spent several hours prayerfully preparing it!

At the end of the service, I was determined not to have to speak to him in public, but after the benediction, Rev. Hayworth walked to the door to greet all his parishioners, so I had no choice. Just ahead of me was Rev. Brinkhill's spinster daughter. She was a long-faced, pale individual who was known to be a scholar of ancient Greek and a recluse. When she shook hands with Rev. Hayworth, she gave him her best, toothy smile and with more words than I had ever heard her utter, praised him for his "truly edifying" sermon. She went on to say her parents would be delighted if he came to tea some time. Rev. Hayworth thanked her politely but did not commit himself.

When it was my turn, I simply said, "Thank you for the sermon." He squeezed my hand as he shook it and said, "Mother would like to know when you will next visit."

"She is very kind," I replied. "Would Tuesday suit?"

"I am sure it would." He smiled and then turned to greet the next person.

After lunch and before the evening service, I rather belatedly visited the Kemps. I took Rex with me, both to give him exercise and for Mr. Kemp's pleasure. It was good to see them settled in the family cottage with their grandchildren around them.

Children appeared from nowhere when they heard Rex was visiting, and chaos broke out until their mother ordered them all into the garden with the dog. Through the window we could hear arguments about whose turn it was to hold the dog's lead.

In the comparative peace, Mrs. Kemp wanted to know all the news from Biggenden and how many times we had blackened the kitchen range.

"We don't do bad fer visitors," she told me. "Agnes, bless 'er 'eart wiv all 'er step-children, 'as been along. En we've 'ad the new parson. En wot surprised us te most wos a call from Miss Brink'ill."

"Miss Brinkhill!" I exclaimed, knowing she hardly set foot out of the parsonage.

Mrs. Kemp nodded knowingly. "But te rumour is, she's got 'er 'eart set on te new parson. Why, she's a-visiting every sick person in te village, en 'efore she never 'ad 'er 'ead owt a book."

I absorbed this information glumly. I had a rival—a rival who was at leisure to busy herself with deeds of mercy throughout the parish whenever she wished. And was a Greek scholar to boot!

I went home, fell on my knees, and begged the Lord once again that my hopes would not be dashed.

It was even harder to concentrate in the evening service as (rather symbolically) Miss Brinkhill was sitting between me and Rev. Hayworth, forcing me to see her ramrod-straight back every time I looked up. Unlike the rest of us who need the occasional shuffle to ease our posteriors on the hard pew, she sat stock-still throughout the service; if I were a young lad, the temptation to poke her would have proven irresistible. Such thoughts are not conducive to good sermon hearing, so I benefited little from the exposition.

CHAPTER 35

THE COMING WEEK LOOKED SET to be another quiet one at Biggenden. The Harringtons had decided that, despite having no un-married daughters they needed to display, they would like to show their faces in London during the season. Mr. Thorpe had no desire to be involved in this outing, but Sophia begged him to come along, for as an engaged woman, she was no longer free to dance and flirt with whomever she liked. Her one pleasure now would be to proudly parade around on the arm of her fiancé. Needless to say, Mr. Thorpe complied, and I was once again the sole inhabitant of Biggenden.

Just as I started to worry that Molly and Clara might get lazy from lack of tasks to do, a heavy parcel from Miss Sophia arrived containing yards of beautiful velvet to be made up into curtains. We were afraid to cut the lovely material, measuring and re-measuring the windows many times before we were confident enough to make the first snip; then our work hours became dominated by the sewing of endless seams. As we sat bent over our work, our tiny stitches mak-ing barely noticeable progress along the seams, the sunshine and the birdsong outside seemed to mock our captivity.

On Tuesday, as soon as the midday meal things had been cleared away and the girls were back to work on the curtains, I took my work pinny off and went upstairs to get changed. Much to my annoyance, the kitchen doorbell rang just as I was ascending the stairs.

*Which trader will delay my half day this time?* I wondered as I, rather irritated, unlatched the door. To my delight it was no trader, but Rev. Hayworth himself.

"Good afternoon, Miss Stubbs," he said. "Today is so beautiful that I could not resist the pleasure of walking to meet you."

"Good afternoon, sir," I replied. "That is very kind of you. Were you visiting parishioners in this neck of the woods?"

"No, alas, I have no such laudable excuse; just the desire to leave my stuffy study and walk with you."

"Then I am greatly honoured." I smiled, noting the twinkle in his eye. "May I detain you for a few minutes while I run upstairs and change out of my work clothes?"

"If you wish, but what you're wearing looks fine to me."

So Rev. Hayworth took a seat in the kitchen, and I rushed upstairs to change. Such was my haste that I misbuttoned the back of my dress, did not realise until I had reached the penultimate button, then had to undo them all and start afresh. *This is why ladies employ maids,* I thought, *to ensure they do not go into important company in a state of disarray.*

I need not have rushed, for re-entering the kitchen, I found my guest browsing through a recipe book.

"You are quick, for a woman," he teased, slamming the book shut.

"And you have an interesting taste in reading, for a man," I replied in the same vein; then laughing, we left the house together.

With our morning's work behind us and the sun on our backs, we were both in a light-hearted and playful mood as we rambled through the lanes. My companion was for trying out a new route, which by accident or design added a few miles to a normally straightforward journey. But neither of us cared, for our conversation was far more wandering, covering all subjects from Bible commentaries to bicarbonate, pulpits to pantries. Our dialogue went smoothly and satisfactorily from serious to playful, from teasing to earnest, then back again without any need of explanation or fear of misunderstanding. With the happy realisation that my opinions, hopes, and fears were truly sought out and valued, and without the fear of the mocking sarcasm I had often experienced with Mr. Thorpe, my heart flourished. The more I learned of Rev. Hayworth, the more my respect and esteem for him grew. The more it grew, the greater was my dread that someone or something could tear this newfound source of joy away, leaving me deeply wounded and desolate.

It was mid-afternoon before we arrived at the Hayworths' cottage. Mrs. Hayworth had clearly expected us long ago, for the kettle had almost boiled itself dry. As we sat down with a cup of tea, Rev. Hayworth explained our new route to his mother.

"Was this an elaborate way of avoiding Miss Brinkhill?" she asked with a laugh.

"No, indeed, but that is not a bad idea," replied her son.

Mrs. Hayworth turned to me to explain. "Poor Jack spends half his life at the moment trying to avoid encountering Miss Brinkhill."

Rev. Hayworth nodded. "Yes, she seems to be in every cottage I visit and every lane I tread. The sick of the village fake their own recovery just to avoid her grim visitations; and if I have the misfortune of meeting her (which happens far too often), I can be sure to receive a long, depressing catalogue of reasons why there is little hope, either for body or soul, for the poor parishioner she has just inflicted a visit upon, despite her best rebukes and warnings."

"Jack's main work has become attempting to give hope to those downcast through the condemning verdict of Miss Brinkhill," added Mrs. Hayworth.

"Miss Brinkhill obviously does not like her father's parishioners, and they do not like her, so I do not understand why she puts both herself and them through these gloomy encounters," Rev. Hayworth said, shaking his head.

"No, I do not know either," I said, secretly knowing that I understood her motives better than either of my companions. Unknown to them also was the relief that the conversation had given me; now that I knew Rev. Hayworth was not enraptured by Miss Brinkhill's strange overtures, I felt sorry for her—well almost.

The unexpected visit from the church warden brought our congenial afternoon to an abrupt end. He was a man to be taken seriously, one who had a high view of his own importance. A visit from him would not be a mere fireside chat, but always warranted the secrecy of the study—away from women's ears. I saw my hopes of an escort home dashed, and not wanting to walk home in the dark, I soon rose to leave. As I was shutting the door, Rev. Hayworth managed to extract himself from his study and see me off.

"This man's ill-timed visit has robbed me of the pleasure of walking you home," he said.

"Yes, it is unfortunate timing," I agreed.

"But may we lessen the pain by agreeing to meet up very soon?" he suggested. "How about Friday?"

"Yes, that will do nicely. I look forward to it," I replied. "And meanwhile, we must be as selfless and dutiful as Miss Brinkhill."

"Don't you dare emulate her," he teased.

"Or you, her father," I replied and departed with a smile playing on my lips.

## CHAPTER 36

I ALMOST DANCED MY WAY home that evening, hugging my conviction that the budding friendship between Rev. Hayworth and I would flower into something beautiful. No true gentleman, let alone a minister, would give a woman such warm encouragements without a genuine desire to woo her. Of course, when I went through the middle of the village, I walked like any sensible person, but the absurd grin stuck to my face was harder to rectify.

Every now and again, a song of silent praise rang from my heart to the Lord who does all things well. Each tree and flower I passed seemed to display the Lord's care and agree with me in praising His goodness. I sailed into the kitchen, glad that the girls had gone home and, having the house to myself, I just pottered about, dreaming, smiling, and singing.

The next two curtain-dominated days dragged past. The sunny weather gave way to heavy rain and high winds.

The weather was not the only unwelcome arrival. On Friday morning, Mr. Thorpe unexpectedly appeared. This was most unfortunate as the two maids were due to have their half day that afternoon, and I was hoping to disappear to the Hayworths'. I saw the latter plan disappear before my mind's eye, for Mr. Thorpe would require an evening meal. I remembered Rev. Hayworth and my parting words, which were spoken in jest but now seemed prophetic, and with an air of dutiful resignation went to find Mr. Thorpe to discuss meal arrangements. Much to my relief, he did not require an evening meal. "I have stuffed myself on eggs and bacon at breakfast time. In fact, I have had so much rich food over the last few days, I would be happy with bread and water for the next week!"

"I trust you had an agreeable time in London, sir?" I asked, having sorted out the meal situation.

"Yes. I pleased everyone—the Harringtons in going to London, and myself in leaving."

"So was it not enjoyable?"

"Oh, in a way it was. The most satisfactory thing was seeing all the young ladies dolled up in their finest outfits and realising that I am marrying the best of the lot."

"That is very good, sir," I agreed.

"But what is this I am hearing about you?" he asked with a raised brow.

Hiding my alarm, I turned to gaze elsewhere. "About me, sir?"

"Yes. Clara says you are courting the curate."

"Then Clara needs her ears boxed," I said, blushing.

"Then you can deny it?"

Instead of giving a sensible reply, I just managed a few *errs* and *umms*. Mr. Thorpe chuckled at my discomfort. I tried to change the subject, but it was rather too obviously linked to the last.

"Before I knew of your plans, sir, I gave both Clara and Molly their half day today."

"That will be no problem," Mr. Thorpe assured me.

"But I too was hoping to have a few hours off, but I can cancel it if necessary."

"No indeed, please go ahead. But what are you doing?"

"Walking Rex," I replied.

"And walking the curate?" he asked knowingly.

"Well . . . yes, sir."

"Actually, I fancy a walk myself," said Mr. Thorpe teasingly. I imagined the three of us walking rather uncomfortably together. "So I'll take Rex with me and leave the curate with you."

"Oh, thank you, sir," I answered, relieved.

"But I want to be properly introduced to this chap before long," he said pompously. "I have a paternal interest in the well-being of my dependents."

I hurried off to get changed and was only just ready when Rev. Hayworth arrived at the kitchen door. As if to illustrate our mood, the clouds broke and the sun shone as we tried yet another route to the cottage. Our long, laughter-filled ramble was rudely interrupted by a heavy shower, so with open umbrellas, we ran, battling our way through the wind and rain.

"I don't know if the weather is for or against us," said Rev. Hayworth with a smile as we shook our umbrellas and removed our dripping coat and shawl.

It did not matter to me about the weather, for the wind and rain beating on the windows only made the cottage seem cosier and more inviting. We sat drinking hot tea as our outerwear steamed themselves dry next to the stove. As I looked across at the bedraggled Rev. Hayworth, his wet hair unruly and extra curly, a huge surge of love for him took the breath out my lungs. How I longed to run my fingers through those curls and ruffle his hair!

I was brought back to reality by Mrs. Hayworth tutting about the price of sugar and expecting a coherent response from me. She was busy making a final batch of elderflower cordial and soon had me involved in sieving the liquid through muslin. Her son disappeared to his study.

Another heavy shower at four o'clock prompted an invitation for me to stay and have soup, bread, and toasted tea cakes before I left. Rev. Hayworth's enthusiastic seconding of the idea removed any resistance I might have had, and I gratefully accepted. While I munched my way through a fruity tea cake that dripped with melted butter, I thought of Miss Sophia in London—dining in ornate houses, mixing with the elite, sampling the finest cuisine—and I would not have swapped places with her for all the tea in China.

When we had finished our simple meal, Rev. Hayworth reached for the large, well-thumbed family Bible and read a short passage from Hebrews. He concluded with prayer, thanking the Lord for our food and for safekeeping during the day, and committing the evening and night into His hands.

After I had helped wash up the crockery, it was time to go. Mrs. Hayworth kissed me good-bye, and her son helped me into my now-dry shawl, saying, "Tonight no church warden will stand in my way of walking you home."

Although it was June, the gloomy clouds brought on an early dusk. We picked our muddy way around puddles and pot-holes. Water meandered along the lanes, washing along gravel, leaves, and debris. We crisscrossed our way through the streams, pausing every now and again to re-channel the flow and break up the leafy dams with our boots. This was just the sort of activity that Bessie and I delighted to engage in as we sauntered along on our way home from school.

As we walked through the village, I tried to describe Pemfield to Rev. Hayworth, but so busy was I with reminiscing, that I did not see a rabbit hole by the verge of the road. My right foot landed in it, but the rest of me continued, causing me to end up flat on my face on the muddy grass. A shearing pain gripped my right ankle.

Rev. Hayworth's face was all concern as he helped me sit up and offered me his handkerchief for my mud-spattered face. I tried to laugh the incident off, but when I tried to get up, the pain in my ankle was so intense I nearly fainted. My ankle was rapidly swelling.

After persuading me it was the wisest thing to do, Rev. Hayworth carefully untied my boot and eased it off my ballooning foot. He then knelt in the mud and let me lean against him while I tried to recover. The thought of his knees getting gradually wetter and colder spurred me into action, and after a while with his support, I managed a standing position. With my arm over his shoulder and his arm around my waist, we made halting and painful progress toward Biggenden.

Just when we thought things could get no worse, the heavens opened and it poured with rain.

"Well, there is nothing else for it," muttered Rev. Hayworth, and with that he picked me up and carried me.

The pain, mud, self-consciousness, and rain combined could not completely eclipse the enjoyable sensation of feeling his strong arms around me. Fortunately for Rev. Hayworth, he did not have far to go, and soon he staggered into the kitchen and, with an air of relief and triumph, deposited me in an armchair near the stove.

I did not know whether to laugh or cry as I tried to express my thanks, but Rev. Hayworth was hardly listening, for he was busy arranging a foot stool, removing my shawl, and finding a cold compress for my ankle. As he was stocking the smouldering fire, the door opened and Mr. Thorpe entered waving a poker from the nearest fireplace.

"I thought I heard intruders," he said, before walking over and introducing himself to the curate.

The two men shook hands, one wearing his soft indoor shoes and looking clean and neat in his tweed jacket, and the other caked in mud and wearing a dripping overcoat.

"What a state you are both in!" exclaimed Mr. Thorpe, rather unnecessarily. "Have you fallen amongst thieves?"

"Not thieves, but a rabbit hole," replied Rev. Hayworth, smiling. "When I was walking Miss Stubbs home, she had the misfortune of stumbling into a rabbit hole and badly spraining her ankle."

"And he has been my Good Samaritan," I added, smiling up at him.

"That is good of you, Reverend," said Mr. Thorpe.

"But, sir, Miss Stubbs is in severe pain and is awfully pale. Do you have any port or the likes that she could drink?" asked Rev. Hayworth.

"Why, of course," replied Mr. Thorpe, and he disappeared from the kitchen to find some.

When we were alone again, Rev. Hayworth squatted down next to me and asked, "How are you feeling now, Rebecca?"

It was a simple question, but the tenderness of his voice and the fact that he had used my Christian name for the very first time filled my eyes with tears and my heart with love.

"Oh, Jack," is all I could utter as I squeezed his arm.

Tears ran down my cheeks as I looked into his kind eyes. I noticed a crust of mud on his forehead and carefully rubbed it off, wiping my finger on my skirt. He reciprocated by rubbing a splatter off my cheek and was just opening his mouth to speak when, proud of his speed, Mr. Thorpe entered the kitchen, waving a bottle of port and three glasses. Jack and I both faked admiration for his swiftness, but whereas Jack looked cool and composed, I felt hot and flustered.

"Do take your coat off and join us for a glass," invited Mr. Thorpe. "Unless, of course, you have signed the pledge."

"Thank you, I would be glad to join you, and no, I am not a teetotaller and see no reason to begin now." Jack smiled back, removing his coat and putting it near the stove to dry for the second time that afternoon.

I pointed out a tin on the side containing a rich fruitcake, and after further instructions where to find a knife and plates, we all settled with our refreshments. Mr. Thorpe and Rev. Hayworth were soon busy discussing the strengths and weaknesses of the various Oxford and Cambridge colleges, but although Jack's conversation was mainly directed at Mr. Thorpe, his eyes often strayed in my direction.

Being unused to strong drink and having been given an overgenerous measure by Mr. Thorpe, I soon began to feel drowsy and distant. Despite being close to the roaring stove, I was still cold and shivering. My ankle throbbed more than I cared to admit.

Jack observed my condition and believed I was in a state of shock. "You need to be tucked up in a warm bed," he said.

The thought of dragging myself out to the closet, then up to bed, especially in my muddy state, seemed almost impossible, and it dawned on me how awkward it was having only gentlemen around. This problem must have gone through Jack's mind at the same time.

Speaking to Mr. Thorpe, Jack asked, "Is there any local woman we could call upon to help poor Miss Stubbs to get comfortable?"

Mr. Thorpe thought for a minute and then snapped his fingers. "I've got just the ticket. I can ask the groom to fetch a carriage to take you home and to fetch a local woman to help Miss Stubbs."

"I do not need a carriage, only the loan of a lamp," objected Jack. "By the time you have hitched the horses up, I could be halfway home. It seems a shame to disturb the groom at this hour."

"*This hour* is only eight o'clock, Reverend, and after all you have done for my housekeeper, it would please me if you accepted my offer."

"Please do," I seconded. "It is still pouring out there."

With that, Jack reluctantly consented. Mr. Thorpe pulled a newly installed bell to summon the groom, and soon all was neatly arranged. Agnes's mother, Mrs. Brookes, was the nearest neighbour. She, along with Violet, came to see what state I was in, and with much friendly sympathy, they organised hot bricks to warm my bed and opodeldoc lotion for the sprain.

Jack looked relieved at the motherly attention I was getting and bade me good night, promising to visit the next day. Mr. Thorpe, on seeing the flutter of womanly activity, vacated the kitchen, leaving the kind ladies to attend me.

I insisted I could help myself, but Mrs. Brookes brushed aside my efforts. Once standing, I was most grateful for her support, because the room spun around before my eyes. Somehow she helped me to the outside closet and then to ascend the stairs. I was for flopping exhausted into bed, but she dismissed Violet, undressed me like a little child, and washed away all the mud. Finally, as if my arms were affected as well as my ankle, she combed my hair before helping me into my warm and cosy bed. I laid back in utter relief. Then, as I tried to express my gratitude to Mrs. Brookes, I burst into tears.

## CHAPTER 37

I HAD A FITFUL NIGHT. The port sent me to sleep, but the pain in my ankle woke me a few times. When awake I was fully alert, my mind whirling with the events of the evening and the firm realisation that Jack loved me. This knowledge was like a warm cocoon wrapped around my joyful heart—a heart almost bursting with love for Jack and thankfulness to the Lord.

It did not matter that I had hardly slept and that my foot was throbbing, for my new happiness gave me as much energy as hours of undisturbed slumber. I knew what Mrs. Brookes was like and more likely than not, I would now be her "project" until I was well again, so to prevent my being a burden to her, I was determined to get myself up and dressed before she came to help. Out of sheer stubbornness I painfully wrestled my way into my clothes, tidied myself up, and descended the stairs on my bottom. Having accomplished that, I soon discovered that most tasks in the kitchen were nigh impossible, so I had to await the arrival of the kitchen maids before the stove could be stoked and the breakfast preparations commenced.

On seeing my swollen and bruised ankle, the two girls rose to the occasion, promised to do all the work, and packed me off to the housekeeper's parlour. The gardener kindly cut me two sticks that were a great help in the coming days.

While Clara and Molly busied themselves with the cooking and cleaning, I continued sewing the endless curtain seams. During the morning, Mr. Thorpe visited my parlour to enquire after my well-being, but he could not resist the opportunity to tease.

"The curate could not keep his eyes off you last night."

I was relieved when he left the house to inspect the crops.

Mid-afternoon the doorbell rang and shortly afterwards, Molly, with a knowing look and a smirk, ushered Jack into my parlour. He had only just sat down when the doorbell rang again and Miss Brinkhill was announced.

My little parlour seemed overcrowded with this third, unwelcome person present. Jack politely vacated the armchair and brought forward the desk chair for himself. When Miss Brinkhill was settled, we all exchanged rather stilted pleasantries. Molly, out of kindness or curiosity, brought in a tray of tea and biscuits. It was a relief to busy myself with the arranging of cups and saucers and the pouring of tea, for a stern silence was radiating off Miss Brinkhill, creating an awkwardness.

After receiving her tea and taking a few polite sips, she broke her silence. "I sympathise with you as regards to your ankle injury, Miss Stubbs."

"Thank you," I replied.

"But I am duty-bound to point out that your accident was a judgement."

"A judgement?" queried Jack.

"Yes, indeed, and out of regard for Miss Stubbs, I felt I should come and reprove her in private, but seeing as you are here too, Reverend, maybe together we can gently point out the error of her ways."

I was speechless, but Jack said, "Kindly explain," in such an icy tone that I shivered.

Miss Brinkhill was oblivious to the ice and continued, "Well, it has come to my attention that Miss Stubbs has taken to loitering in the dark with an unknown male."

I put down my saucer with a clatter, but she went on. "And indulging in unseemly physical contact."

I sat forward to offer some incoherent reply, but Jack silenced me by putting his hand on my arm.

My accuser continued, "And, I am sure you will agree, Rev. Hayworth, such behaviour is unbecoming for a church member, and it is up to the likes of you and me to uphold the standards of the church."

"Yes, indeed it is," replied Jack fiercely. "And the protection of parishioners from malicious slander and gossip is also my duty, so bearing that in mind, I would like to inform you of a few salient facts, Miss Brinkhill. Firstly, it may interest you to know that it was *I* you saw 'loitering in the dark' with Miss Stubbs."

Miss Brinkhill's shocked reaction was most satisfactory.

"Furthermore, it was I who had his arms wrapped around her. Let me ask you, Miss Brinkhill, is there anything 'unseemly' about helping a friend along the road when she is hurt? Can one not help an injured person in such a situation without the tongues of village gossips wagging?" Here he paused, then said slowly and emphatically, "Especially if the injured person just happens to be the woman you have every intention of marrying?"

Miss Brinkhill's ramrod body almost leapt out the chair. "Marry? But she is a servant!"

Jack sprang to his feet. "And so am I! I am a servant of the Lord. So we are ideally matched."

"But she is ignorant!"

Jack was looking so fierce that it was my turn to lay a restraining hand on him. "Then he can teach me," I said, but this was unheard as Jack answered at the same time.

"Ignorant? Then I am ignorant, for I find Rebecca my equal."

Because Miss Brinkhill looked so defeated, I had a little sympathy for her.

"Wait until I tell my father," she threatened as she stood up to leave.

"Yes, please tell him, for we need someone to marry us," replied Jack, somewhat cheekily.

At that, she flounced, wet eyed, out of the room, slamming the door behind her.

Jack sat back in his chair and said, "Phew," and we both laughed rather nervously. I suddenly felt very shy.

"I am sorry," said Jack, taking my hand. "That must be the most unromantic marriage proposal in history."

"But the most exciting," I offered with a smile.

Then he got down on one knee and said, "My dear Rebecca, would you do me the honour of becoming my wife?"

"I would be delighted," I replied, and before I knew it and despite my ankle, he had removed me from the armchair, sat himself in it, and had me on his lap.

## CHAPTER 38

MOLLY AND CLARA FOUND MY engagement slightly unfathomable. Their reaction was an amusing mixture of bewilderment and envy as they tried to understand how a spinster housekeeper and a greying minister could possibly fall in love. Romance seemed impossible at the grand age of twenty-one, and courting a curate did not come into their definition of fairy-tale love. But in this they were totally wrong; being in love and engaged to Jack was utterly romantic and exciting.

Mr. Thorpe's initial reaction to the engagement was to worry that I would leave Biggenden earlier than arranged. Only after he had received my assurance that I would stay until he returned could he give his congratulations, but he was far too busy preparing for his own wedding to be interested in hearing our plans.

The villagers' reaction was also cool. They could approve of a parson in a monk-like single state, or in a well-established family state, but a preacher on his way from one of these positions to another seemed somehow indecent. And to show any sort of enthusiasm or passion about the journey was positively scandalous. But none of this did anything to detract from our intense enjoyment, and the two months between our engagement and wedding flew by in an exciting whirl.

Mr. Thorpe left Biggenden to get married in early July. The only indication we had that the nuptials had taken place was a package of dried up wedding cake that arrived a week later. Within a fortnight of his departure, the first influx of new staff and crates of Mrs. Thorpe's possessions arrived.

The new housekeeper was exactly as one could expect, seeing as she had been hand-picked by Mrs. Harrington. She was well into her middle years, broadly set with a determined gait that silently proclaimed "I know best." She immediately made it abundantly clear that my reign was over, my contribution or ideas were superfluous, and that I was no longer needed. Had I not been so occupied with Jack and wedding preparations, I would have felt hurt and offended; had I not promised Mr. Thorpe to stay until his return, I would have gladly left immediately. But as it was I duly vacated the housekeeper's parlour and made myself scarce. My reduced role consisted of caring for Rex and lending a listening ear to Clara and Molly as they poured out their frustrations at the regime change.

In fact, thanks to the battle-axe new housekeeper, I had a most relaxing summer ever and was able to spend a great deal of time at the Hayworths' cottage or enjoying long walks with my fiancé and Rex. Mrs. Hayworth welcomed me into the family with all her generous heart. The Lord had fulfilled His promise of "putting the solitary in families."

Mrs. Hayworth threw her all into helping us plan the wedding, declaring it was like being the groom's mother and bride's mother in one, and she was certainly as organised and productive as two ordinary women. By now her eyesight was so much improved that she telegrammed her ophthalmologist, begging his permission to return to normal activities. His cautious reply stated that a gradual return to normal was recommended. His notion of gradual was probably vastly different from hers, but thankfully she had no ill effects from her exertions. Having fitted herself with a wide-brimmed straw hat, she was out into the summer sunshine and off.

I introduced her to Mrs. Brookes, who became a firm friend and ally in organising the wedding breakfast. Mr. Brookes, in his master's absence, proposed that the threshing barn be used, and he organised some farm labourers to clean it out. Remembering the cosiness of the harvest supper there, I was very happy with the arrangement and hoped Mr. Thorpe would not feel we were presuming too much on his kindness.

Mrs. Hayworth also started packing her boxes with as much pleasure and enthusiasm as she had only recently unpacked them, for she declared she would now go and live with her daughter, Elisabeth. She had lived with her and her family for many years and only moved in with Jack to have peace and quiet while recovering from her cataract operation. I wondered how busy and chaotic Elisabeth's household was, if moving parish and house with Jack was considered "peace and quiet"!

Jack and I did not want her to feel obliged to move out, but she would not hear our arguments, insisting that newlyweds needed time alone together. Indeed, she often took herself off upstairs to have an early night or to do some sorting out in a poorly disguised attempt to give us time alone.

Right from the start, Jack introduced family worship to our evenings together; we took it in turn, the one reading from Scripture and the other praying. This was a precious new way of becoming closer to each other and the Lord, a habit we hold dear to this day.

I wrote a long overdue letter to Uncle Hector, informing him of my romance and engagement, to which I had an effusive reply, playfully chiding me for being a "sly puss" and insisting on giving me away. I was unenthusiastic at the idea but realised someone had to walk me down the aisle, and he was my closest male relative. Jack encouraged me to accept by pointing out how much pleasure it would give the old man, so I agreed and started enquiring into finding suitable lodgings for Uncle Hector over the wedding.

Every now and again, in planning our future, I had to pinch myself to make sure this was really happening to me and was not just a beautiful dream. My heart was overflowing with gratitude to the Lord for His amazing goodness to me. Now I could thank Him for all the prayers He had left unanswered about Mr. Thorpe and how He had planned something so much better for me.

Almost every afternoon, Jack and I would meet and take Rex for a long walk. We sometimes wandered along the River Medway, sometimes through the woods or through the lanes. On a few occasions, we hitched a lift on a cart going to Tunbridge and spent some happy hours roaming the town or exploring the ancient Norman motte-and-bailey castle. Whether to shield us from gossiping tongues or to enjoy her newfound freedom, Mrs. Hayworth wisely suggested she join us on our day trips as a chaperone. And what a wonderful one she was! Cheerfully perched next to the driver on the cart, adorned with her inevitable straw hat, she was visible for all to see; but once we arrived in Tunbridge, she invented some business to do in town and disappeared. We rarely saw her until the return journey, when, full of her day in town, she would delight us with descriptions of what she had done and seen, making our excursions seem very leisurely, if not lazy, in comparison.

My memory of that summer is one of brilliantly sunny days and peaceful evenings sitting in the Hayworths' back garden. Just looking around their little cottage gave me a thrill. Within weeks I would be the mistress of the house; as I looked at the cooking range, I imagined myself preparing meals for my husband. Every pot and pan seemed to be charmed with romance. I even felt excited when I saw the mangle outside the back door, at the thought of washing my husband's clothes! Jack seemed equally keen, for he set to work making a handsome wardrobe to house his wife's clothes.

We had no idea how long we would be in the village, as no one was quite sure how Rev. Brinkhill's leg was progressing, but the uncertainty of our future just added to the excitement. I would have gladly set up home in a tepee or igloo, so long as Jack was by my side and the Lord was directing us. Jack laughed when I shared this idea with him and could not decide whether I would make a sweeter squaw or Eskimo!

I had intended to make my own wedding dress, but when Uncle Hector sent me a large banker's draft, I decided to forgo tradition, probably incurring the scorn of the ladies' sewing guild, and had the gown designed and made by the friendly dressmakers in Broadstairs. This arrangement involved a three-night stay with Miss Miller, which seemed an awfully long time away from Jack, but by careful planning, it coincided with his London trip to escort Mrs. Hayworth to her ophthalmologist, making it more bearable.

Once I was back in Broadstairs, I thoroughly enjoyed my time with Miss Miller, who, as it was in the school holidays, had time to join me on long coastal walks. Twice a day I went for a dress fitting and was always delighted to see the progress and admire the intricate details. The dress transformed me from an ordinary, everyday girl into a fairy-tale bride, making me feel both elegant and pleasantly demure. Miss Miller and I repeatedly expressed our amazement that only four months since our parting, I should be back in order to purchase a wedding dress—for myself! We rejoiced in the Lord's goodness, for, rather than being jealous of my prayers being answered before hers, Miss Miller saw it as a great encouragement as to how the Lord overrules events in our lives in order to give us the very best.

August fled by and September raced along, bringing back to Biggenden the well-travelled Thorpes. Once I had handed Rex over to his owner and witnessed their joyful reunion, I felt I had fulfilled my obligation and was free to leave the house. Mrs. Brookes kindly volunteered to let me lodge with her for the week between the Thorpes' return and my wedding. Most of my belongings were already at the Hayworths' cottage, so all I had to do was to pack my case and walk out. The staff was so busy making the newlyweds comfortable and preparing for the forthcoming arrival of Mrs. Harrington that no one even noticed my departure.

Miss Miller had declined my invitation to the marriage; the start of a new term was the ideal excuse to miss a social occasion where she would know only one person—but Uncle Hector was installed in the best (and only) inn the village boasted of.

I was rather overwhelmed as the Hayworth clan gradually gathered at the cottage for the wedding. They were all very nice and welcoming, but the very knowledge that they were gathered on our behalf suddenly made me feel shy and slightly trapped. As they all chatted in the now stuffy and overcrowded living room, I slipped out to the kitchen to wash up.

"When did you sneak off, my dear?" asked Jack as he put his arms around my waist.

"Only five minutes ago, I thought I would not be missed," I confessed.

"You needn't be here working."

"But I prefer it."

"As the bride-to-be, you should be out there in the thick of it."

"I'm sorry," I said, my eyes filling with tears. "But I have never had a large family before, and it will take a bit of getting used to. I don't know all the fun little stories that you are recounting to each other. I don't know your family traditions and jokes."

"Ah, Rebecca, it is me that is sorry," sighed Jack, looking remorseful. "You have been thrown into the deep end, and I should have been more attentive."

He picked up a tea towel and started drying up, but before long we were interrupted.

"Ah, what a sweet scene of domestic bliss," teased Jim, my brother-in-law-to-be as he bounded into the kitchen. "I am sure I could find you a flowery pinny if you want one, Jack."

"Don't trouble yourself," Jack replied with a smile.

"Sorry to tear you from your work, but I was hoping you two would give me a guided tour of your parish. I am especially keen to see the famous rabbit hole."

We all laughed, and I quickly dried my hands. Talking was always easier when accompanied by walking.

The night before the wedding, I found it hard to get to sleep; the bed was comfortable, but my mind was too busy. This would be my last night sleeping alone, and that raised a few anxieties—not the sleeping component of the arrangement, obviously, but . . . I tried to reassure myself by thinking of all the odd, ugly, and unlikely couples I knew (each village has a few) and told myself, "if they can do it, so can we." But better than that, I prayed to God, whose wisdom had designed the marriage union—every part of it.

Before I slept, I shed a few tears because my parents would not be sharing the momentous day ahead with me. Just then I would have appreciated a reassuring chat with Ma. I wondered if, up in heaven, they would know I was getting married, or whether all earthly events are hidden from the saints. But at last I slept and on waking felt refreshed and cheerful.

Mrs. Brookes sat me down to a good breakfast, which I merely picked at. After leisurely ablutions, I was helped into my wedding gown by Mrs. Brookes and Violet. I flushed and tingled when I realised it would be Jack helping me to remove it later. Clara ran across from Biggenden and arranged my hair elegantly in a style that would not be spoiled by the veil. By the time the ladies had finished beautifying me, I felt as ladylike as Mrs. Sophia Thorpe and smiled as I imagined her mother's disapproval at such a lavish gown for a person of my lowly rank. I was delighted by the details, lace, and tucks of the dress that perfectly suited my figure and gave me new confidence.

Of course, even for a wedding, Uncle Hector would avoid walking any distance, so at the appointed time, he arrived in a hired carriage, adorned with flowers on the lamps, to pick me up and escort me to church.

I had always irreverently imagined Rev. Brinkhill conducting our wedding service in his bed cap and nightshirt, so was pleasantly surprised to see him upright and fully robed at the lectern, although not even a wedding service could remove his stern and disapproving look. But when the gallery band struck up, the handsome man waiting at the end of the aisle turned his head and grinned encouragingly as I walked toward him. The look of love and appreciation in his eyes helped to banish any lingering maidenly fears.

Uncle Hector's puffing and wheezing progress down the aisle made me wonder if he would make it. I imagined abandoning my bouquet and carrying him, and so, instead of uplifting thoughts about the solemn vows I was about to make, my mind was full with ridiculous images of staggering under his corpulent weight. Thankfully, we arrived safely, and Uncle Hector sank heavily and gratefully into a creaking pew, while I took my place alongside Jack.

With a funereal air, Rev. Brinkhill began the "Dearly beloved, we are gathered here . . . " business and droned his way through the marriage service. This was as we had expected, for as Jack had earlier explained, "We have to ask him. We know he will do it badly, but we will be married, and he cannot interfere with our joy." So, as we sat, hand in hand, listening to the monotone sermon on the trials and tribulations of married life, we squeezed each other's hand at each mournful warning and tried to maintain appropriately solemn faces.

Rev. Brinkhill could not stand for long, and it was beneath his dignity to preach sitting down, so much to our relief, his exposition was considerably shorter than normal. Finally the last hymn, "Now Thank We All Our God," was announced, which we all sang with feeling and hearty gusto; all, that is, except Uncle Hector, who having roared out the first line, succumbed to a coughing fit that lasted until the benediction.

The church bells pealed as we triumphantly left the building as man and wife. I had expected a quiet wedding, but the churchyard was packed with friends, Hayworths, and villagers wanting to throw confetti and wish us well. The whole crowd then proceeded down to the threshing barn, where a scrumptious lunch had been prepared. No one seemed to know or care who was invited and who not, but all joined in and none were excluded; well, almost none, for Mrs. Sophia Thorpe had excluded herself. Apparently, she had decided attending a former servant's wedding was beneath her dignity and would set an "unusual precedent." Her mother admired her principled stand, but her husband did not and briefly dropped in to shake Jack's hand, sample the cider, and give us his best wishes.

After the customary mingling with the guests and speeches, I sat close to my husband and surveyed the happy scene in the barn. Mr. and Mrs. Kemp were silently munching wedding cake in one corner, Mrs. Brookes and Violet were bustling about serving tea as Mr. Brookes tapped a new cider barrel. Agnes happily fussed around her brood of children, and her girth looked suspiciously as if she might soon be adding another to the number. Molly and Clara were flirting playfully with the farm hands, making me wonder how long they would stay in domestic service. Rev. Brinkhill had retired to bed, but his daughter was sitting bolt upright on a bench, looking as if she had severe indigestion.

I had feared that the dust of the barn would set off Uncle Hector's chest complaint, but one glance in his direction reassured me. He sat, tankard in hand, chatting animatedly to a group of older men. I could not hear his words, but could imagine him describing how he helped to run the country. Between the groups of men, women, youths, and families ran various children, some only newly acquainted but all joining in a lively game with no regard for their smart wedding outfits.

Amid the chatter and laughter, my mind wandered back over the last few years of my life—from Pemfield vicarage, to becoming a housemaid, then the unexpected move to Biggenden as a housekeeper. *And now I'm a wife! I've gone from being Rebecca Stubbs, the vicar's daughter, to becoming Rebecca Hayworth, the vicar's wife!* I did not know what the future held, but I knew the God who holds the future and that I could trust Him and His unfailing promises. My heart swelled with gratitude and joy at His goodness to me.

Jack put his arm around my shoulders, interrupting my musings, and drew me toward him. "Shall we go, Mrs. Hayworth?" he whispered.

I smiled and nodded my consent, and then, having bade all our friends and relatives good-bye and amid cheers and whistles, we left the barn and walked home together.

*If it is well told and to the point, that is what I myself desire; if it is poorly done and mediocre, that is the best I could do.*
Apocrypha, 2 Maccabees 15 v 38

For more information about

# Hannah Buckland

and

*Rebecca Stubbs: The Vicar's Daughter*
please contact:

hannahebuckland@gmail.com

For more information about
AMBASSADOR INTERNATIONAL
please visit:

*www.ambassador-international.com*
*@AmbassadorIntl*
*www.facebook.com/AmbassadorIntl*